In the

Shadow

of the

Dragonfly

In the

Shadow

of the

ragonfly

M. Jean Pike

Black Lyon Publishing, LLC

IN THE SHADOW OF THE DRAGONFLY
Copyright © 2008 by M. JEAN PIKE

Our books may be ordered through your local bookstore or by visiting the publisher:

www.BlackLyonPublishing.com

Black Lyon Publishing, LLC
PO Box 567
Baker City, OR 97814

This is a work of fiction. All of the characters, names, events, organizations and conversations in this novel are either the products of the author's vivid imagination or are used in a fictitious way for the purposes of this story.

ISBN-10:   1-934912-07-7
ISBN-13:   978-1-934912-07-2
Library of Congress Control Number: 2008931669

Written, published and printed in
the United States of America.

Black Lyon Literary Love Story

For Marjorie—my sister, my friend.

Book One

Hope

Chapter One

August, 1984

It was hands down the best day of Ted Hanwell's life. This thought kept him lying awake, his heart overflowing and his mind racing with tasks to be completed before the incredible concept became a reality. *A father*, he thought. *I'm going to be a father.*

Georgie stirred beside him. He rolled onto his side and watched her face in the shadows, drinking in the sheer wonder of her.

My wife. The mother of my child.

As if on cue, she opened her eyes. Smiling, she ran her fingers over his biceps and chest, then slid them lower as her lips closed around his nipple. Groaning with pleasure, he drew her to him and kissed her. Gazing into her eyes, he knew no man had ever cherished a woman more.

"Can you believe it, Ted?" she whispered. "My God. I'm still in shock."

His hand traveled to her abdomen, still soft and flat. "Me too, baby."

The street lamp outside the window reflected the mist in her eyes, making them shine. Her voice caught. "I can't believe we're finally going to have our baby."

Feeling his heart constrict, he slid his arms around her. Sweet Lord. Had a man ever died from sheer love for a woman?

"What do you mean, finally? We haven't been trying that long."

"Yes, we have. You just didn't know it."

Laughing softly, he pulled her closer. He breathed in the soap and water freshness of her skin and thought how young she still was. He'd married her two years before, when she was twenty-one and he was thirty. By then he'd already loved her for a decade.

"Dana made labor sound like hell," she said abruptly.

"Dana could make a trip to Disney World sound like hell."

"You won't leave me, will you? If I don't get my figure back?"

"Never."

She snuggled closer, smiling a mysterious little smile.

"Hey there, Georgie girl?"

"Hm?"

"You won't get as big as Dana, will you?"

"I might."

"Yikes."

"Ted, be nice. You know my sister hasn't had it easy."

He made a face.

"Ted!"

"I'm sorry, Georgie. I have a tough time feeling sorry for a woman—a smart woman like Dana, who lets herself get suckered by some traveling salesman and then uses it as an excuse to hate all men everywhere forever."

"She doesn't hate all men. She doesn't hate you."

"I'm so blessed," he muttered.

"You're so mean."

"I'm sorry." He kissed the tip of her nose. "Let's not talk about Dana any more."

"I just feel sorry for her, that's all," Georgie said, staring at the ceiling. "She was lonely. And Derk was so nice looking."

"Yeah, well nice looking doesn't translate into nice any more than southern translates into gentleman. I think I tried to tell her that."

"I know you did."

"I hated that jerk."

"Me, too."

"I mean, think about it. Who but your sister gets married, pregnant, and divorced within three months?"

"Let's drop it, Ted."

"All right."

"She doesn't hate you, though."

"She did her damndest to keep us from getting married. There must have been a reason."

She smiled wickedly. "Maybe she wanted you for herself."

Ted grasped his throat and made low, gurgling noises.

Laughing, she grabbed for his hands. "Ted Hanwell, I told you to be nice."

"Oh, I intend to." He kissed her, long and hard. "I love you, baby. Do you have any idea how much?"

By November, the skin around Georgie's belly was stretched taut and a pleasant fullness padded her features. She sat on the futon in Ted's office, huddled beneath a blanket, her book of baby names open in her lap. She read aloud to him as he went over his spread sheets.

"How about Freya? It means goddess. Or Fulvia," she let the word roll off her tongue. "The blonde."

"I don't know, Georgie," he said, not looking up. "Don't you think the other guys would pick on him?"

She threw the book down. "You know, Ted, you could consider the possibility that your son might turn out to be a girl."

"Mm hm." Damn. The figures were down this quarter. Where could he cut back? Supplies?

"You won't love it, I guess. If it's a girl."

He heard the tremor in her voice and quickly shifted his attention back. "Of course I will."

"But you want a boy. You'll feel like I let you down if I don't give you a son."

He kneaded the knotted muscles at the base of his neck. Damn. He really needed to have the book work on his accountant's desk by morning. Sighing, he set down his pen. "Sweetheart, boy or girl, I swear it doesn't matter. Just as long as it's healthy. Ten fingers and ten toes, right?"

Georgie's expression brightened and she patted the space beside her on the futon. "Come and help me, then. The ultrasound's tomorrow. If they can tell us what sex it is I want to be ready with a name."

Moments later he stood behind her, massaging her shoulders and looking into the book. "I thought we liked Noah. Didn't we say Noah?"

"For a girl, though." She flipped through the pages. "We haven't even talked about girl names."

No, they hadn't. But Ted got the sinking feeling they were going to now, and probably for the rest of the night. He glanced longingly at the open ledger on his desk, then sighed again and let it slip through his hands.

•

"Ted!"

He bolted up in bed and groped for the clock. Three AM.

"What's wrong, Georgie?"

"It came to me. Just now, while I was sleeping."

He blinked and rubbed his eyes. "What came to you?"

"Our daughter's name! It's Jenna."

"Jenna?"

"You don't like it?"

"Sure I like it. It's just ..." He fought to clear the static from his brain. It was three o'clock in the morning, for Christ's sake. He didn't even know his own name.

She tore back the blankets and eased herself from the bed.

"Where are you going?"

She padded from the room and returned moments later with the book of baby names. She flipped through its pages, then smiled in triumph.

"Jenna. It's Arabic. See, it means small bird."

"All right. We'll have a small bird."

"Ted, I can feel her," she whispered, wide eyed, running her hands across her middle. "I can feel her tiny wings inside me, beating against my heart."

This settled, she slipped peacefully back into sleep.

•

The examining room seemed smaller the next day, almost too small to hold the anticipation and nervous tension that bounced around its sterile boundaries. Georgie gripped Ted's hand as the nurse applied the cold, pink jelly to her stomach.

"Ted," she whispered, squeezing his hand. "I think I'm gonna pee my pants!"

Moments later Georgie's doctor appeared, wheeling a cart that held the ultrasound equipment, and Ted's excitement mounted. For Georgie the pregnancy had been real for weeks, since she felt the first stirrings of nausea and the tenderness in her breasts. Now it was his turn for a dose of reality.

The doctor flipped a switch and placed a small transducer on Georgie's stomach, slowly moving it back and forth. "It'll be just a minute, folks ... Here we are."

The monitor yawned and came to life, revealing a gray and black half moon, which he identified as Georgie's uterus. He pointed the end of a marker at the screen. "Here we can see the spinal column. Here the heart, nice and strong. The bladder ..."

Ted stared at the small gray blobs and tried to make them seem like a child.

"Doctor Ryan?" Georgie literally trembled with excitement. "Can you tell us what sex it is?"

"Hm. I'm afraid not. It's hard to tell with the legs drawn up like that." Ted studied the screen, trying to see legs in the blobs, feet and the beginnings of tiny toes. One blob in particular looked promising. It was darker than the rest, situated in the bottom corner of the half moon. He and the doctor seemed to notice it at the same moment.

"What's this?" he asked, pointing.

The doctor squinted at it. "I don't know." He stared at it for several moments, then abruptly turned to leave. "Sit tight."

As he left the room Georgie gave Ted a nervous smile and reached for his hand. They sat without speaking, watching the screen until Georgie's doctor returned, followed closely by a technician.

"... appears to be some sort of mass."

The technician introduced herself before turning her attention to the screen. She studied the images for a long moment.

"I think it would be wise to set up some tests."

A chill passed over Ted. "What tests?"

"A scan, to start. A biopsy, possibly a fetoscapy."

"Why? What's wrong?"

"Probably nothing. A swollen lymph node, a benign tumor, perhaps."

Ted tried to speak but could only manage a hoarse whisper. "A tumor?"

"It's probably nothing, Ted," Doctor Ryan said. "Let's run the tests before we worry." His words sounded hollow, and Ted couldn't help notice the worried looks that passed between him and the technician.

They didn't talk about the mass on the way home, or later that evening as they sat poring over the ultrasound pictures. They spoke instead of the spinal column, the bladder, the heart. Good and strong, hadn't Doctor Ryan said that? Both were careful to avoid the miniscule shadow in the corner, both terrified of its implications.

They didn't talk about the mass for five days, until once again they say face to face with Georgie's obstetrician.

"Ted. Georgiana." He sighed. "I'm afraid it's bad news. The biopsy showed the tumor to be malignant."

Every ounce of blood in Ted's body rushed to his head. "Cancer?" he croaked.

"I'm afraid so."

He clamped his hand down on Georgie's, struggling to choke back the bile that rose up his throat. "How is that possible? She's kept her checkups, there was never any sign of … of anything like this."

The doctor sighed again. "Sometimes, in rare cases, a pregnancy can bring cancer on. Hormone levels change, there's a shifting in the regular blood flow patterns. If a woman has any predisposition at all, a pregnancy can accelerate it."

Ted buried his face in his hands. "Oh, God."

"I'm sorry. I truly am."

No one spoke for a long moment, until Georgie's voice, strangely calm, broke through the silence. "What'll we do?"

The doctor hesitated. "The safest course of action would be to remove the tumor immediately."

"But what about the baby?"

"We'd have to abort the fetus."

"Then we'll hold off until after she's born."

"Your due date is five months from now."

"I'm aware of that."

"An awful lot can happen in five months, Georgiana. Changes in blood flow patterns could cause the cancer to spread."

Ted moaned as another wave of nausea hit.

"And besides," the doctor continued, "depending on how rapidly the tumor grows, we may not have the luxury of another twenty weeks. Frankly I don't know how long the two can coexist in the uterus."

Georgie stood. "We'll hold off."

Ted laid a hand on her arm. "Georgie."

"Ted, I'm ready to go."

The doctor gave Ted a sympathetic nod. "You'll want time to talk over your options."

Ted pushed the words past the lump thickening in his throat. "How soon could you do the ab—"

"Ted! I said I'm ready to go."

They drove home in silence. Ted stared at the road ahead, knowing by the defiant tilt of her chin that talking to Georgie now would get him nowhere. His mind chewed furiously on the possibilities, rationally and carefully trying to work out a solution. Every problem had a solution. It was just a matter of finding it.

At home, Georgie went to bed and stayed there until dinner time. That evening he found her in the nursery, painting faces on the teddy bears she'd stenciled above the crib. He stood in the doorway and watched her work, his heart breaking into a hundred jagged pieces.

"What are you doing Georgie?" he asked quietly.

She turned with a smile. "I wanted to finish this before I'm too big to reach."

He stepped into the room, took a breath, expelled it softly. "Georgie ..."

She turned back to her work. "Ted, don't."

"We need to talk about this. Ignoring it isn't going to make it go away."

Ignoring him, she painted a pink smile on a panda bear.

"I think we should go ahead and let them re—"

"No."

"Georgie, the cancer could spread. You heard what he said. In five months your whole body could be full of it."

"I don't care."

"You don't care?" He strode to where she stood and pulled her roughly into his arms. "I watched my mother die of cancer. I can't let it happen to you."

She stiffened against him. "We'll wait until after the baby is born."

He counted ten, resisting the urge to shake her. "By then it might be too late."

Seeing his own terror reflected in her eyes, he relaxed his grip and pulled her to his chest. "We can have another baby. Later. Maybe next year. Honey, I—"

She jerked free, eyes flashing. "How can you say that?"

"I'm only saying it wouldn't—"

"Now that you've heard her heartbeat and seen her little toes, how can you stand there and talk to me about another baby? Ted, there is no other baby!" She burst into tears, burying her face in his chest.

"Georgie, please." Blinking back his own tears, he stroked her hair. "Everything I have ... Everything I am, it's all about you. I can't lose you. I'd rather die."

"You won't lose me, Ted," she whispered against his chest. "It'll be all right. I promise."

As the weeks crawled past it became painfully obvious that it wasn't going to be all right. They'd gone for a second opinion, and then for a third. Each doctor and every test pointed to the same catastrophic ending.

Most days Georgie didn't have the strength to get out of bed, and when, for Ted's sake, she tried, she walked with an exhausted, shuffling gate, each step leaving her breathless. At the end of her second trimester she was admitted into the hospital. Ted stayed by her side, holding her hand and staring vacantly out the window. His business was falling apart, but he couldn't make himself care. Not when his entire life was vanishing before his eyes. He sat in the grim shadows of her impending death, watching her face grow paler with each new day, and knew he was losing the most beautiful thing he'd ever had...

He was twenty-one when he met Georgie. New in town, he was working as a shop clerk at his uncle's hardware store on South Main Street. Georgie was a girl of twelve, tagging along as her father ran errands on Saturday afternoons.

"The son I never had," he joked, affectionately patting her head.

Her fascination with tools had been an amusement to Ted, her blonde curls and sky blue eyes, an enchantment.

At fifteen she started coming by the store without her father, to say hello or to ask Ted's advice about boys, and he felt a subtle shift take place inside him.

At sixteen she became an obsession. Half girl, half woman, she was like poison ivy beneath his skin—a flower too delicate to pick, but too beautiful not to want. And so he waited. And while he waited, he planned. He built an empire from the basement up, his own construction company; its foundation, his reputation for excellence and integrity. Each drop of sweat that fell from his brow was mortar, each completed job, another brick in the framework of his dream.

That was the year the new expressway came through and Mt. Bishop began to die. People said he was crazy to start a business there. Every third building on Main Street was empty. The owners would sell them cheap, but nobody wanted to buy. Nobody except Ted Hanwell. He knew it would be a gamble, but to leave the garden would be to lose his chance at the exquisite flower that bloomed there and so he dug in his heels. Another day's work. Another drop of blood. Another contract. All ribbons on the gift he would one day lay at Georgie's feet ...

In her thirty-fifth week of pregnancy, Georgie's team of doctors decided to perform a C-section, and directly afterward, remove the tumor. On a blustery March morning Ted stood beside her bed and waited for them to come for her.

She gave him a wan smile. "It'll be all right."

"Of course it will."

A desperate prayer shrieked inside his head, a dog whistle wail that only he could hear. *Let her be strong enough for this. Let her make it through. Dear God, don't take her away from me.*

A nurse entered the room, her casual manner indicating that it was just another day, just another surgery. "Are you ready to go, Mrs. Hanwell?"

Georgie nodded.

"Nurse," Ted said. "I want to go in with her."

"No, I'm sorry. That's out of the question."

"Please." He heard himself begging, suddenly fearing that if he let Georgie go alone he'd never see her again.

"I'm sorry Mister Hanwell. Under the circumstances it wouldn't be wise."

He heard the firmness in her voice and knew that to insist would only upset his wife. He stood back, heart breaking, as the orderlies transferred Georgie to a gurney.

"Ted?" Georgie whispered.

"What, baby?"

"I love you. More than anything."

He pulled her close and whispered into her hair. "Oh, Georgie ..." His voice cracked and his throat ached with the effort of holding back tears. "I love you, too." It wasn't until he knelt, alone and broken in the small hospital chapel that he let his tears flow.

An hour later a nurse sought him out. He was deep in thought and her soft voice startled him. "Mr. Hanwell?"

He anxiously searched her face.

She smiled. "You've got a beautiful little girl out here."

He continued to stare, holding his breath while he waited for more information. When none was offered he gripped the back of the pew and asked, "How's my wife?"

"She'll be in surgery for awhile yet. Would you like to come and see your daughter?"

He followed her down the corridor, not hearing or comprehending her cheerful descriptions of the baby's birth weight and size. She led him to the nursery window and pointed to a small cubicle shrouded in plastic. "That's her."

He peered at the small pink body, bundled in a blanket and cap, and at the equipment that sustained her fragile life. "Is she all right?"

"She's fine. The equipment is precautionary. It simulates the warmth of the uterus. She's in a little cocoon of sorts."

"Oh."

"Would you like to go in and see her, maybe hold her hand? They say a baby thrives on touch."

When he'd washed with antibacterial soap, she gave him a sterile gown and guided him to the side of the cubicle. His hands shook as he placed them inside. He stared in wonder at the tiny fingers curled around his thumb, at the rose petal lips, so much like Georgie's. Her beauty was too much for him. Turning away, he blinked back tears.

It was eleven days before Georgie got to hold her child. She sat in her hospital bed, propped up with pillows and surrounded by a tangle of tubes and monitors. As she cradled the baby to her breast, Ted caught his first glimpse in weeks of the woman he loved. His Georgie, with sparkling blue eyes and a radiant smile. He sat by, silent, knowing the moment was as sacred as life itself. Finally Georgie tore her gaze from her child.

"Isn't she beautiful, Ted?"

He managed a smile. "Just like her mother."

She tried to sing a lullaby and succumbed to a fit of ragged coughing. Ted moved quickly to her side. "Are you all right, baby?"

She drew a long, rattling breath. "I'm fine."

He willed the words to be true, though he knew in his heart they weren't. The tumor had been successfully removed but as predicted, the cancer had spread and now ran rampant throughout her body, sucking her life away, one whispered breath at a time.

He laid a gentle finger across his daughter's cheek and looked back into Georgie's eyes. "Jenna, then?"

"No."

"No?"

"Hope, Ted. I want to call her Hope."

By the end of April, when the alliums and the purple hyacinth burst into color beneath her window, Georgie was too weak to lift her head from the pillow. Ted sat beside her and listened to the labored sound of her breathing, knowing their time together was almost spent. Opening her eyes, she spoke his name. He reached over and pushed her few remaining strands of hair from her face. "What, love?"

"I want to talk to you about Hope."

"All right."

"Dana—" She tried to sit and surrendered to a fit of coughing.

"Lay back, sweetheart."

She collapsed into her pillows, her face damp with sweat. After a long moment she spoke again. "Dana wants to help. She said she and Jared would come and stay at the house for awhile, take care of the baby while you put the business back together."

He sighed. He hadn't known Georgie was aware of how bad things had gotten. He was down to two crews with barely enough work to keep them busy. "Georgie, let's not talk about—"

"Ted." She mustered a small measure of firmness. "It would be just for a little while. Just until I'm better."

The tears that were never very far away threatened and he turned his face from her.

"Hope's ready to be released. It would help me a lot to know that the two of you were being taken care of." When he didn't answer she continued, "Dana is a good person, Ted. Strong, like you."

"Oh, Georgie ..." His voice cracked with the effort of holding back the words he ached to say. *Baby, and I'm scared. I can't do this.*

"Ted, I'm so scared."

He wrapped his arms around her. "Me too, baby."

Clinging to each other, they wept without shame for a lifetime of dreams that would never be fulfilled.

Chapter Two
April, 1985

Ted felt like he was spinning his wheels and getting buried in the mud. He sat in his office, trying to bring order to the chaos of payroll sheets and new tax regulations strewn across his desk. He opened an invoice from Jansen's, wincing when he saw the cost of the materials for the motel job in Conway. He'd low-balled in order to get the bid. A huge mistake. The job seemed cursed from day one and after paying his men he'd be lucky to break even.

Setting the statement aside, he rubbed his tired, aching eyes. Opening them again, he focused on a silver-framed photo of Georgie, suntanned and smiling on a wind-swept beach. Georgie. God. Had it only been a year? It seemed an eternity since he'd held her, a lifetime since they'd snuggled together in their bed, whispering late into the night. It was the little things he missed the most.

The thoughts were painful and he firmly pushed them away, concentrating instead on his paperwork. At least he wasn't operating in the red anymore. Thank God for that.

He became aware of a dull aching sensation in his stomach and idly wondered how much time had passed since Dana poked her head in and told him dinner was ready. An hour? Two? The house had grown quiet and he listened intently to the absence of sound. Some time ago he'd heard running water. That would have been seven thirty. He could set his watch by Dana's routine. The children were bathed at seven-thirty, had stories and prayers at eight, and were in bed, lights out, at eight-thirty sharp.

He heard a soft knock before the door opened and Dana stepped into the room. "I brought you a plate."

He looked at the steaming slices of beef, the potatoes smothered in gravy, and fleetingly wondered how such different women could have sprung from the same gene pool. Georgie had been hard put to scramble an egg, whereas Dana turned out these nightly masterpieces seemingly without effort. "Thank you, Dana."

She set the plate before him and lingered, like she had a speech to make and was rehearsing her lines. Uncomfortable, he scoured his mind for a conversation piece. "Are the kids in bed?"

"Yes, but I doubt Hope will sleep. She's lost the moon."

"Oh dear."

Dana referred to the tattered yellow doll his daughter slept with. A gift from the hospital nursery staff, she'd never passed a night without it.

"Ted? Maybe you could look in on her later, if you're not too busy."

He heard a subtle note of reproach in her voice and bristled. Though she never said as much, Ted knew Dana didn't approve of his parenting skills. Or rather, his sorry lack of them. She thought he spent too much time on business and not enough on his daughter. Her disapproval troubled and irritated him. Damn it all, he was doing the best he could. Did she think it was easy operating a business in this dried-up excuse for a town? Keeping his anger in check, he stood. "Of course."

"After you've had your dinner, I meant." She turned to leave, adding softly, "It's after eight. You must be famished."

Later, as he headed down the hallway to Hope's nursery, he paused to look in on his nephew. Jared lay sound asleep, his body curled into a fetal position. He looked small and vulnerable and Ted felt an unwelcome twinge of guilt. It couldn't be easy for him, not having a father.

He thought of the way Jared's eyes followed him around a room, studying his every move. How he'd returned from the store with Dana the day before with a new ball and shown it to Ted, his eyes asking the question his lips hadn't had the courage to form. Play with me? But there were phone calls to make, jobs to set up …

Turning to leave, Ted caught sight of a hump beneath the quilt, a fuzzy yellow hand peeking out from the corner of the bed. He pulled back the blankets to reveal Hope's moon.

He looked questioningly into Jared's sleeping face. Surely at five years old the boy was beyond the need to sleep with a stuffed doll. Had he hidden it there to torment his baby cousin or had there been another reason? He held the doll in his hands, running his fingers over its worn surface as he contemplated the small act of cruelty.

When he reached her room, Hope was asleep. He laid the doll beside her and lightly touched her baby white curls. It was the greatest paradox he knew of. Hope was his biggest source of joy and his deepest source of pain.

When he returned to his office Dana was waiting for him. She rose from the futon when he entered and Ted again got the uncomfortable feeling she had something on her mind. He hoped she wouldn't make an issue of the lack of time he spent with his daughter. He wasn't up to defending himself that night.

"Ted, there's something I've been wanting to talk over with you." She gestured toward the open ledger on his desk. "If you're not too busy."

Damn. She was going to call him out. He reached for his coffee cup and took a lukewarm swallow. All right. He'd let her have her say.

"Not at all. What's on your mind?"

She picked up his paperweight and studied it before setting it back on the desk. "I got word last week that my renters are moving out at the end of the month. I'm considering going home."

He sank woodenly into his chair. It was the last thing he expected her to say. He thought the arrangement was working out, hadn't even considered the possibility she might want to return to her own home.

"Of course, Dana. If that's what you want to do."

He took a long, hard look at her, noticing the tiny lines around her eyes, the beginnings of silver in her hair. She was thirty-four, the same as him. What was the matter with him? He should have known the arrangement wouldn't be permanent, that sooner or later she'd want real male companionship, a chance to find a father for her child.

As if reading his thoughts, her cheeks reddened. Her gaze rested for a moment on Georgie's photo, then dropped to the floor. "I don't know whether you've been aware ... People in town are starting to talk."

He saw the flags of color on her cheeks deepen to crimson and suddenly he understood.

"I don't care so much for myself, but Jared will be starting school in the fall. I'm afraid of what he might hear. I've tried to raise him with certain standards ..." Her voice trailed away.

"I'm sorry, Dana. I didn't know."

"It'll be hard for the children. They think of each other as brother and sister."

He sighed. "Yes, I guess they do."

"I've been giving it a lot of thought, and—" She pulled in a breath and then her words came out in a rush. "Ted, I'd like to adopt Hope."

His coffee leapt over the side of his cup and splashed across his ledger. "What?"

"You're a busy man. A little girl needs certain things, certain training."

The words brought him to his feet. "Absolutely not."

"You could see her whenever you wanted to," she added hastily. "I'd never try to keep her from you."

He fought a losing battle with his anger. Who was she to sit in judgment over him, to so generously offer to train his daughter like a circus pony? "The answer is no," he said, struggling to keep his voice even.

"I'm not implying any negligence on your part, Ted. I know how hard it is for you. I thought it might make things less complicated if I were to—"

"What part of no is it that you don't understand, Dana?" he thundered.

Time seemed suspended. When he continued to glare at her, she drew herself up. "Fine. The Stillsons won't be moving out until the first. I'll stay until then, if that's alright." Without waiting for a response she turned and marched from the room.

For the rest of the evening and the entire day that followed Ted thought about her proposal. Maybe she was right. What did he know about taking care of a little girl, about her needs and what it would take to guide her into womanhood? He was the first to admit his ignorance, still ... He loved his daughter more than life. She was all he had left of Georgie, the only tangible evidence that remained of their love. But how could he run a demanding business and raise a toddler single-handedly?

The thought filled him with dismay. His mind wound slowly down the avenues of possibility, searching for a solution. What could he say? What could he do to make Dana want to stay?

In the end there was only one solution and Ted knew it. For three days he wrestled with the idea. On the fourth day his decision was made. For better or worse. That evening he walked purposefully down the hallway to Dana's room. Seeing the soft pool of light beneath her door, he raised his hand. It hovered in mid air. *Georgie ... forgive me.*

He pulled in a breath and knocked.

Soft footsteps approached the door, and then it opened and he and Dana were face to face. He'd never visited her room before, and her eyes betrayed her surprise. "Ted?"

"Can I come in for a minute, Dana?"

She clutched her terrycloth bathrobe close around her and stood aside to let him enter. Once inside, he did a double take. He hadn't been in the room since it was Georgie's home gym. Now it looked more like an upscale hotel room. Where there had once been rubber mats he now saw pastel throw rugs, and where heavy nautilus equipment had stood there was a brass bed and a velvet slipper chair. A cherry cabinet held fussy vases and fluted candlesticks of sparkling crystal.

"What can I do for you, Ted?"

He faced her, shoulders squared in determination. "I've been thinking about what you said."

Her eyes bore into his face. Only the tight clasping and unclasping of her hands on the throat of her robe betrayed her nervousness.

He cleared his throat. "I've been trying to decide on the best course of action. For all of us."

"And?"

"I—" The words stuck in his throat. He took a breath and forced them out. "I thought that maybe we—you and I, that is ... could—" He cleared his throat again. "Dana, would you consider marriage?"

Shock registered on her face before she looked away.

"I'd adopt Jared, of course. Raise him as my own son. If that's agreeable to you."

It seemed like a lifetime before she spoke, and when she finally did, her words were a whisper. "It's agreeable."

He thought with irony how different a proposal it was from the urgent plea he'd offered her sister.

"All right, then. Do you want to make the arrangements or should I?"

She met his gaze briefly before looking away. "I'll make them."

"Good." He shifted in his shoes. "Just let me know."

He lay in his bed later and thought how Georgie would have laughed. How she would have lay beside him, shaking with giggles at the thought of something so outrageous. He and Dana.

"God help me," he muttered.

He rolled onto his side, neither amused nor repulsed. It didn't matter either way whether he stayed single or married. In his heart he would never belong to anyone but Georgie.

He and Dana were married on the second Saturday in August in a simple ceremony at the Mt. Bishop town hall. Dana wore a plain ecru gown and carried the spray of roses Ted bought at the Village Florist's. He stood beside her, sweating beneath his sports coat while he mechanically recited vows he was too numb to feel. Loving and cherishing another woman were no longer an option, but he would do his best to honor her and make a decent life for her and her son.

That night she inconspicuously moved her things into his bedroom. He lay beside her in the darkness, sickness swirling in his gut, knowing she expected him to consummate the marriage and he couldn't.

For the next two weeks they lived a strained, polite existence. She prepared his favorite meals, took care to iron the wrinkles from his work shirts, and had fresh pots of coffee waiting for him every morning when he awoke. She spoke to him with courtesy and respect, and not once did she look him in the eye. Ted sensed her disappointment and couldn't blame her for it. He felt like a failure and he knew that marrying her had been a terrible mistake. His days became something he merely tolerated, and his nights, something to dread.

On the first of September he had the dream again.

Georgie, or a vaporous, white-shrouded apparition of her, stood just outside his reach, enveloped in a thick blanket of fog. He walked toward her, unable to see her face but knowing her instinctively. His heart pounded as he walked closer. With trembling hands he reached for the veil that covered her face and pulled it away. She was radiant.

Georgie. He reached for her. *Oh Georgie, how I've missed you.*

As always, she vanished the moment he spoke her name.

He lay inert, drenched in sweat and sorrow, moaning her name. Through his pain, he heard the sound of gentle words whispered against his ear and felt the comfort of warm arms wrapping his body. Desperate for the solace they offered, he moved into their circle and stayed there the entire night.

When he went down to breakfast in the morning Dana wouldn't meet his eyes. They were awkward together, focusing their attention on the children. He watched as she poured Jared's milk, as she cut up Hope's eggs, and thought how unfair life had been to them all.

Finally she came to his side, her hand brushing his shoulder as she refilled his coffee cup. He felt a distant, unmistakable yearning and quickly opened his newspaper. "I see the circus is coming to town this weekend," he said. "Maybe we could go on Saturday."

He looked up to see every eye at the table focused on him.

"But Saturday's a working day," Jared said.

Ted smiled. "I don't think the world would come to an end if I took one Saturday off, do you?"

The boy beamed. Ted saw the look of pleased surprise that passed across Dana's face and knew he had a lot of catching up to do.

•

It was nearly ten o'clock when he got home from work that night. The job hadn't gone well and he'd stayed to oversee the finishing work himself. Dana was in bed reading, and slid her book beneath the pillow when he came into the room.

"Are you hungry?" she asked, pushing back the blankets. "I'll go and warm your plate."

"No, sit still. I grabbed a sandwich at the diner."

She tucked the blankets back around her. He sat on the edge of the bed and pulled off his shirt, and then his pants. He felt her eyes on him and was suddenly as embarrassed as a freshman in the gym locker room. When he slid beneath the sheets, she reached for the lamp switch.

"You can keep reading, Dana. The light won't bother me."

"No, it's all right. I don't want to read any more tonight."

He lay beside her in the glow of the street lamps, studying the outline of her cheek and remembering how good her arms felt around him. The memory awakened a desire he'd thought dead and buried. Slowly, cautiously, he reached across the space between them.

Her body was pleasantly round, her skin warm and smooth beneath his hands. He brought his lips to hers in a gentle kiss. Sensing her hesitation, he opened his eyes and gazed into hers.

"Ted," she whispered. "I know I can never be what she was to you."

He laid his fingers across her lips. "Shh."

He closed his eyes and kissed her again. And then slowly, tenderly, and like a virgin, he made love to her.

Chapter Three
August, 1988

"You stupid little bastard! How many times have I told y'all not to play with the goddamned stove?"

"I wasn't playin', Mama. I was just—"

"Give me that." Yanking the worn dish cloth from his hands, she slapped at the hazy air until the smoke detector ceased its shrieking. She grabbed the handle of the red hot fry pan and howled in pain as an angry red welt appeared on her hand. As the pan clattered into the sink, she turned to glare at him, her eyes still swollen with sleep.

"Look at this goddamned mess!"

Gray stared at the cracked linoleum beneath his bare toes, wishing she'd hit him and be done with it. He could bear anything except Mama's anger.

"Think I don't have anything better to do than clean up after you?"

He lifted his gaze to the sink, where the fry pan hissed angrily beneath the leaky faucet. On the counter beside the stove lay a charcoaled lump of bread and melted cheese, his failed attempt at supper. He'd seen Joe Diamond, the cook at the diner, make the sandwiches a hundred times. He thought he knew how to do it.

"Look at you," she said in a harsh whisper. He saw the familiar look of hatred come into her eyes and couldn't bear it. He flinched when he felt her cold hand on his chin, jerking it upward to meet her icy gaze. "You're just like him, aren't you? You've got his eyes, stone cold gray. The same color as his soul."

"I'm sorry, Mama."

"I could have done better, you hear me? I deserved a hell of a lot more than this."

"I'm sorry, Mama."

"I'm sorry, Mama," she mocked. "Get out of my sight. I can't stand to look at you." Yanking him by the arm, she dragged him from the kitchen and pushed him out the front door. He heard it slam behind him, and then the sliding of the deadbolt, and sank down on the stoop, wondering how long Mama would stay angry this time.

Shadows fell, and then darkness. Children deserted the broken sidewalks and the fancy ladies in short skirts and high heeled sandals took up their positions on the corner of Fox and McAdams Streets as Dragonfly Court put on its nighttime face.

Across the river, the Dragonfly Hotel sat like an angry god, casting its long, dark shadow over the grimy housing project. Gray watched as the hotel emblem flickered to life; a red and silver dragonfly, its barbed tail poised to strike. He shivered in the humid Alabama air.

Mama had forgotten about him, must be. His stomach ached with hunger and he had to go to the bathroom, but he dared not knock on the door and reawaken Mama's fury. Pressing his ear to the window, he listened intently to the silence. It'll be all right, he told himself. The emblem was lit. Mama would soon be going to work.

His gaze once again traveled to the old hotel where his mother worked the night shift as a call girl. His friend Jody said that made his mama a whore. He said call girl like it was something lowdown and dirty, but Gray couldn't see the shame in it. He pictured his mama sitting behind the big desk in the lobby, answering the telephone and writing down reservations. It seemed to Gray that was at least as respectable as emptying wastebaskets and scrubbing toilets, like Jody's mama did down at the Super Seven.

He held his water until it hurt, then walked quickly toward Ho Chan's Chinese Buffet. Barefoot, he was careful to avoid the broken glass and rat turds that littered the alley. Outside the back door of Ho Chan's there was a big, red overflowing dumpster. Gray stepped behind it and lowered his zipper.

When he'd finished peeing he walked to the corner to investigate the pay phone where he and Jody once found two dollars in change. Maybe he'd get lucky again and find enough to buy an egg roll at

Ho Chan's. His footsteps stopped short, all thoughts of egg rolls fleeing, when he spied a dead cat in gutter. It was spooky black, its mouth open to reveal two rows of tiny fangs, as if it had died in the heat of battle. Fascinated, he poked at it with a stick. "Not so mean now, are ya boy?"

Hearing approaching footsteps, he ducked into the doorway of an abandoned dry cleaner's, watching, wide-eyed, as a drunk ambled past. He counted twenty, then sprinted back up the alley toward home.

The sound of low, female voices carried to him from the corner. Glancing over, he saw the silhouettes of the fancy ladies, the tips of their cigarettes glowing red in the dark.

"Gray Baldwin, is that you?"

Recognizing Wynetta's voice, he strode toward her. He liked Wynetta, liked the soft brown color of her skin and the deep, musical sound of her laughter. Of all the fancy ladies, she was his favorite.

"Hey Miz Wynetta," he said shyly.

"Boy, what are y'all doin' out here so late?"

He shrugged.

"Where's your mama?"

"She's home."

Reaching in her pocket, she produced a pack of bubble gum. She removed a square and handed it to him. "Be a good boy and go on home now. This ain't a safe place for a little boy at night."

Savoring the gum's sticky sweetness, he trudged homeward. When he reached the apartment he saw Mama on the stoop and his heart leapt.

"Mama?" he bleated. "Were y'all looking for me?"

"Well, there's my baby. What are y'all doin' out here?" Her voice was soft and far away and as she gathered him up in a hug she smelled her sweet scents of perfume and whiskey and he knew she loved him again.

What seemed all too soon she planted a kiss on his forehead and pushed him away. "Be a good boy now and go inside. Mama has to go to work."

"Okay."

"Don't let anyone in, you hear?"

"I won't, Mama," he promised, but she was already gone from

him, walking across the alley, black dress swaying and silver heels clicking as she went.

Gray watched TV until his eyes felt heavy. Curled up on the pull-out sofa, he drifted off to sleep until the sound of canned laughter blended with sirens and urgent screams in the alley outside, jarring him awake. Blue and red lights strobed across the paneled walls and he sleepily went to the window and peered out.

The police cars and rescue vehicles in front of the hotel filled him with a vague uneasiness. He didn't like cops. Cops were bad people, mean. Mama told him time and time again if he saw one to look the other way. Cops would lock a person up for no good reason and throw away the key, like they'd done to his daddy.

Out in the street he saw a blue-clad cop talking with Jade Parma, the hotel owner. Jade gestured wildly, shaking her head as she pointed to his apartment building. Turning, the cop looked in his direction and an ice cold chill shuddered through Gray's body. Snapping off the lights, he raced to his hiding place in the back of Mama's closet. Stumbling over shoes and purses, he parted hangers filled with dresses and burrowed far into a back corner.

He heard the sound of thunderous pounding on the front door before it splintered open. He sucked in a breath when heavy footsteps entered the apartment.

"Gray Baldwin? Where you at, boy?"

His heart pounded ferociously as he squeezed himself farther back into the dark.

"Gotta be here somewhere," a deep voice said. "Gray Baldwin? Come on out!"

Room by room, he heard them searching for him. Within moments the light snapped on and Gray saw the cop from the alley enter mama's bedroom. Through the broken slats in the closet door he saw blue-clad legs and a holstered gun. He squeezed his eyes shut against his sudden terror.

"Gotta be in here somewhere," the cop said. "We've looked everywhere else. Christ, would you look at this shit hole."

The cop opened mama's secret drawer and rifled through it, upsetting her underthings. Gray winced, knowing how mad his mama was going to be. She'd made him swear never to open that drawer, never even to look at it. He watched as a meaty hand pulled out mama's cigarettes, her pipes and baggies. He watched, astonished, as the hand removed a large roll of money and shoved it into a blue pocket. His breath rushed out of him, despite himself. He'd never known his mama was rich.

Without warning the closet door burst open.

"Gray? I know y'all are in there, boy. There's no use tryin' to hide. Come on out now."

As the cop pawed through mama's clothes, Gray's mind raced with plans for escape. If he could make it past the cop and out the back door he could disappear into the alley and wait until mama came to find him.

With this thought firmly in mind, he sprang from his hiding place and bolted out the door. Halfway across the room the other cop intercepted him.

"Woah there, little man. What's your hurry?"

Finding himself wrapped in a pair of colossal arms, Gray shrieked with rage. Turning his head, he sank his teeth into one of the oversized biceps. Shouting obscenities, the cop threw him to the floor and slapped a pair of handcuffs on him.

"You're cuffin' him? Little bit of a thing like that?" the other cop asked.

"The little prick bit me. Lookit this. I'm bleedin'."

The cop propelled him through the apartment and shoved him into the back of the police car.

"You're gonna be sorry," Gray shrieked. "You never shoulda took my mama's money."

"You keep your mouth shut."

"She's gonna be madder than hell."

"Listen here," the cop said, his face inches from Gray's. "I didn't take nobody's money, and even if I did, your mama ain't gonna do a damned thing about it. She's down at the county coroner's office, dead as a doornail."

Gray stared at the man in shocked silence, trying to picture his pretty mama grotesque and bloated like the cat in the gutter beside the dumpster. It was a lie. It had to be. Hot tears sprang to his eyes and he blinked them back.

At the police station, an old, gray-haired cop with a shaggy white beard insisted they remove the handcuffs. He gave Gray a bottle of soda and a stale doughnut and sent him to a lumpy sofa in the corner to wait.

Gray stared at the barred windows and at the Wanted posters that lined the walls, and tried to fathom what he'd done wrong. He thought of asking the old cop, who sat at a battered desk, eating a doughnut with one hand while he pecked at the keys of a typewriter with the other. But Gray had learned early on that when in trouble it was best to say nothing at all.

The heat of the room, coupled with the late hour and the hypnotic clacking of typewriter keys made him sleepy and he felt his eyelids droop.

The morning sun had just begun to streak the sky outside the window when an old woman hobbled into the station. Through half-closed lids, Gray studied her plum body and kindly face as she and the cop spoke in low, murmuring voices.

"Gladdy, I was hoping it'd be you they sent. Thanks for coming."

"Glad to do it, Will. Is this him?"

"That's him. A real wildcat. Ain't but eight years old. Scratched the dickens out of Ben Jamison's face when he was tryin' to bring him in."

"He was afraid, I'm sure, a big man like Ben coming at him. His mama's dead, then?"

For the second time, Gray was overcome by a wave of shock. He struggled to block out their whispered voices.

"Drug lords came down … Dragonfly Hotel … Shot her dead. Just a case of the wrong place at the wrong time."

"Oh, the poor, sweet babe. Does he know?"

"Actually I was hoping, I'm not good with kids and, well, I was kind of hoping you'd break it to him, Gladdy."

Gray heard shuffling footsteps and then felt a warm, rose-scented hand on his forehead. "Gray? Can you wake up, child?"

The kindness in her voice seemed genuine and he desperately wanted to respond, but couldn't. He was paralyzed, overwhelmed with fear and grief and so he lay beneath the scratchy blanket, eyes sealed tight against the world as mama's words whispered inside his head.

"Stupid bastard. Stupid little boy …"

Chapter Four
June, 1989

Gladdy Parker awoke at 6:45 on the morning of her seventieth birthday. She lay in bed until 7:00, allowing herself the luxury of an extra fifteen minutes to celebrate that she'd cheated death out of another three-hundred, sixty-five days. Her sixty-ninth year had been a good one, all things considered.

She heard the crunch of tires in the driveway and soon after that, the steady clink-clink sound of metal tapping metal. Pushing herself to the side of the bed, she lifted a corner of the curtain and watched, kneading the swollen stiffness from her hands. Clink-clink. Clink-clink. When she could no longer bear it she let the curtain slip back into place. She knew two things for certain on that mild June morning. One, that the arthritis would be the end of her. And two, that Gray Baldwin was not going to understand the perky red For Sale sign at the end of the driveway.

Easing her aching limbs over the side of the bed, she winced at the stabbing pain in her knees. With pained but determined steps she inched down the hallway, stopping outside the boy's bedroom door. When she poked her head in, Garvey, her aged golden retriever, glanced up from his place at the foot of the bed and wagged his tail. Gladdy pressed a solemn finger to her lips and the dog laid his head back down on the boy's feet. Her glance moved tenderly over the sleeping child. Nothing in her thirty-six years of providing foster care had prepared her for the ferocity with which she loved him.

He stirred and rolled onto his side, then sank quietly back into sleep. Gladdy closed the door and resumed her slow journey to the kitchen. As she clung to the banister, her fingers lovingly traced the smooth spots where the varnish had worn thin over the years by more than fifty pairs of little hands. She shook her head. Thirty-six years. If only she could buy a few of them back for Gray's sake.

An hour later she looked up from the stove to see him standing in the doorway. Startled, she nearly dropped the plate of hash browns she'd prepared. "Goodness, Child. You move as quietly as a cat. Sit down, now. I've got our breakfast ready."

He shoved his chair back from the table and sat. Gladdy hurried through her morning prayers. Gray was more robust and a good ten pounds heavier than he'd been the year before, still … She watched as he shoveled a forkful of sausage into his mouth. The boy had a hunger inside him and she doubted whether all of the kettle cakes in Alabama could have filled it. A pang of sadness overtook her. She would have given anything to spare him what was coming. Better to get it over and done with, she told herself.

"Gray, darlin'?"

He glanced up expectantly and Gladdy averted her gaze. Lord, this is not going to be easy. "I've got something' I've been meanin' to talk over with you."

He swallowed a mouthful of sausage. "Yes, Ma'am?"

The abrupt jingling of the phone spared her. She moved across the room to answer it and moments later settled into a conversation with Patsy Taylor, the minister's wife. Gray finished his breakfast, cleared the plates from the table, and stacked them in the sink. He hesitated in the doorway for a moment, then gathered up his egg basket and went outside.

Gladdy hobbled to the window and watched as he trudged across the yard, Garvey close at his heels, as he carried a bucket of meal to the handful of chickens that still inhabited the henhouse.

Her gaze traveled to the pond where a lone pair of geese sailed across its rippled surface. She could almost hear the shrieks of laughter, almost see, if she squinted, the shadows of the children who used to play on the old tire swing. Lord, but she was going to miss this place …

•

When he'd fed and watered the chickens, Gray retrieved his egg basket from beside the door and reentered the chicken coop.

"All right, boy," he said to the dog. "Let's try and get this over with quick so we can go swimmin'. I'm hotter than hell, aren't you?"

The dog answered with a wag of his tail and followed Gray inside.

He shooed the chickens from their little boxes, laughing when they tried to peck his hands. He'd been afraid of them at first, but Gladdy showed him early on how to get the eggs, how to show them who was boss. He wiped the sweat from his face with his sleeve, thinking how good the cool water would feel. He still couldn't believe he had his very own swimming hole. Truth was, he couldn't believe a lot of things, but that didn't make them any less true.

He knew the farm was only twelve miles outside the city, but his new life with Gladdy seemed a million miles away from the one he'd shared with Mama at Dragonfly Court. Mama …

He closed his eyes and pictured her pretty blonde hair, her red mouth. The tearing pain of months ago was now a dull ache. The truth was he liked Gladdy better than his mama. He liked sitting down at the supper table to fried chicken, or honey glazed ham, instead of canned ravioli or nothing at all. He liked having a regular bedtime, and had even gotten used to not having a television. He'd come to look forward to evenings, when Gladdy would read to him from *Swiss Family Robinson* or *Moby Dick*.

He'd come to the farm not even knowing his alphabet. Mama never cared if he went to school or not, so he usually didn't. Gladdy taught him to read and it opened a whole new world to him. She also took him to the big whitewashed church on Sunday mornings and taught him how to pray. He liked listening to Pastor Taylor's sermons about the depth and breadth and height of God's love. Mama's version of God was some sort of big, cosmic cop. Better to stay out of His way, Mama said, and hope He didn't take no notice of you.

Swinging his basket of eggs, he headed back toward the house, stopping when he noticed the sign at the end of the driveway: For Sale. He stared at it in disbelief. "It's gotta be a mistake," he whispered.

Hurrying to the house, he noticed a shiny blue car in Gladdy's driveway. A man and woman wearing good, Sunday clothes stood at the edge of Gladdy's vegetable garden. He raced past them and onto the porch, banging through the front door. "Gladdy! Gladdy!"

Gladdy hobbled to the living room, wiping her hands on a dishcloth. "What is it, Child? What's wrong?"

"There's a sign out by the road, a For Sale sign."

He studied her face, waiting for a puzzled expression to appear, for her to confirm there'd been a mistake. Before she could answer there was a sharp rapping on the door and she limped across the room and opened it.

"Yes?"

"Sorry to bother y'all, Ma'am," the man from the garden said. "I'm Ron Robinson, this here's my wife, Sweetie. We was drivin' by and couldn't help noticing' the sign out front. We've been lookin' to buy a farm and this place looks like just what we've been wantin'."

Gray stared at him, going numb.

"Sweetie here was wonderin' if it would be all right if we came in and had a look around?"

"We're not sellin' our house!" Gray yelled. "We're not, are we, Gladdy?"

"Hush, Child."

He couldn't bear Gladdy's words, or the sternness in her voice. His stomach started to churn as fear slithered through his insides. Dropping his egg basket, he raced out the door and across the yard, not stopping until he reached his favorite hiding place in the woods.

It was almost dark when Gray finally returned to the house. Gladdy warmed his dinner plate and sat in the living room, reading her Bible and trying to gather her thoughts while ate. After he'd had his bath, she joined him in his room to listen to his prayers. It wasn't until he'd settled into bed that she finally spoke. "Gray, I know y'all must be wonderin' about what happened today."

"Who were they, Gladdy? Are they gonna take our house away?"

She took a breath and slowly released it. "They're going to buy it, Gray. They're looking for a place to raise their family. It warms me to think this old house will have a family again."

He stared at her with his beautiful gray eyes, drinking in her words, trying to understand. "The truth is I'm gettin' old, Gray. I just can't keep up with this house any more. It's time for me to let it go. Can you understand that?"

"I'll help you, Gladdy," he said in a rush. "You don't have to sell it."

She saw the stricken look in his eyes and it caused an aching deep inside her. She'd never intended to keep him this long. Lord knew she had enough on her plate with her body deteriorating like it was, and she, barely a year into widowhood. It was high time she let someone look after her, or so Margo said, and Gladdy had just begun to let herself believe it.

But then a call came in one late August night; a boy needing help. It was only for a day or two, the County reassured her, a couple of weeks at most. But the department of Social Services had been hard put to find a placement for him. Sad as it was, there just weren't many families willing to take in a small boy with a tainted past. Unless you counted the places that were no more than work farms, their charges no more than unpaid laborers.

When Freida Farley contacted her in September with a possible placement, Gladdy had been anything but relieved. She knew the boy was too fragile. A sapling bent under a weight of sorrow too heavy for him, she knew that to uproot him again so soon would be to break him. Who better to school and nurture the child, she argued, who better to bring him up to his potential than she? And the overburdened system had been all too willing to leave him in Gladdy's capable hands. But now her recalcitrant hands betrayed her, betrayed them both.

She pulled him close and hugged him, savoring the joy he brought her old heart, wishing there was another way. "Go to sleep, Child. We'll talk about it in the mornin."

With Gray safely tucked into bed, Gladdy hobbled to the living room to return Margo's phone call. As they talked about her upcoming move to Margo's townhouse in Birmingham, Gladdy tried to make it seem real.

"Are you sure the Robinson's will wait till the first of the month?" Margo asked.

"They'll have to. I've made it a contingency."

"Will you be all right until then, Mama?"

Gladdy smiled, warmed by Margo's use of the word. Margo was her first foster child and what Gladdy had not received in monetary recompense, all those years ago, she'd been given back a hundredfold in loyalty.

"I'll be just fine, darlin."

Margo's voice brimmed with excitement. "We've got your room all ready. I was going to save it for a surprise, but I just can't wait to tell you. Tom's built on a little Florida room. If y'all didn't know better, you'd think you were back in the country."

Feeling a pang of loneliness for the farm, Gladdy forced the words past the lump in her throat. "Well that's just wonderful, Margo. I can't wait to see it."

"I'm awful sorry about Gray. I wish we had room for both of you."

"Gray will be fine," she said with a confidence she didn't feel. "It's time he was around other children his own age."

"You've done more than your share, Mama. You can't be a mother to the whole world."

"No," she repeated softly. "I can't be a mother to the whole world."

With her face to the window, and her ear intent on her conversation, Gladdy was unaware of the small shadow that crept silently back up the staircase.

•

On the last night in June Gladdy threw a small celebration. She baked Gray's favorite cake and decorated it with all of the letters of the alphabet. Garvey sat at the table beside Gray, lapping milk from a cereal bowl, his one good eye fixed on Gladdy in anxious disbelief. She patted his head, trying not to think about the fate that awaited her dear, old friend, come morning.

Later she followed Gray to his room and sat at the end of his bed while he recited his prayers. When he'd finished she placed a small, clumsily-wrapped package in his hands. "I got you a little somethin', Gray. I hope y'all will keep it with you in life as a reminder of our time together."

He loosened the wrapping and opened the box, then removed the shiny silver cross and held it in his hand. "Thank you, Gladdy."

He held it for a long moment, running his fingers over the smooth metal before slipping the chain around his neck.

"One thing y'all will always have with you, Gray, no matter where this ol' life takes you, and that's the love of Jesus. Try to remember that, all right?"

"Yes, Ma'am."

"A man of many friends comes to ruin, but there is a friend that sticks closer than a brother. The book of Proverbs, chapter eighteen and verse twenty-four." She drew him to her, so close she could almost feel the breaking of his heart. "Y'all are a good boy, Gray Baldwin."

"Yes, Ma'am," he whispered.

"Some day you'll be a real good man. Jesus loves you, Gray. So much."

He held the cross in his hand as the words echoed inside his head. For Gladdy's sake, he tried to believe them.

•

He didn't cling to her, nor did he cry or throw a tantrum when it was time for him to go. He stood beside her on the porch, gripping Garvey's collar as the dark sedan crept slowly down the driveway. His anxiety was betrayed only by his sharp intake of breath. Gladdy placed a reassuring hand on his shoulder as they waited.

The social worker stepped from the car, already rumpled and tired despite the early hour. "Mornin', Gladdy."

"Good mornin', Freida."

"This him, then?"

Gladdy's hand tightened protectively on his shoulder. "Yes, this is Gray."

Her eyes swept over him appraisingly. "Ready?"

He turned to Gladdy only once and she knew the silent, heart wrenching plea in his eyes would haut her for the rest of her days. She bent to kiss his cheek and took a small measure of comfort in the sight of the silver chain glinting beneath his collar. "I love you, boy," she whispered.

"G'bye, Gladdy."

He gave Garvey a last, fervent hug and stepped from the porch. Gladdy watched as he climbed into the passenger seat of the waiting sedan. He turned his face away from her, but not before she saw his tears, the damp brown smudge left on his cheek as he wiped them away.

That night when she was alone and the house was darker and quieter than ever she could remember, Gladdy Parker forced herself to her knees beside his bed and whispered a prayer for the boy who was nobody's child.

Chapter Five
November, 1993

Hope clung to the waistband of her father's jacket as Jared smirked at her from the doorway. She wouldn't give up, wouldn't let Jared win. "I want to go with you, Daddy!"

He dropped to a squat and gently took her face in his big, strong hands. "Not this time, baby."

Hot tears spilled onto her cheeks. "Why not?"

"This is Jared's day, Hope. Remember last month we went to the Ice Capades, just you and me?"

She remembered it well. It had been one of the best days of her life. For as long as she lived, Hope would remember the figure skaters in their glittery leotards and the way the silver blades of their skates sparkled on the ice, the beautiful music that played as Crystal Rose came out for her finale. But now that all seemed like a distant memory.

"You don't want to go to an old football game," he said, patting her head. "You'd be bored silly."

"Would not!"

"Honey ..."

Her chin quivered.

"Oh, Hope ..."

She saw his resolve weakening and knew if she kept at him just a few minutes more, he'd give in. "Please, Daddy."

"That's not fair!"

She threw a hate-filled glance at Jared, who clutched his scarf and the Buffalo Bills cap daddy had bought for him. "This is supposed to be our day, Dad. Just the guys."

Hope's eyes narrowed to angry slits. *He's not your Dad*, she thought.

"He's right, Ted." Dana's voice crept from the hallway behind her son. "Fair is fair."

Feeling her anger seep up from her toes, Hope glared at Dana. *And you're not my mother!*

She turned back to her father with a last, tearful plea. "Daddy, pleeease?"

He stood and she knew the decision was made. She'd lost.

"Not this time, Hope. You'll have more fun here, baking cookies with your mother."

Stamping her foot, she ran from the room, pounding up the staircase and slamming her bedroom door. She threw herself across the bed and gave in to frustrated tears. She didn't want to make any stupid old cookies! She wanted to go to the city and sit beside daddy under the woolen blanket and soak up the excitement of a real football game. She wanted to eat popcorn and hot dogs and see the pretty cheerleaders right up close. She made a fist and struck her pillow. It wasn't fair.

She heard Dana's footsteps in the hall and quickly brushed away her tears. Dana knocked on the door. When Hope didn't answer, she poked her head inside.

"Are you ready to get started?" she asked cheerfully, as if she hadn't just ruined Hope's whole life. When Hope glared at her, Dana sighed. "All right, Hope. If you'd rather stay up here and continue your tantrum, you may. But if you change your mind I'll be down in the kitchen making cookie dough. I'd really like your company."

She closed the door and Hope heard her footsteps creaking back down the staircase. She buried her face in her hands and cried again, this time in sadness. She'd looked forward to the baking all week. She and Dana had gone to the store the night before and bought new cookie cutters and real cream butter, and now the whole thing was ruined.

"What makes me do it?" she sobbed. "What makes me act so mean?"

She stared down the street as if that would somehow bring her daddy back. The deal was, one month daddy would take her someplace special and the next month he would take Jared. It was fine when it was her turn. But when she saw them packing the cooler, laughing and having fun, she got swept away with jealousy.

Rising from her bed, she reached underneath and pulled out her box of secret treasures. She lifted the lid, smiling when she saw that nothing had been disturbed. Her hands glided over the treasures, taking pleasure in the feel of them, in the sheer joy of owning them. Selecting the silky red underpants and bra set, she rubbed their softness against her cheek. Dana made her wear white cotton underpants and matching undershirts, but some day she would wear pretty things like this. She smiled just to imagine it, but then a small shadow crossed her face. She hadn't meant to steal them, exactly ...

She'd been playing hide and seek at Morgan's house and found the set under Mrs. Foster's bed. She'd only meant to look at them, to hold them in her hands. But when Mrs. Foster came and chased her out, she shoved them down the front of her pants, not wanting to give them up.

She thought how pretty Morgan's mother was, and how full of fun, and felt a stab of guilt that she hadn't given the panties back. The guilt felt so bad she almost couldn't enjoy them any more.

Replacing them in the box, she brought out the bottle of cherry red nail polish Dana said she was too young to wear. She scowled. When she was a grown-up she would wear it every day, along with loads of mascara and shiny gold bracelets, like Mrs. Foster wore.

She rifled through her treasures until she found the one she was looking for. Pulling it carefully from its envelope, she stared at it, just as she had every single day since her father gave it to her.

She stared in awe at the pretty pink mouth and the sky blue eyes, the same color as her own. She felt the longing and pride that came with knowing this pretty lady had once held her and loved her, and as unbelievable as it seemed, had actually been her very own mother.

Her glance caressed the woman's golden curls and pretty, blue dress. She was certain the lady in the picture would have let her wear the cherry red nail polish. Her resentment flared again. Why had her daddy ever married an old stick in the mud like Dana, anyway?

And Jared ...

Daddy had so little time to spare as it was. Why should she have to share him with Jared, who wasn't really her brother at all?

Somehow it just didn't seem fair.

An emotional chameleon, her thoughts returned to the color of guilt. Dana had come to take care of her, daddy said, to love her and help daddy make a new family.

She looked at her treasures until she felt better again, then tucked them back in the box and went downstairs. Dana was as tough as an overdone roast when it came to the rules, but she was also quick to forgive. She sniffed the air as she walked, testing it for the scent of Dana's sugar cookies. When she reached the kitchen she saw that Dana had not started baking at all. She sat in the breakfast nook reading a book, and shoved it into her handbag when she saw Hope in the doorway.

"I thought you'd be baking," Hope ventured.

"I've been waiting for you. Are you ready now?"

Hope wavered for only a second, then ran to Dana and wrapped her arms around the comfort and the sheer dependability of her.

Chapter Six
July, 1996

It was the worst job ever. Gray thrust the end of his shovel into the mound of chicken dung and pitched the load into the wheelbarrow beside him. A half dozen more trips to the compost heap and he'd be done. With this job, anyway.

He pulled a frayed, red bandana from the pocket of his jeans, then rested his weight against the shovel and wiped the rivers of sweat from his face. Despite the gaping holes where the clapboard hung at crooked angles, the walls of the chicken coop seemed to suck in the heat and hold it fast, denying even the tiniest of breezes entry.

He gazed with longing at the patches of blue sky visible through the gaps in the roof. He hated the chicken coop worse than anyplace else on Earth, hated the heat and the filth of it, and the stench that rose up from the floorboards and made him want to puke.

He turned back to his work, stopping again when a mouse darted from its corner and ran across his shoe. It perched there for a moment, wrinkling its small pink nose in curiosity at the hole where his sock came through. Then, as if noticing for the first time there was a human attached, it scuttled to an opposite corner and dove beneath a pile of straw.

Gray chuckled. "It's all right, little fella. I won't hurt you none."

Tying the bandana around his nose, he lifted out another shovelful of dung. The Herbert's farm wasn't any worse than the other places he'd lived. In most ways it was a whole lot better. At least Drew and Lorna gave him enough to eat and didn't dole out beatings like they were his weekly allowance.

He frowned. As bad as some of the foster homes had been, he

would have stayed at any one of them rather than keep moving around like he did. Even a bad home where he felt he belonged would be better than none at all. Most of the families got rid of him because he was too small for the rugged farm work required. For the Lawrences, his last foster family, he'd been too big. Go figure.

His frown deepened when he thought of Jackie and Jim Lawrence. They'd been decent to him, damned near kind, until his fifteen-year-old body began to swell with hard work and testosterone. Then everything changed. He remembered with shame how they started watching his every move, how they seemed to weigh every word he spoke to their beautiful thirteen-year-old daughter, Alyson.

Closing his eyes, he conjured up her jade green eyes and the auburn mane that fell to her waist. Laying down his shovel, he maneuvered the wheelbarrow out into the afternoon sunshine. Jackie and Jim needn't have worried. He never would have touched Alyson. Girls were a source of terror for Gray. A tantalizing mystery, they invaded his thoughts a hundred times a day, disturbed his sleep at night and filled him with a fierce and hungry desire he couldn't begin to understand. But he never would have had the courage to act on that desire.

He steered the wheelbarrow over to the compost pile. Tipping it on its side, he raked out the manure and spread it over layers of banana peels and eggs shells. Damn. How could a body eat anything that grew from this stinking pile of shit?

He whistled as he worked. After this he'd have to help paint the front porch, then they'd probably want him to finish weeding the vegetable garden. And then with any luck he'd have an hour or two of freedom.

He picked up his pace, thinking of the Civil War novel he'd bought at the used book store. He'd take it out to the orchard where he could sit in the shade of the peach trees and read without interruption.

His gaze wandered across the gently rolling landscape. Instead of the run down farm, he imagined a stately plantation where cotton fields rang out with Negro spirituals, and lords and ladies drove along the tree-lined paths in horse drawn carriages …

"Hey, Baldwin! Y'all are pitchin' that shit like a woman. Put some muscle into it, if ya got any."

His decorous world shattered, Gray looked up to see Curly

Dennison, a four-year veteran of the farm, leaning against the fence, a surly smile on his face. He sighed. It was a look he'd seen enough times to know the boy who wore it was looking for trouble.

"What's the matter, pansy?" Curly jeered. "Y'all afraid a getting' them dainty little hands of yours dirty or something?"

Gray's anger spread through his system like poison. He fingered the silver cross beneath his shirt, trying to calm himself, telling himself some guys just didn't know any better. Curly was just an ignorant moron.

He gave the compost pile one last pass with the rake and turned the wheelbarrow back toward the chicken coop. Curly leapt from the fence and planted his foot squarely in front of the wheel.

Though small for his age, Gray squared his shoulders and looked the other boy in the eye. He'd learned a long time before that to back down meant certain death in a new foster home.

"What's your problem, Curly?"

"I got no problem, pansy. Just makin' sure y'all are pulling your weight around here, that's all."

"Get outa my way."

"Get outa my way," he mimicked, giving the wheelbarrow a forceful kick. Gray set down the handles, every muscle in his body tensed. If it was a fight Curly wanted, he'd surely give him one.

Lorna Herbert's voice cut through the thickness of the air, granting him a reprieve. "Boys! Drew! Lu-u-u-nch!"

Drew Herbert and his foster wards emerged from the field and lumbered toward the house. Glancing in their direction, Curly gave the wheelbarrow a last, fierce kick, overturning it into the compost heap. Laughing, he swaggered toward the house. Gray lifted the handles from the manure and wiped his hands on the back of his pants.

"Dumb S.O.B.," he muttered.

He felt the weight of Curly's stare on him all through lunch. He was definitely looking to start something. What or why, Gray couldn't be sure, but if he'd learned anything in his fifteen years of life, it was that some people didn't need a reason for their meanness. Only a target.

He was relieved when Drew paired him for his afternoon chores with Ace Javitz. He liked Ace. Big and dark, and as lethal in his quiet as the calm before a cyclone, Ace got a person's respect with one look into his coal black eyes. Equal only in their number of years, Ace was everything Gray would have liked to be.

As they walked to the barn to retrieve their paint buckets, Gray chanced a glance at Ace from the corner of his eye. In contrast to the gold talon that glinted from his eyebrow, Ace had a jagged, lightning streak scar that ran the length of his face. Silver against the darkness of his skin, the scar added to the mystery of him, the subtle quality of danger that spoke of a life of turbulence Gray could only guess at.

They worked side by side into the afternoon, painting the spindles of the weathered porch. Gray ventured a comment now and then about the hotness of the day or the brightness of the sun, but when each offering was met with a grunt or stone cold silence, he gave up.

He looked up, tensing, when Curly appeared, carrying a large metal pail filled with blueberries. He stomped up the steps and sent the pail crashing into the side of Gray's head.

"Aww, gee. Clumsy old me," he said, smirking.

Gray pressed his hand against the stabbing pain and fought a losing battle with his anger.

"Hey, look at the professor with the paint all over his pretty little hands. Guess y'all are finding out you ain't no better'n the rest of us poor slobs, ain't ya, pansy boy?" He grabbed an empty pail from the porch and strode back to the berry patch. Gray jammed his brush into his paint can using more force than he'd intended. It tipped sideways and fell from the railing, half of its contents pooling out onto the ground.

"Damn!" He quickly righted the pail, then addressed Curly's retreating figure. "Dumb S.O.B."

Ace dipped the end of his brush into his can and spread an even layer over the spindles.

"That dude just don't like me," Gray muttered. "I never give him any reason."

Ace dabbed at a drip of paint, then stood back and studied his work. "He like you just fine," he said breezily. "I expect that's what his problem is."

Gray stared at him, his brush hovering in mid-air. "What do you mean?"

Ace dabbed at the railing again. "You the professor. You figure it out."

Gray saw the smirk on Ace's face and a slow realization dawned. "Naww," he said, incredulous.

Ace shrugged. "Alright."

Straining his eyes in the direction of the berry patch, Gray watched Curly busily filling his pail. He'd never known any gay guys before but Curly sure didn't fit the image. He was big and tough, masculine. Curly was the kind of guy who kept girls like Alyson Herbert starry-eyed and blushing. "Well I'll be damned," he said softly.

"He's always giving trouble to the new ones." Ace's glance swept over him from head to toe. "'Specially your kind."

"I ain't that kind!"

Ace laughed. "That don't matter none. Won't keep his skinny ass from crawlin' into y'all sleeping bag some one of these nights to try and find out."

Gray gaped at him in horror. "He wouldn't do that."

Ace shrugged again and turned back to his work. "Trouble with y'all is they ain't no meanness in you. Makes it easy for guys like him." He flicked his paintbrush in the direction of the berry patch. "Like like stealin' the shoes off a blind man."

"I ain't so nice. Least I ain't gonna be, he comes crawlin' into my bed." Gray spoke with conviction, but as he worked, his mind filled with anxious thoughts. Curly was a lot bigger than him. What if Ace's prediction came true?

"Damn," he said softly. "I hope he don't make it rough for me. I was hoping to stay on here."

Ace grunted.

"Don't you like it here, Ace?"

"I don't like it nowhere I ain't my own man," he said, his dark eyes seething with quiet anger. "Doing white folks' dirty work and cleaning up after they damned stinkin' animals. I hate it." He glanced toward the house, lowering his voice. "Gonna take myself off as soon's I work out a way."

Gray gaped at him. "Where are y'all gonna go?"

He shot another hurried glance at the house. "Gonna take myself up north."

The way he said it, up north, was as if he'd spoken of Eden itself.

"Up north? What the hell you wanna go up north for?"

"Shh!" His savage look silenced Gray in an instant. "Because they give a man a chance to be a man up north, without automatically thinkin' he's pond scum just because his skin's too dark." His expression softened. "I hear they got fishin' boats in Maine where you can throw down a net and come up with a lobster the size of a man's leg."

"We got fishin' boats right here in Alabama," Gray said.

"Y'all ain't hearin' me, son." Ace gave Gray a look of contempt that chilled him to the marrow. "But then I wouldn't expect a young golden boy like y'self to understand how it is to be black and ugly in the goddamn heart of Dixie."

Gray thought for a long time before answering. He didn't understand, but the last thing he wanted was to make an enemy of Ace. "You try and run off, they'll send you up to The House just as sure as I'm standin' here."

"Not if they don't catch me, they won't. Anyway, The House ain't no worse than here. It's just a different kind of prison, that's all."

Gray shuddered, remembering horror stories he'd heard about the county juvenile detention center. "I don't know about that, Ace. Seems to me there's some prisons a whole lot worse than others. Least here we got plenty of food and fresh air, and—"

"Shhh!" Ace pressed a finger against his lips and indicated Lorna's shadow in the doorway. "Shut up now," he whispered. "I ain't gonna talk about it with you no more."

Gray turned back to his work and Lorna's shadow retreated.

"Ace?"

"What?"

"Do you really think Curly'll make it rough for me?"

"Yup."

He ran his paintbrush along a spindle. "Did he make it rough for you when you first come here?"

"Hell no." Ace sat back on his heels and studied Gray's face. "I could take care of it for you."

Gray felt instant, lightheaded relief. "You could?"

"I could, but it'd cost you."

"Cost me what?"

"Y'all get five bucks a week pocket money, right?"

"Right."

"If I fix it for you, I get four bucks a week. Y'all can keep one for yourself."

"What am I gonna do with a buck a week?"

Ace shrugged. "Don't seem like too much to ask. You pay me four bucks a week and he leave you alone. I guarantee it."

Gray thought about it for all of ten seconds. He liked to go to the used bookstore in town on Saturdays and was slowly building his own library. He'd have to kiss that goodbye. But it would be worth the money not to have to watch his back. "Alright," he said. "You got a deal."

Ace stood and strode to the berry patch. Gray sat back on his heels and shaded his eyes with his hand. He saw Curly glance in his direction, then raise his hands in a gesture of surrender. Ace returned moments later, a satisfied smile on his lips.

"Did you fix it?"

"Yup."

"What'd you say to him?"

Ace's smile broadened. "I told him y'all was mine."

Gray's heart sank to his feet. "No you didn't."

"Hell yes, I did. He thinks y'all belong to me he ain't gonna mess with you."

"But now he thinks I'm queer," Gray wailed. "Word'll get out and they'll all be thinking' it."

"Why y'all worry so much what everybody thinks?"

Gray stared at the ground. "I dunno."

"Long as he thinks you're mine he leave you be. You want me to go back out there and tell him different, I will." He thrust his finger in Gray's chest. "But if he come crawlin' into your sleepin' bag tonight, which he will, you on your own." He jammed his paint brush into the bucket. "I ain't gonna help you again."

Gray was instantly repentant. "Ace?"

"What?"

"Thanks for fixing it."

"You welcome," he said grudgingly. "Now shut up and let's get this damned thing finished so we can go fishin'."

Curly didn't speak to him, or even look at him for the rest of the day, but not taking any chances, Gray moved his sleeping bag into Ace's room that night.

Not really a bedroom, Ace's "crib" was an enclosed porch with oversized screened windows that looked out over the peach orchard. Up until six months before it had been Curly's room, but an agreement had been reached between the two the day Ace arrived on the farm, or so Ace said.

Gray looked up at the sprinkling of stars in the sky and thought what an unlikely match it was. He hadn't had a real friend since he was seven years old and Jody King was his best buddy. It would be nice to have someone to talk to. Especially someone as smart as Ace.

"I wish there was some girls around the place," he said wistfully.

Ace snorted. "Just as well they ain't."

"It'd just kinda make it nicer if there were."

"No it wouldn't."

"Don't y'all like girls, Ace?"

Ace rolled over to face him and Gray saw his eyes glittering in the darkness. "I like 'em fine, in they place."

"I guess you probably been with a lot of 'em."

Ace shrugged. "Not a lot."

"Some, though."

"Yeah."

Gray sighed. "I wish I had. I wish I was with one right now. A real pretty one with nice big tits."

Ace shook his head. "You'd be better off savin' them wishes of yours."

"I know, but …" Gray sighed again. "It gets to aching me sometimes, wonderin' what I'm missin'."

Ace's voice took on an edge that surprised Gray. "What y'all are missin' is a whole lot of aggravation for what satisfaction they is in it." He lowered his voice, muttering, "Expect a man to sit up and beg for it, then they want you to perform like you was some goddamned trained monkey. Gets so a man couldn't do it if he wanted to."

Gray stared at him, wide-eyed. "What do you mean?"

"You'll find out. Take my advice, don't go fallin' in love with no woman."

"Why not?"

"Cause they more trouble than they worth, that's why. And

besides that they ain't a damned one of 'em that'll tell a man the truth. Eat your heart right out and then they sit there pretty please askin' for your soul. Loving a woman, that's a one-way ticket to hell."

He took Gray's hand and abruptly shoved it between his legs. "You give 'em this, though. Give it to 'em as hard and as often as y'all get a chance, but this…" He moved his hand and placed it over his heart. "Do yourself a favor and keep this back."

He peered at Gray intently, then dropped his hand and rolled over to face the wall.

"Ace?"

"Yeah?"

"Y'all must've got hurt pretty bad, didn't you?"

"Shut up and go to sleep."

•

July melted into August and before Gray knew it summer had slipped away. On the night before the new school year started he set out the sneakers Lorna had bought him and the one new outfit. He held the shirt to his face, savoring the newness and the crisp, black fabric beneath his fingers. He was looking forward to going back to school. He'd be a sophomore this year, and he welcomed the challenge of new classes.

The next morning, though, as he stood in front of the bathroom mirror and pulled a comb through his newly shorn curls, Gray felt sick to his stomach. What if he didn't get on in the new school?

Ace stood beside him at the sink, drawing a razor across his face and watching Gray from the corner of his eye.

"You working' awful hard at that for what little bit of hair y'all got left."

Gray set down his comb and stared at his reflection. He ran his fingers over the faint golden stubble on his chin and decided to leave it alone. "I wish you were goin' with me, Ace."

"I already told you they don't want me in they damned schools. Gave up on me a long time ago."

"I could help you catch up. Wouldn't take no time at all."

"Schoolin' ain't in me like it is, you. It'd just be another prison."

Underwood High School was a three-story red-brick building that sat on a knoll above the river. It was old and rundown and it became clear to Gray on his first day that the cliques were well formed and impenetrable. He watched the other students flock together in the hallway and knew that just like everywhere else in his life, there would be no niche at Underwood he could squeeze into.

He dove headfirst into his classes, telling himself he didn't care. Who needed them anyway?

He was cursed with Geometry and Biology, but thankfully there was English and American History to balance the scales. Grace Stacy, his English teacher, was a bookish woman of forty. She wore wire glasses and drab, ankle-length skirts, and the fact that she singled Gray out as her favorite on the first day did little to improve his popularity.

At the end of his first week he stood in the back of Ms. Stacy's classroom and drank in the selection of books, arranged alphabetically on the book cases. His to borrow, she'd told him with a smile, as many as he wanted. If that wasn't enough to lure him to class every day, there was the added bonus of Cerise Barnhardt. Like her books, Grace Stacy preferred her students arranged alphabetically, which put the brown-eyed beauty in the seat directly ahead of Gray's.

Day after day he sat behind her, obsessing over her sweet-smelling perfume and the gentle curve of her shoulder, the mane of chestnut-colored curls that would one day be held captive in a silver clip, and the next, free falling down her back. He found himself constantly daydreaming, wondering whether her skin was as soft as it looked, and what mysteries she hid beneath her tight black pants. That she didn't know he was alive did little to stop the graphic fantasies that played out daily in his mind.

He talked about her incessantly.

"Can't be all that good, is she?" Ace grumbled, long since tired of the subject and losing patience with his friend's infatuation. "Y'all makin' out like she's one of Charlie's goddamned Angels, for chrissakes."

"I'm telling you, Ace, she is. You ain't never seen a girl as pretty as Cerise."

"Prettier they look the meaner they are. Y'all take my advice and don't go after them pretty ones. It's the ugly ones that's easy. Go after the ugly ones and they so damned grateful they let you do whatever you want."

"I don't want no ugly girl. And besides, I'm not gonna go after Cerise. I just like thinking' about her's all."

"Hmmph."

Ace's disapproval hung thick in the air for a long moment.

"Hey, Ace?"

"What?"

"If a guy was wanting to go after a chick, how would he go about it?"

Ace told him there would be signs if Cerise was interested and Gray spent the remainder of September watching for them.

By October he'd worked up enough nerve to say hello, and his sole reason for getting up in the morning was that Cerise might smile at him that day, or say hello back.

On a balmy Friday in the middle of October Gray asked the Herbert's for permission to study at the public library after school. He had a Geometry exam coming up and the noise at home made concentrating impossible.

He sat in the cool quiet of the century-old brick building until late afternoon, working and reworking equations until they swam before his eyes. Finally he closed his book and stretched his arms. Maybe too much quiet ain't good either, he thought. Remembering a sub shop he'd seen down the street, he decided to take a break and walk down for a soda.

He strolled down the sidewalk, whistling as he went. It felt good to be out in the fresh air, to be a real person and not just another student or a foster care ward. As he neared the sub shop he inhaled the tantalizing scent of baking pizza and his mouth began to water. He hadn't had real pizza since God knew when. You couldn't count the boxed kind with the cardboard crust Lorna treated them to once a month. He reached into his pocket and pulled out a handful of change. Damn. Not nearly enough. The tune he was whistling died on his lips when he glanced into the large front window and saw Cerise inside.

He backed up a step and leaned against the building, his legs rubbery and unable to support his weight. He shot another glance in the window, just to be sure.

She sat at a table in the window with a her majorette friends. He couldn't see her entire face but would have known the chestnut curls and the gentle curve of her cheek anywhere. He sucked in a deep breath, pulled a comb through his hair, and went inside.

He heard the laughter and buzz of girl chatter the moment he opened the door. He chanced a glance and saw that the table opposite hers was empty. Taking another breath, he strolled to the counter and ordered his drink. He'd take it to the empty table, he decided, where he could watch her without being obvious. The abrupt music of her laughter caused his heart to hammer in his chest. He paid for his soda and turned, almost dropping it on the floor. Cerise Barnhardt was standing right behind him and she was smiling. "Well hey there, Gray."

He cleared his throat. "Hey, Cerise." His voice had deepened in pitch more than a year ago, but now to his embarrassment it cracked like a twelve-year-old's.

"I've never seen y'all in here before, have I?"

He allowed his eyes a third of an instant to travel down the tight black sweater and over her low rise jeans. "Umm, n-no, I … "

"I didn't think so." She smiled, her gaze sweeping to her friends and back again. They rested on the Geometry book in his hand. "You should come out more often, do a little socializing instead of just studying' all the time."

He wasn't sure what he said, or whether he answered her at all. He didn't hear the eruption of giggles when she returned to her friends, or know that he'd walked back to the library until he found himself sitting at the table. All he knew was that she smiled at him. That as surely as if she'd painted it in neon and worn it on a sandwich board, Cerise Barnhardt had given him a sign.

Chapter Seven
November, 1996

On the first Monday in November, Gray rose from his bed before the sun came up and padded to the bathroom. Retrieving his razor from its shelf in the medicine chest, he carefully lathered the soft whiskers on his chin.

Whisking them away, he peered at his reflection. Pale gray eyes stared back from dark ringed sockets. He hadn't had a decent night's sleep since Cerise smiled at him in the sub shop. Ace said it sounded like he might have a shot and Gray made up his mind to find out.

He played out the scenario a thousand times, a million ways, until he got it right. He thought of the twelve dollars in his sock drawer and mentally weighed it against the cost of a pizza and two sodas.

He gained and lost his nerve a hundred times before the last bell of the day rang. Cerise stood at her locker, laughing with her friends. He drew a shaky breath and approached her. *It's now or never, Baldwin,* he told himself.

He waited in agonized silence for her to turn around. At first it seemed like she never would, like he'd stand there forever, a sick knot of dread aching in his guts. Finally she slammed her locker door and turned and they were face to face. With a look in her eyes he was struck dumb.

"Excuse me, Gary," she said, brushing past him.

Gary? He moistened his lips with his tongue, then swallowed, desperate to make intelligent words come out of his mouth.

"Cerise, can I talk to you for a minute?"

She glanced to where her friends waited then back into his eyes, her brows lifted in impatience. Suddenly the timing didn't seem right. Suddenly she didn't seem as friendly as she had before. Her eyes weren't as warm and her smile not as bright. He jammed his hands in his pockets. The timing wasn't right, but how could he turn back now?

"Uhm, I was just thinking', if y'all ain't busy sometime, maybe ... uhm ... " He felt a blush burn across his face and hated himself for it. He glanced at the empty space between the lockers and noticed a fly caught in a spider web, and had never felt more sympathetic toward anything in his life. He cleared his throat and tried again. "What I mean is—"

"Gary, are y'all trying to ask me out?"

"My name is Gray," he said softly.

She laughed, but it wasn't the gentle melody from the sub shop. It was like the sound of clashing cymbals. It caused his hands to tremble in his pockets. He looked into her eyes again and the look of pure meanness he saw there turned his insides to mud.

"What do I look like to you, Gary?"

Oh, baby, please. Please don't talk so loud.

He felt the blood drain from his face as his eyes dropped to the floor. Searching his mind for an answer, he found only a deep, dark abyss of nothingness. "I don't know."

The cymbals crashed. He dug his fingernails into his palms and braced himself for the full impact of her rejection.

"I'm a majorette, Gary. Do you know what that means?"

He stared at his feet, dizzy, afraid he'd be sick. "Nope."

"It means I don't go out with no homeless bums!" Laughing, she sauntered away to rejoin her friends. Half way down the hall she turned back. "Especially the ones who stink like cow shit!"

He was dizzy, spinning. His vision was blurred and his head clouded with vague impressions; smiles, smirks hidden behind hands and notebooks. Laughter swelled around him, echoing from the lockers and the ceiling and the walls. Hanging in the very air he breathed. The air he couldn't breathe. Oh, God. He couldn't breathe. He was nothing. He was less than nothing.

That night he lay in the darkness, licking his wounds and trying to recover. Ace remained silent, but Gray could tell by the quiet rhythms of his breathing that he was awake. When he could no longer contain them, his thoughts became words and crept out of the shadows.

"My mama used to say all the while how it was a mistake I ever came into this world. I guess she was probably right."

It was a moment before Ace spoke. "Turned you down, didn't she?"

"Yeah."

Ace sighed and propped himself on his elbow. "Y'all takin' it too hard, Gray. So you didn' get this one. You'll get another one, that's all."

Gray dared not respond. He lay in silence fighting tears. No way would he let Ace know he was crying over some stupid chick.

"You okay?"

He nodded, knowing Ace couldn't see him in the dark but not trusting his voice. He felt Ace's hand, rough with work but strangely tender as it traced the damp tracks of his tears.

"No you ain't."

"Ace ..." He choked out his friend's name, took a quivering breath and gave up the fight, collapsing in sobs. He felt Ace's arms go around him, his big hands moving gently through his hair.

"I know, Gray. I know."

Burying his face in Ace's rock hard shoulder, he wept.

•

He hadn't done his homework in a week. Even the glossy new copy of Upton Sinclair's *The Jungle* Ms. Stacy gave him could not arouse his interest, so Gray wasn't surprised, that Monday afternoon in November, when Grace Stacy asked him to stay after class. "I'd like to talk with you about something, Gray."

"Yes, Ma'am." He shifted his books against his thigh, feebly working out an excuse. He decided not to bother. What did it matter anyway? What did anything matter?

She reached into a file folder and pulled out one of his essays, cradling it against her breast. "It's rare that I see this quality of work, Gray. Especially from a sophomore. Your insights are just ... startling."

As he listened to her words the realization dawned that it was not the reprimand he'd expected, but praise.

"Gray." She reached out and touched his arm. "I really hope you're starting to give serious thought to college."

He looked at her in surprise. "College costs a lot of money, don't it?"

"Well, yes, it does, but there are grants available, scholarships. I'm sure you could qualify for some of them. I'd be glad to help you with the forms, when the time comes."

Her voice faded as his mind began to reel. He'd never seen college as an attainable possibility before.

"Anyway," she said, removing her hand, "what I wanted to talk with you about today is the school newspaper, *The Smoke Signals*. We have space open and I was hoping we could get you to fill it."

He stared at her blankly. "With what?"

"It could be anything you like. Poetry, book or movie reviews, student life articles. I'd give you complete freedom."

When he didn't answer, she persisted. "I really think your writing would be an asset to the paper, Gray. And it would look good on your college application. What do you say?"

"I don't know."

"Promise me you'll think about it."

"All right. I'll think about it."

In the days that followed he thought about little else. He went over his entry again and again, agonizing over each word, rewriting it until he was satisfied. Putting his thoughts into words helped to ease the sting of the humiliation Cerise Barnhardt had dealt him.

At two, forty-five on the last Friday in November he hurried to the classroom that served as print shop for the school paper. The deadline was three o'clock. He'd hand in his entry before he lost his nerve.

He reached the classroom and found the door locked. He hesitated for a moment, and then slid his entry beneath the door with a sense of relief. It was done. Heading to the bus loop, he whistled a small tune. He'd be anxious to see what Grace Stacy had to say, come Monday.

He noticed the patrol car in the driveway from a half mile down the road. His mouth went dry as he thought out each possible scenario that would necessitate a police visit to the farm. He stepped from the school bus and slowly followed the other boys into the house.

Drew sat on the sofa in the living room talking to two uniformed officers. Gray's heart skipped a beat when he realized they were talking about Ace. They turned when the door closed behind him, their faces unsmiling. Drew stood. "Gray, these boys'd like a minute of your time."

White spots swam before his eyes. At the officer's command, he sat. He heard the chipped ice sound of the cop's voice and tried to focus on his words. "I understand y'all were friends with Ace Javitz?"

Were?

"Yessir."

"He run off this morning,' but I guess you probably already knew that."

"No, Sir."

"Uh-huh. I don't suppose y'all would have any idea of where he took himself off to?"

Gray hesitated, his mind filling with pictures of clear blue skies and of crisp, northern air. Of gulls rising and falling on the wind above deep blue waters. He hesitated just long enough that the cop knew he was lying.

"No, Sir."

The other officer stepped forward. "Bein' a minor he's still the legal responsibility of this county. Lot can happen to a young boy out there on his own. If you know where he might be, I suggest you tell us."

The words surprised and angered Gray. He had a tough time thinking of Ace as a young boy, and who were the county workers to treat people like their own private property? He lifted his chin in defiance. They could go to hell. Gray Baldwin didn't rat out his friends.

He sat, silent, throughout their questioning, until they finally gave up, then walked woodenly to his room, empty now except for his clothes and two sleeping bags in the corner. Although Ace's belongings hadn't amounted to much, the room seemed barren without them. He slid down onto the floor. Hugging his knees to his chest, he stared out the window at the miles of country roads beyond the orchard. Ace was his only friend in the world and the sickening realization that he was alone again flattened him like a wrecking ball. He stared at Ace's empty sleeping bag. *How come you didn't even say goodbye?*

Stretching out on his sleeping bag, he rested his head on his pillow. As he ran his hand along the cool floorboards, he felt it. His fingers closed around it and he slowly pulled it from beneath the pillow. Opening his fingers one at a time, he smiled. There, glinting in the waning afternoon sunlight was Ace's gold talon. It was as good a good-bye as any.

Later, he tried to ignore the excited whispers as the other boys trooped into the house for dinner; whispers of how Ace would be shot for certain, how he'd be caught and sent up to The House. He scrubbed his hands until they stung, reminding himself that Ace was smart. He'd never get caught. Never in a million years.

After a silent meal, he scraped the plates and carried them to the kitchen. Normally he hated K.P. duty, but that night the chore was a welcome diversion. As he carried the last of the silverware from the dining room, he was dismayed to see Curly standing in the kitchen, wearing a dish towel on his arm and the old, familiar smirk on his face.

"Guess y'all done lost your best friend, ain't you, pansy?"

Gray turned to the sink and filled it with warm, soapy water. Seconds later Curly was behind him, his breath a hot, disgusting surprise on the back of Gray's neck. "Cheer up, professor," he said softly. "Ain't nobody ever told you there's more than one fish in the sea?"

Gray seethed with anger but remained silent.

"I know y'all like 'em dark, but I got a stick of pure cane sugar here and I bet y'all are gonna love it."

Sliding his arms around Gray's middle, he jerked him backward. Curly's arousal outraged and sickened Gray. He pulled free of Curly's grasp and whirled to face him. "Don't touch me!" He jabbed his finger in Curly's chest. "You keep your goddamned filthy hands offa me, you hear?"

Curly's expression betrayed hurt and anger.

"What's the matter, Gray? Ain't I your type? Ain't I big and black and stupid enough for ya?" He gave Gray a shove, and Gray felt an unshackling take place inside of him, a loosing of the pain and rage that had been building for fifteen years.

"You'd better shut your goddamned mouth!"

Curly got in his face, a twisted smile on his lips. "Or what, huh? What do you think you're big enough to do about it?"

Gray drew back his fist and with a fierceness he didn't know he possessed, sent it crashing into Curly's mouth. Curly hit the floor and sat for a moment in dazed silence. He touched his fingertips to his bleeding lips, staring at Gray in disbelief. "You little son of a bitch."

Recovering with lightning speed, he lunged at Gray and grabbed him around the middle, pulling him down to the floor. Gray heard the crunch of bone on bone as Curly's fist connected with his face. Once. Twice. Three times. He heard the torrent of filth that poured from Curly's mouth and clamped is eyes shut against the raging pain in his head. They flew open again when he felt the cool, sharp blade of Lorna's butcher knife against his throat. Curly's face, red and sweaty and twisted with rage, was inches from his own. "Say your prayers, Baldwin," he hissed.

Gray swallowed and felt the pressure of the blade digging deeper into his flesh. He stared at the end of the knife, too terrified to plead for his life. A picture of his mother danced before his eyes and he fleetingly wondered if she'd be happy to see him again, or if she'd even remember him, after all this time ...

Fear made him lightheaded. What would Curly tell them, he idly wondered. In seconds he would be drowning in his own blood, messing up Lorna's spanking clean floor tiles. What would she have to say about that?

"You ready to die, Baldwin?"

Curly shoved the blade against Gray's throat until a thin bead of blood appeared. Gray swallowed, closed his eyes, wet himself. *Oh, God. Oh, God. Our Father, Who art in heaven ...*

"Y'all ready to go and meet your—"

"Curly, Gray, stop that this instant! Drew!"

Curly dropped the knife when Lorna's voice shattered the quiet. Gray saw the murder in his eyes instantly turn to fear. Then Drew was there, pulling him off and giving him a sound shaking. "What's goin' on out here?"

"He come after me, Drew. I didn't give him no reason. Just come right after me with Miz Lorna's knife. I was defendin' myself."

The farmer looked from Curly to Gray.

"I swear it, Drew!" Curly was whining, near tears. "I wouldn't lie to you. Here, ask Benny. He'll tell you how it was, he saw the whole thing."

Drew let go of Curly's shirt and looked to the small, raven haired boy with dark rings encircling the most haunted eyes Gray had ever seen.

"That right, Benny?"

The boy's glance darted from Curly to Gray, and then down at his shoes. "Yessir," he whispered.

Drew waved an angry hand at the crowd of boys who had gathered in the doorway. "Y'all get out!" he barked. "There ain't nothing to see out here." He pulled Gray to his feet. "I been good to you, boy, but there's limits to a man's goodness. I won't have no violence in my home."

He walked Gray to the cellar door and shoved him through it. "You can sleep out here until you learn how a man settles his differences."

Gray heard the door slam behind him and sank down on the steps. He laughed, harshly and without humor. "Well here I am again, on the wrong side of a locked door, and damned if I know the reason for it."

Through the door, he heard muffled voices in the kitchen for what seemed hours before the house filled with silence. He wrapped his arms around his torso. Only then did he realize he'd wet himself.

He cradled his throbbing head in his hands and thought how close he'd come to dying. His life had been spared on a whim of fate. He wondered about that for a moment, wondered whether he even cared. Maybe he'd have been better off dead. What good was a life like his anyway?

He heard a faint scuffling at the bottom of the stairs and peered into the shadows. Rats. They'd come when he was asleep, crawl over his body, sniff at his hair and skin. Drawing his knees closer to his chest, he tried to think what Ace would do if it was him. He reached in his pocket and let his fingers close around the talon for a moment before pulling it out and studying it. Being Gray Baldwin had never brought him a day of satisfaction his whole damned life. From now on he would be Ace Javitz.

He jammed the talon through his eyebrow, crying out as it punctured his skin. Bracing himself, he pushed, stopped, pushed again. Grinding his teeth together, he pushed harder until the dull, throbbing pain in his eyebrow blended with all of his other pain and finally the talon was through.

He leaned his head back against the door. Pain was a good thing.

For as long as it lasted it would remind him of what happened to nice guys. Until they finally wised up.

Sometime in the night he drifted into a fitful sleep. When he opened his eyes again a tiny stream of light filtered through the crack beneath the door. He smelled coffee and bacon and cigarette smoke and stretched his arms to try and relieve the cramping in his legs and shoulders. A ripple of pain spread across his face.

Moments later he heard voices in the kitchen and the sounds of chairs being scraped back from the table. Finally he heard footsteps drawing near the cellar door. When it opened Drew stood on the other side.

"Come on up here, Gray."

As he walked past, Drew looked at him and quickly averted his gaze. "God A'mighty," he said softly.

When Gray had eaten his solitary meal, Drew once again appeared in the kitchen. "Go upstairs and get your things. You'll be leavin' today."

Gray felt his breakfast rise to his throat as he awaited some further explanation. When none came he went quietly to his room and stuffed his clothes into his back pack. He stopped in the bathroom to wash up and immediately knew the reason for Drew's shocked expression. His left eye was nearly swollen shut from Curly's beating, and his cheek was encrusted with dried blood. He washed his face, savoring the cool agony of the cloth against his wounds.

Downstairs he found Drew and Lorna waiting in the living room, along with a man he knew instinctively to be a county social worker. Drew stood. "I'm sorry, Gray. I just can't let you stay."

Gray's impulse was to throw himself at the farmer's feet and beg him to reconsider, but an eerie calm settled over him and he remembered he was Ace now; cold and hard and able to take anything life and the county could dish out.

The social worker was quiet for much of the drive. Gray sat beside him, angry and fearful until at last the other man broke the silence.

"Got a couple out in Westbrook eccentric enough they want to take in a teenaged boy. You're the only one handy that don't have a history of drug abuse or violence. Till today, that is."

Gray listened, hope rising like a thin curl of smoke around his heart.

"Y'all can spend the weekend at the shelter, and I hope to God that face of yours'll be cleaned up by Monday. The Masons were real clear about not wanting anyone violent." He stopped at a red light and turned to Gray. "Y'all are gettin' a hell of a break and I hope you know that. You screw up again, I'll haul your ass up to The House myself."

Gray turned and stared out the window. Don't matter where you land, son, Ace's voice whispered. They all just different kinds of prisons ...

•

SMOKE SIGNALS FROM UNDERWOOD HIGH
Volume 12, Issue 3
Poet's Page

Cloud

It's black. It's white. It shades the night,
the harvest moon, the satellite.
Obscures the sun and drinks the heat,
no Mother Earth beneath its feet.
And passing through
it rains on me, it rains on me
it rains on you.
Till on the wind it rides again
to shades of where the shadows fall,
the white winds call (called out again)
Unfettered. Wild. I'm like a cloud,
nobody's fool. Nobody's child.
No wrong. No right. No splintered light
falls to the ground. Into the night,
the falcon's flight is
silent. Broken. Crashing down,
fallen angel hit's the ground, I
hit the ground running.
But here I'm dancing out of step.
And here I'm singing out of tune, and
here I'm speaking out of turn, and here
I'm baying at the moon. Silent

Angel. Fallen. Wild.
Nobody's son.
Nobody's saint.
Nobody's child.

—Gray Baldwin

Chapter Eight

December, 1996

She's as changeable as the winter skies. One minute dark and brooding, and the next, filled with sunshine and giggles, Dana thought, sliding a chocolate cake into the oven. Her glance slid sideways to where Hope sat, staring out the window. One didn't have to dig very deep beneath the family tree to see where Hope inherited her temperament. Georgie had been anything but predictable. Hope was the picture of her mother, but where Georgie had been snips and snails and puppy dog tails at age eleven, Hope was one-hundred-percent girl. She thought of the mascara and lipstick she'd found in Hope's backpack earlier that week. *Eleven going on twenty-five*, she thought. *Lord, give me patience.*

The abrupt ringing of the phone scattered her thoughts. Hope scampered off to answer it and Dana could tell by her hushed secrecy that it was her best friend, Morgan Foster. Moments later Hope returned.

"Mom, can I go sledding with Morgan?"

Dana felt a stab of disappointment. Ted had taken Jared to a hockey game and she'd hoped for some quality time with her daughter. She'd bought felt and sequins at the craft store thinking she and Hope could spend the morning making angels for the Christmas tree. After that, she planned to take Hope shopping at the mall.

"Please?"

Dana sighed, knowing that to impose quality time on the girl would only result in animosity. "Yes, you can go. But be home in time for dinner."

Hope raced back to the phone. Moments later Dana heard her

footsteps pounding up the stairs. When Diane Foster's SUV pulled into the driveway, twenty minutes later, Dana stood at the window and watched as Hope bounded into the back seat and rode away, laughing. She felt the pang again. Disappointment, she thought, but something else, too. Loneliness. She spent entirely too much time alone.

As much as she'd missed her teaching job, it seemed like a Godsend when Hope and Jared were small, not to have to go out to work. Ted Hanwell's home had been a haven of security. But now that the children were older and didn't need her as much, the walls seemed to close in around her and her haven felt more and more like a prison.

She sat down at the table and opened the romance novel she'd picked up at the supermarket. Opening to where she'd left off, she let herself be drawn back into the story. She read eagerly, chiding herself for the secret thrill the book brought her. A former English Literature instructor, her love of the written word was no secret. Her passion for romance novels, however, was. The books filled a need that went deep to her core.

As she read the words of passion, she became so engrossed in the story that she almost didn't hear the buzzing of the oven timer. Jumping up, she quickly pulled the cake from the oven and inspected it. Not burned, exactly, but not as perfect as it could have been. She tipped it upside down onto a cooling rack, then cut a generous wedge, set it on a plate, and carried it to the table. Pouring a glass of milk, she returned to her book.

He reached for her, hands caressing her silken skin as his lips whispered down her neck and came to rest on the perfect roundness of her breast, his golden prize ...

Shivering, she resolutely dumped the milk back into its carton and wedged the slice of cake back into place. Eating wasn't going to solve anything. And chocolate cake certainly wasn't going to transform her body into anything Ted would consider a golden prize. And besides, there wasn't a food in the world that could satisfy when a woman's hunger went deeper than her taste buds.

She ran her hands across her middle, wondering when the benefits of her nightly exercise routine would begin to show. She'd lost another three pounds this week. That made twelve in all. Her smile and frown came almost simultaneously. She still had a long,

long way to go.

Scooping up her book, she stuffed it into a drawer. She wouldn't try to lose herself in someone else's pleasure, either. She'd go out, enjoy the fresh air and the glorious sunshine.

An hour later she was plodding through the mall, contemplating gifts for Ted and the children. She stopped when a navy blue sweater in the window of The Men's Shoppe caught her eye. It would compliment the blue in Ted's eyes, she thought, and the sturdy line of his shoulders. She shivered, wondering if she would ever become immune to his good looks, to his powerful, masculine maleness.

After purchasing the sweater, she ducked into a video store and bought Jared and Hope each a DVD. By that time a headache was creeping up the back of her neck and she decided she'd done enough shopping for the day. A glance at her watch confirmed that it was getting late. Leaving the mall, her eyes were drawn to the window of Victoria's Secret. She stared wistfully at the lace camisole featured in the display. *How many more sit-ups before I'd look good in something like that?*

Unable to tear herself away, she walked up to the window and stared into the store. She felt a mixture of anger and embarrassment when she saw the slim, pretty women who were walking around inside. Glancing at the lacy garments, it occurred to her that these were the sort of things Georgie would have worn around the house, even made Ted's dinner in. She would have met him at the door and with one look at her in this camisole he would have— *Stop it, Dana!* she told herself. *You're a far cry from Georgie, and standing around feeling sorry for yourself isn't going to change that one bit!*

Closing her eyes, she tried to recapture her earlier good feelings. Georgie would have been dynamite in any one of these garments, no doubt about it. But as for cooking Ted's dinner, she'd probably not once in the two years they were married put a digestible meal on Ted's table, God rest her soul. Cooking was the one area in which Dana didn't have to worry about pleasing him. That had to be worth something, didn't it? In a moment of insanity she forgot her embarrassment, lifted her chin, and marched into the store.

Driving home she still couldn't believe she did it. Her hand slid across the seat and into the pink-colored bag. The feel of the creamy satin beneath her fingers gave her goose bumps. The salesgirl had been a pro. It would have taken no less than the miracle she was to find something as beautiful and sexy as this negligee that a woman didn't have to be anorexic to fit into. *Good Lord, Dana, thirty-eight dollars for a tiny scrap of lace and you'll never have the nerve to put it on!*

She arrived home just in time to tuck the gown in her dresser drawer and slide a casserole into the oven before Hope returned from her sledding outing. "Did you have a good time?" she asked cheerfully.

"Yep."

Her cheeks were rosy with cold, and looking closer, Dana couldn't help notice the smudges of lipstick and mascara that lingered on the girl's face, despite her obvious attempts to remove them.

"Were there boys there, Hope?"

Hope rolled her eyes and copped the indignant tone Dana had come to know so well. "I can't help who was there, Mother."

Seeing Ted's truck pull in the driveway, Dana made a mental note to save the discussion for later. "Why don't you go and wash up, and then help me set the table."

Ted and Jared entered the house, brimming with cheer and male bonding and Dana was warmed through by the sight of her family gathered at the table. She did her best to seem interested as Ted and Jared recapped the highlights of the hockey game. She watched her husband's face, ruddy and relaxed, and thought what a treasure he was.

Overcome with emotion, she excused herself and hurried to the kitchen where she gave in to a brief, unaccustomed shower of tears. Ted Hanwell provided her with a lovely home and with security. He didn't beat her or fool around with other women, which was more than a lot of women could say. Why couldn't she be satisfied with what she had, instead of allowing herself to bleed internally for a passion he couldn't give?

Her first husband lied to her, made wild promises in the dark that were forgotten with the first cold rays of morning light. He'd taken her heart and her trust fund and left without a backward glance. At least Ted was honest about what they had, a marriage of convenience and nothing more. She wiped at the last of her tears. Damn that silly novel.

Later that night she sat in front of the television, thoughts of the nightgown swimming in her head. She remembered with a thrill how soft the fabric felt against her skin, how sexy it made her feel. When she could no longer stand it, she announced she was tired and slipped unnoticed from the room.

Drawing a bath, she sank down into the water, savoring its vanilla almond luxury, then scrubbed her skin with pumice until it tingled. She took her book from beside the tub and reread the last chapter, then she toweled off, put on her new negligee, slipped into bed, and waited.

Some time later she heard Ted say goodnight to the children. Her heart skipped like a pony when he finally entered the bedroom.

Foolish! she chided herself, while at the same time she trembled with anticipation.

She glanced up from her magazine as he shed his robe, peeping like a voyeur at his muscular legs, the shape of his buttocks, and knew that she would never get used to his good looks. When he climbed in beside her she closed the magazine and let it drop to the floor beside the bed.

"Go ahead and read, Dana," he said. "The light won't bother me."

"No, it's all right. I'm finished."

He smiled at her and kissed her cheek and disappointment coursed through her. She'd learned to read his signals long ago. A kiss on the cheek meant he wasn't feeling amorous. With a pounding heart she turned her face so their lips brushed and when she chanced a look into his eyes, saw surprise and amusement.

"I thought you said you were tired."

Her cheeks burned. "I'm not tired anymore."

"Oh."

Smiling again, he reached across her to turn off the lamp. The scent of his after shave filled her senses, nearly making her dizzy. He lay back down and slid his hand to her thigh. When it made contact with the creamy satin it hesitated, then slowly moved across it again.

"What's this?"

"I bought it at the mall today."

He reached for the lamp switch and the room flooded with light. She died a hundred times as he pulled back the blanket. His eyes moved over the negligee as if he'd never seen one. She burned with shame, feeling more naked than ever in her life.

"It was silly of me."

"No it wasn't."

The firmness in his voice stood in sharp contrast to the gentle pressure of his hand on her cheek as he forced her to meet his eyes. He sighed. "Dana, I know I haven't been much of a lover to you—"

"Ted, please don't think that. You've always left me … satisfied."

"But?"

Her cheeks flamed as she pulled the blanket close around her.

"Hey." His fingers traced a slow path down her cheek and then slowly inched the blanket back down. "You don't have to be embarrassed." It was the tender, soothing voice he often used to placate his daughter. "You're my wife. And I love that you wore it for me."

"Ted, I—"

His lips covered hers, gently at first, and then with more pressure as his hands traveled over her body. He moaned softly as he filled his hands with her breasts. His lips moved down her neck, and then she felt his tongue slide beneath the lace.

As her hands moved slowly down his back he inched the silken straps from her shoulders and then her breasts were exposed and rigid before him. She reached for the lamp switch but his hand shot out and curled around her wrist.

"Leave it on."

She lay back again, embarrassed but thrilled that the blatant evidence of her desire was pleasing to him. His lips covered first one breast and then the other, teasing until she was wild with need.

She lay beneath him, trembling, as he slid the negligee over her head and let it drop, unneeded, to the floor. His hands separated her thighs, and then he was between them, pulsing with a need of his own. It was then that she remembered her book. "Ted, wait." She pushed him away. "Lie on your back."

And then she was above him, cradling his hips. She took him into her hands and guided him inside. When she looked into his eyes she saw that they were not closed, as they usually were when he made love to her, but burning back into her own, moving from her breasts to her eyes, and back again. He gripped her thighs and rose swiftly, almost violently, to meet her. He crashed into her again and again, alternately moaning and whispering her name. She felt the absolute joy of his maleness filling her with an urgency she'd never felt in him before until finally his body shuddered and released her.

She slumped against him in the relief of spent passion. She turned off the lamp, then moved back into the warmth of his embrace. She drifted into a satisfied sleep, hearing him completely though he hadn't spoken a word.

Chapter Nine
December, 1996

Life was going to be easy now that he'd slipped into Ace's skin. Gray started in the mirror on the first Monday in December. The ugly purple bruises on his face were reduced to faint yellow welts, but more than that, the subtle hardness in his eyes said his naiveté and striving after love and acceptance had faded, too. He didn't care about those things any more.

He didn't speak to the social worker during the twenty-minute drive to Westbrook, but when they pulled down a tree-lined street and stopped in front of the Tudor mansion he turned to the other man in disbelief. He'd known the Mason's were rich, but surely there had been a mistake. Gray Baldwin didn't get breaks like this.

As if echoing his thoughts, the older man checked the address on his paperwork and nodded. "Yep. This is the place all right."

Gray collected his back pack and followed him up the cobbled path to a set of leaded glass doors. After ringing the bell, they stepped back to study the house. "In case you don't know it, you're gettin' a hell of a break," the social worker said. "These are decent people. For some insane reason they want to take you in. If y'all are as smart as they say you are, you'll stay in line."

Gray heard footsteps approaching from inside, and then the door opened and he was face to face with the richest woman he had ever seen. Forty something, he guessed, but dressed a whole lot younger. His eyes made a quick journey down her body, evaluating the faded designer jeans and tight fitting sweater. Her hair was artificially blonde and her face expertly made up to disguise years of baking in the Alabama sun.

"Good mornin'." She extended her hand first to the social worker and then to Gray. "I wasn't expectin' y'all quite so early. Lord, I haven't even put myself together yet."

The lie was gently and laughingly spoken from full, dark lips, and the sound of her voice was as sultry and caressing as the manicured hand that clasped Gray's own. His eyes made another lightning quick journey over her body, and then seeing he'd been caught looking, crashed to the ground.

The social worker cleared his throat. "Kendra Mason?"

She smiled brightly. "That's right. And this must be Gray."

He looked back into her eyes and saw that she hadn't been offended by his indiscretion, rather, pleased by his wholly male appraisal. Reminding himself he didn't feel things like embarrassment anymore, he squared his shoulders. "Yes, Ma'am."

"Come on in, darlin'. I'll show you to your room."

His bedroom was bigger than most houses he'd lived in. Kendra pulled open the closet doors to reveal racks of clothes, the price tags that hung from them revealing her exquisite taste.

"We picked up a few things for you," she said. "They didn't give us much to go by as far as your personal tastes … " Her eyes moved surreptitiously over his shabby clothes. "If there's anything in here y'all don't like, why you just put it aside and we'll take it back."

He nodded, hoping he didn't look as awed as he felt. There were more clothes in the closet than a person could wear in a lifetime.

When she finally left him alone he once again opened the closet door. He put his hands on all of the fabrics, read each of the labels. South Pole, Dockers, Tommy Hilfiger … He steeled himself against the gratitude that welled up inside him. He hadn't asked for any of this, had never asked to become some rich woman's charity of the week, in a league with Greenpeace and the National Endowment of the Arts.

"Save the whales. Save the manatees. And save the sorry ass of Gray Baldwin," he muttered, pulling the door closed.

The mansion and the new wardrobe were just the first of his surprises. He stood at his bedroom window at five, forty-five and watched as a metallic green Chrysler pulled in the driveway. He knew instinctively that the large man who stepped out was Burdette Mason, the corporate giant. He watched with curiosity as the man tucked in his shirt, smoothed back his thinning hair and strode toward the house. Moments later, Gray heard him enter the foyer, and stood in tensed silence waiting to be called downstairs.

Burdette "Buddy" Mason was as large and untidy as his wife was petite and perfect. Gray shook his enormous hand, surprised that it was not the soft executive's handshake he'd expected, but a firm, callused grip that spoke of years of physical labor. He looked into the laughing eyes and couldn't help but like the jolly corporate giant just a little.

Kendra insisted they celebrate Gray's arrival at The Yankee Court, the most exclusive restaurant in Westbrook. Gray sat at the table feeling as stiff as the linen napkin in his lap. He counted no less than six forks on the table beside him. As Buddy and Kendra sipped their chardonnay and made married conversation, Gray stared at the silverware, no clue what he was supposed to do with it all.

Kendra did her best to include him in her conversation but Gray barely responded to her questions. He struggled through the meal, measuring each bite of food he took, painfully careful not to slurp or spill.

Halfway through the entrée, a couple named Rhoda and Stephen Marks joined them at their table. The wealthy investor and his wife studied him, asking a million questions he couldn't answer and Gray felt their keen disapproval beneath their smiling veneer. He shifted in his chair, feeling like a square ball in their croquet set. They could go to hell. He wasn't buying into their phony act.

When they realized Gray wouldn't play their game, the couple set their sites on Buddy. Gray listened with interest to the comments Buddy made, silently cheering him on. He was civil and polite on the surface, but when thought about, his words were obvious barbs. Gray's finely tuned ear picked up a subtle tone of mockery in Buddy's speech and he knew Rhoda and Stephen Marks had met their match.

Finally Buddy stood. "I need to visit the washroom, if you'll all excuse me."

Fearing Stephen would target him in Buddy's absence, Gray stood quickly to his feet. "I'll go with you, Mr. Mason."

He followed Buddy through the restaurant, staying close in his shadow, as if that would shield him from the whispers and curious stares of the other patrons. Was he dressed wrong, he wondered, or did it show on his face that he was a punk impersonating a prince?

Once they were safely behind the oak doors, Buddy turned to him. "I'm sorry about this, kid," he said. "If it'd been left to me I wouldn't have put you through it."

Gray shrugged. "It don't bother me none."

"Are you sure?"

"Yessir."

"Good."

With this settled, Buddy let loose the loudest release of gas Gray had ever heard. "Damn, that's a relief."

Gray stared at him in disbelief. His face broke into a grin, and then a chuckle. When Buddy broke wind again, Gray nearly doubled over with laughter. "Damn, Buddy, I wish—" He paused to catch his breath. "I wish y'all would've given me some warnin'."

"I did give you some warning."

"Well hell, I thought y'all were apologizin' for havin' such obnoxious friends!"

Buddy hooted. In that moment Gray glimpsed beneath his prosperous exterior and saw a man as down to earth as Alabama clay. He chuckled again. The guy was Chevy Chase in a Georgio Armani suit.

Buddy clapped him on the shoulder. "I like you, boy," he said. "Now let's get the hell outta here."

As they walked from the rest room Gray quickly crawled back into his shell of aloofness. No way would he let this corporate clown know how much he was already liked and respected.

Like everything else in his new life, Westbrook Academy was outside anything in Gray's range of experiences. In addition to the state-of- the-art computers and lab equipment the school had an Olympic-sized swimming pool, which Gray took advantage of nearly every day.

He wandered through the halls and found himself welcomed rather than singled out for ridicule. Now that he wore the right clothes and lived in the right neighborhood he was accepted, even though he was still the same old Gray Baldwin. No, he corrected himself. The old Gray Baldwin would have been grateful for the crumbs they threw. The new Gray was cool and silent as steel. A man to be respected and even feared.

As much as he enjoyed swim class, it was The Sophomore Literary Group that was the high point in Gray's week. On his second Friday at the academy he arrived late and saw that his usual seat was occupied by a girl named Alexis he recognized from his biology class. He hesitated for a moment before sliding into the seat across the aisle. She leaned toward him and whispered, "Am I in your seat?"

He shrugged. "It don't matter none, darlin."

He had not meant to call her darlin', and the fact that he'd used the endearment surprised him as much as it did her. Her face broke into a dimpled, heart-melting smile.

They were studying the works of Thomas Wolfe and though he had a binder filled with notes, Gray found himself unable to contribute even one intelligent comment. His thoughts returned to Alexis' smile as often as his eyes did the sheer nylons that encased her lovely legs. When she smiled at him again he retreated behind his notebook like a snake to the shelter of a rock. He sat through the rest of the discussion aware of nothing but the uncomfortable snugness of his pants.

Alexis returned to the discussion group the following Friday. The more she spoke the more obvious it was to Gray that she hadn't done the required reading and wasn't the least bit interested in Thomas Wolfe. She started sitting next to him in biology class as well, and he watched every move she made through a thin veil of ambivalence.

By the end of December, she was hanging around him all the time, making small talk and dropping hints about parties and school dances. He dodged her with the skill of an Old West gunfighter, telling himself it was an ambush, that she was trying to coax him out into the open so she could shoot him down in cold blood. No way he'd make that mistake again.

On the day before Christmas break he found her waiting for him at his locker. When her fingertips brushed his arm he felt hundreds of electrical currents course through his body. "Hey, Gray? I was wonderin' ... Are y'all doing anything special for New Year's?"

He shifted his books and shrugged. "I don't know. Why?"

"Well, the thing is, I'm having a party. Nothin' real fancy. I was wonderin' if maybe y'all would like to stop by for awhile?"

He considered the invitation for all of thirty seconds, considered her raven-black hair and her soft, dimpled cheeks. Then he looked away. "I don't think I can make it."

"Oh."

Her expression betrayed a disappointment so genuine that he fought the urge to reconsider.

"All right, then. Maybe next time."

With what remained of her dignity, she turned and walked away.

Alone in his room that night he thought about how pretty she was and tortured himself with wondering what it would feel like to kiss her, to hold her in his arms and press his body tightly against hers. Rolling over, he told himself he'd done the right thing by turning her down. Like Ace said, girls were more trouble than they were worth. There wasn't a damned one of them that would tell a man the truth.

Chapter Ten
January, 1997

On the first day of the new year the temperature in Westbrook dropped to a chilling 38 degrees. Kendra lay in bed recovering from the corporate bash the night before. By mid-afternoon it became apparent to Buddy and Gray that they were on their own for dinner. At two o'clock Buddy rolled from the couch, rubbed his generous middle, and yawned. "Well, let's go and see what we can find in that kitchen of hers."

Gray trailed after him and stood looking over Buddy's shoulder into the cupboards. There were dozens of bottles filled with herbs and plastic containers labeled with words like wheat germ, barley flour, and bouillabaisse. Buddy removed the cover from a rectangular jar and stared at the tangle of thin, green pasta inside. He turned back to Gray. "I don't suppose y'all know the magic formula that turns any of this stuff into food."

"No, Sir."

"Me either." He snapped the lid back in place and grabbed his jacket. "Let's go."

Within minutes they were wandering the aisles of the supermarket, and in the tradition of hungry, clueless men, began haphazardly filling their cart.

"Doughnuts are good," Buddy said. "Y'all like doughnuts?"

"Yeah, I like 'em," Gray said, ducking when a box of Freihoffers came hurling toward him. He bent to pick them up.

"How about chips?" Buddy asked. "You want Doritos or Cheese Doodles?"

"Don't make no difference to me." He sprang after the two bags of chips that sailed through the air. "I wish you wouldn't—"

"How about soda?"

"Buddy, quit it!" He laughed, barely catching the two-liter bottle of soda Buddy tossed in his direction. "Don't, now. I ain't gonna catch nothing else." As he said it, he leapt for the bottle of Club soda Buddy threw.

"I know what we're forgetting. Bacon. And eggs. Might as well think about tomorrow's breakfast, too, if I know anything about my wife."

He strode down the aisles, oblivious to Gray's protests as he tossed various food items over his shoulder. Gray followed behind with the cart, dodging and catching with the skill of a linebacker. Finally Buddy stopped in front of the dairy case, scratching his head as he scanned the labels.

"Jumbo," he finally said, removing a carton of eggs from the cooler.

"No! Don't!" Gray said. When Buddy grinned wickedly, he folded his arms across his chest. "Go ahead. Throw 'em. I'm telling' you, I ain't gonna catch 'em."

"Yes, you will."

"No, I won't." He stubbornly stood his ground while Buddy shook the carton of eggs at him. "Yes, you will. Know how I know?"

"How?"

"'Cause underneath that tough-guy act of yours there's a decent kid who wants to play by the rules."

Gray watched as the eggs came at him, seemingly in slow motion. At the last moment he made a grab for them, but not quickly enough.

"Aww, man ..." He bent over the gooey mess. "Now look what y'all did."

He glanced up to see that Buddy had disappeared. In his place stood a chubby, angry woman. With her stout body and pronounced overbite, she looked like a human bulldog. His glance went to her smock, where the name Bitsy was embroidered in black lettering. Below it, the words: *Proudly serving you for twelve years.*

"I'm sorry," he stammered, "I—"

"Joe!" she bellowed. "Wet spill, aisle three!"

"I'll be glad to pay you for 'em."

"You bet you will!" She stood there staring at him for a full sixty seconds before she turned and marched away.

He found Buddy in the deli, salivating over a display of rotisserie chickens. "Ever smell anything as nice as those?" he asked. "Y'all like rotisserie?"

 Gray gave him an icy stare. "Yeah, I do. And by the way, thanks for makin' me look like a fool."

Buddy grinned. "I proved my point, didn't I?"

"You proved nothin'. Now I can see why Miz Kendra don't take you shopping. Made me look like a fool, and now ol' Bitsy's into me for a buck and a half."

Buddy suppressed a smile. Despite himself, Gray grinned and gave him a shove.

Buddy shoved him back. "I wouldn't do it to Kendra."

"I know you wouldn't. Wouldn't dare!"

"You're right."

They laughed for a moment, and Buddy said, "Hey, I'm sorry I made you look like a fool."

Gray cracked a smile. "No you ain't."

After the deli clerk boxed up their chicken, they proceeded to the check out line. "I am," Buddy insisted. "And just to prove it, I'm gonna square you up with Bitsy."

"Well that's real big of you, Buddy." Gray heaped the items onto the conveyor belt, enjoying the moment of bonding until a soft voice spoke his name. "Gray Baldwin, it is you. I thought I saw y'all in the dairy section."

He glanced up to see Alexis standing in front of him and gave her a tight smile.

"Are y'all having a nice vacation?"

He thought how he'd spent New Year's Eve alone in the giant house, so bored he'd resorted to channel surfing on the Mason's big-screen TV before finally going to bed before midnight.

"Sure."

She lowered her gaze. "That's good."

She made a heroic attempt at small talk while her items were being bagged, then stood in embarrassed silence. "Well, I expect I'll be seeing y'all in school next week."

"I expect."

"Well … 'bye now."

As she walked from the store, Buddy gave Gray another shove, his eyes wide with disbelief. "What in hell's half acre is the matter with you, boy? You got cramps in your brain from all that readin' you been doin'?"

"What do you mean?"

He gestured toward the door through which Alexis had disappeared. "That little darlin' is crazy over you, and you barely gave her the time of day."

Gray shrugged.

"Damn. You're a mean little shit, aren't you?" He shook his head. "When I was your age I loved them soft little critters. Loved as many of 'em as I could get my hands on."

Gray shrugged again and waited while Buddy paid the bill. They were almost to the car when Buddy spoke again. "I guess you mean to tell me you don't."

"Don't what?"

"Love them soft little critters," Buddy said impatiently.

Gray lifted two shopping bags from the cart and set them in the back seat of Buddy's Chrysler. "Not much."

Buddy hesitated, and in a voice only half joking, asked, "Y'all don't like boys, do you?"

Gray faced him, eyes narrowed. "I don't love nothin', Buddy. Male or female."

Buddy was quiet for a moment, contemplative. "How about metal?"

"Huh?"

"Come on. There's something I been wanting to show you."

They pulled from the lot and headed across town. When they reached Forrester Products, the giant corporation owned by Kendra's father, Buddy maneuvered the car through the maze of side paths and pulled up in front of a small cinderblock outbuilding. Letting the engine idle, he turned to Gray. "This is my best-kept secret. I want it to stay that way, all right?"

"All right," Gray said, burning with curiosity.

As soon as Buddy pushed open the door Gray's senses were assaulted by the scents of grease and motor oil. Buddy flipped on an overhead light. In the center of the room was a mustang convertible, or what was left of one, sitting on concrete blocks. The motor had been torn out and its pieces lay scattered on the floor.

Gray's eyes swept across the room. Everywhere he looked there was work in progress. His gaze took in the piles of dirty rags, the dark puddles of grease, and the tools that lay in haphazard order all around the garage. "What is all this?" he asked.

"My heart and soul, boy."

An aura of maleness permeated the room, so strongly there might as well have been a sign on the door: No Women Allowed! Or rather, Gray thought, no wives.

"You mean to tell me Kendra don't know about this place?"

Buddy smiled. "She knows I have a place somewhere, but she don't know exactly where it is. If she did, she'd be wanting to come in and clean up. Hell, she'd be putting lace doilies on my work bench."

Gray grinned.

"Nope." Buddy moved to the mustang and lovingly ran his fingers over the hood. "Man's gotta have something he keeps back for himself." He added wistfully, "There was a time I got paid good money to play around with an engine."

Suddenly Gray understood the work roughened hands, the mannerisms that suggested a life lived outside the ivory tower.

"Y'all were a mechanic?"

"Yup."

"And now you're pushin' a pencil, and you hate it."

Buddy didn't bother to deny it. "That's right."

"Then why do you do it?"

He smiled; the small, sad smile of a man caught in a crucible. "Because I love her. Because it was the only way I could have her." He turned back to the car, his hand once again caressing the hood. "Hell, once I agreed to be her daddy's hand puppet, they had me outta my coveralls and into a suit quicker'n a man can piss."

Gray stood silent in the solemnness of the moment, watching Buddy's hands move to the door handle, the broken taillight. "Man's gotta have a place he can be himself. A place he can go to forget his worries for awhile. A place he can be a man." He faced Gray again, his expression dead serious. "This is my place, Gray. The piece of myself I keep back. My sanity. Can you understand that?"

Gray nodded, all at once feeling weighed down. Buddy's words merely echoed those Ace had spoken months ago. Love was a trap to be avoided at all costs. He sighed and as his breath pulled away from his body, he felt the last of his illusions go with it.

"Come over here. This is what I wanted to show you."

He walked to the corner where Buddy lifted a sheet away from what he assumed would be another spent piece of metal. Drawing nearer, he saw it was a motorcycle. A black motorcycle with wide whites and a set of full, if dented, fenders. A chill passed through him.

"Picked this little darlin' up at an auction in Augusta," Buddy said. "A 1966 One-Fifty Honda Dream. She's a rare beast."

Gray stared at the motorcycle as if mesmerized.

"Some poor bastard took a spill on her ten years ago and locked her in a warehouse. She ain't run since."

"What's wrong with her?"

"I dunno. Probably more than would be worth fixing." He shrugged. "I keep her around anyway. Reminds me of a bike I had when I was about your age."

Gray stood beside the motorcycle, unable to stop touching the handlebars, the cracked leather seat.

"She ain't one of them crotch rockets y'all are so crazy about these days, but I expect she's still got plenty of piss and vinegar left in her."

Buddy draped the sheet back around the Honda and Gray reluctantly let his hands fall away.

"Somethin' about a bike," Buddy continued. "You wrap your legs around a good bike, it can be more satisfying than a woman, some ways." He gave the sheet a pat. "You don't have to worry about performing, or whether y'all are pleasing her, don't even have to worry about where you're going. Just sit back and let her take you." A few moments passed as the two stared at the mound beneath the sheet, and then Buddy said, "Let's get outta here."

Heading home, it was clear that Buddy's thoughts were still on the motorcycle. "Maybe y'all could come down with me sometimes, help me work on her a little."

Gray's head snapped in his direction. "I'd love it. I mean, I don't know nothing' about motorcycles, but I'd sure be willin' to learn."

Buddy reached over and slapped his arm in a gesture of male camaraderie. "Just remember... she finds out about it, and ..." He drew his finger across his throat.

Gray couldn't stop thinking about the motorcycle. It loomed larger than life in his memory as he lay awake night after night, haunted by the sense of freedom and power he'd felt just being in the same room with it. He thought about it long and hard, imagining what it would feel like to be on it, racing through the countryside, the wind slapping his face. He waited, every day that passed an eternity, for Buddy to bring it up again.

Chapter Eleven
May, 1997

Hope couldn't remember when she'd been more excited. She sat between her parents at the dining room table, gaping at the piles of brochures daddy brought home with him that evening. He'd decided it was time the family went on vacation, and now her mind was boggled by all of the choices, and by the possibility of getting out of Mt. Bishop for a whole week. It was only the twelfth of May. How could she possibly wait until July?

"How about Colonial Williamsburg?" her mother said, leafing through a pamphlet. "It looks fun and educational."

Hope shot an anxious glance at her father. To her, vacation meant big cities and fancy restaurants—excitement. Definitely not education.

"New York City!" she shouted, before he could answer. "I want to see the Statue of Liberty and Times Square. I want to shop at Saks Fifth Avenue!"

"New York City," Jared scoffed. "Why don't we just buy four one-way tickets to hell instead?"

"Jared," her father warned. "Hope's allowed her say, the same as you."

When Hope stuck her tongue out at him, Jared stuck up his middle finger. "Daddy, Jared just—"

"Actually I was thinking of something a little more relaxing," her father said. All eyes turned to him expectantly. Having finally consented to take a week off from Hanwell Contracting, they knew the final decision would be his.

"What were you thinking, Ted?" her mother asked.

"How about Lake Erie?"

It was not a question, Hope knew, but a decision and her heart sank to her shoes. She wasn't into water any more than she was education.

"There's a resort town about a half hour outside of Cleveland. It's less than two hours' driving distance from here. We could rent a cabin for the week." His eyes moved down the page. "There would be something for everyone. Cleveland has the Rock and Roll Hall of Fame, the Cleveland Museum of Art, trendy shopping districts. And for quiet days, the resort offers fishing, boating, parks ..." His hand reached across the table, covering mother's. "Moonlit swimming."

"Stop that," she said softly. A blush spread across her face, but Hope could tell she was glad he said it. She and Jared looked at each other and rolled their eyes, for once united. They hated it when their parents got dopey. It was a complete mystery to Hope. An iceberg when it came to rules and regulations, mother was as slushy as ice cream when it came to dad.

"What kind of shopping?" she asked, her lips gathered in a pout.

Her father smiled. "Well, let's see here ... It says jewelry and clothing outlets, shoes ..."

"Okay, I'll go."

He turned to Jared. "What say you, Sport?"

Jared shrugged. "I don't care."

"It's your vacation too, Jared. Speak now or forever hold your pizza."

"Could we really go on a fishing boat? Just you and me?"

"You bet we could. According to this brochure they have some of the best fishing in the state."

"All right. I vote yes, I guess."

Hope lay in her bed that night, still thinking about the vacation. She wished she were going to Cleveland with Morgan and Mrs. Foster, instead of Mother. Mrs. Foster was so much cooler.

She already knew how it would be. Mother wouldn't let her out of her sight the whole time, and there would be no chance of meeting any cute boys. And because she couldn't swim, she'd get stuck going to museums while Jared hogged up all of daddy's attention, just like he always did.

Oh, how she hated him.

Chapter Twelve
May, 1997

Kendra looked as smug as a walker hound that had treed its first raccoon. Gray glanced up from his dinner more than once to see her watching him, an undercurrent of energy glittering in her sea green eyes. He shifted in his chair, knowing the electricity he felt was directed at him, but for the life of him not knowing why.

It wasn't until the plates were cleared away and she and Buddy lingered over coffee that she finally came out with it. She ran her fingertip along the rim of her coffee cup and daintily cleared her throat. "I have a bone to pick with you, Gray Baldwin."

He shot an anxious glance at her face and was relieved when the thin line of her lips softened in a smile. "How could you not have told us tomorrow is your sixteenth birthday?"

"I dunno. Just didn't think about it, I guess."

"Well, lucky for you, I did think about it. Wait right here."

She left the room and he looked to Buddy for a clue, but his friend only lifted his shoulders and smiled. Moments later Kendra returned carrying a cake blazing with sixteen candles. When she and Buddy broke into song Gray stared at his hands in embarrassment.

Kendra smiled at him again. "We'll have to celebrate tonight because Buddy'll be leavin' for Chicago first thing in the mornin'. Make a wish, now."

He stared blankly at the cake, knowing there was nothing left to wish for, nothing more he deserved or wanted. Nothing, that was, except … His thoughts went fleetingly to the Honda, shrouded and forgotten in the corner of Buddy's workshop. He closed his eyes and blew out the candles.

When they'd finished their cake, Kendra left the room again, this time returning with a large box. Once again Gray felt flames of embarrassment color his face. Aside from the silver cross that hung from a chain around his neck, it was the first real present he'd ever been given. He lowered his eyes so she wouldn't see how badly he wanted it, whatever it was.

"Y'all didn't have to get me somethin," he said softly.

Buddy slapped playfully at Gray's head. "That's what I tried to tell her."

His hands trembled slightly as he lifted the cover from the box. Removing the tissue paper, he sucked in a breath as one by one he pulled out the books. Thomas Wolfe, John Steinbeck, and Upton Sinclair. Edgar Alan Poe, D.H. Lawrence, and Ernest Hemmingway. His own personal library of books, all leather bound and all in perfect condition. He ran his hands over the covers, staring at them until he trusted himself to look at Kendra. "I don't know what to say."

"It wasn't anything, Gray. I picked them up in an old barn outside of town. Fact is, I'm almost ashamed to give them to you, as little as I paid for them."

He looked away, knowing the lie was meant to save his pride. The books were first edition and must have cost her a fortune. "A thing don't have to be expensive to be good," he murmured.

"Well now, I guess you're right," she said, as if the thought never occurred to her.

He took the books to his room later and studied them, not so much reading them as savoring the feel of the worn and yellowed pages, pages that spoke of other hands holding them, owning them, just as he owned them now.

He awoke the next morning to the sound of voices in the driveway beneath his window. Looking out, he saw Buddy pack his suitcase into the trunk of the Chrysler, and he knew by the slow way he moved how much Buddy hated the corporate conventions.

Pulling on a pair of jeans, he hurried downstairs to say goodbye. He stood at the edge of the driveway, staring at his feet as Buddy gave Kendra a lingering kiss, then shoved his hands in his pockets and walked up to the car window. "Have a good time, Buddy," he said.

Buddy snorted. "Yeah." Then he smiled. "Have a good birthday, kid."

"I will."

When Kendra disappeared behind the patio doors Buddy spoke again. "Close your eyes and put out your hand."

Gray hesitated for a moment, then did as Buddy instructed. When he felt the warmth of Buddy's skin merge with cool metal, his eyes flew open. "Buddy, I can't let y'all—"

"Shhh. Don't say anything, just put it in your pocket. When I get back we'll see if we can't get her running."

Without another word he backed from the driveway, leaving Gray to stare after him, the key to the Honda clutched tightly in his hand.

He was relieved when he got home from school and saw the note propped beside his place at the table. Kendra's rolling cursive informed him she was volunteering at the art gallery and he would find his dinner in the crock pot. He'd had visions of Kendra "surprising" him with dinner at one of her five-star restaurants and didn't think he could stomach it without Buddy to take the stiffness out.

He lifted the lid on the crock pot and sniffed the herb and spice scents of cooking meat, then set it back in place and carried his back pack to his room.

He worked uninterrupted until six o'clock, when his hunger drove him back to the kitchen. He ladled out a plateful of stew and carried it to the table. The solitude was a welcome change. Not that he didn't like Kendra, but it was awkward without Buddy.

When he'd finished a second helping of stew he rinsed his plate and set it in the dishwasher, then returned to his room to finish his homework. The key to the Honda sat on his desk and he stopped now and then to touch it, barely able to believe the motorcycle was really his.

By nine o'clock he'd finished his math assignment and read ahead three chapters in his history book. Rubbing his eyes, he closed his books and went back downstairs. He turned on the television and began to surf through the channels, but finding nothing of interest, turned it off and returned to his room. Not knowing what to do with himself, he stripped to his shorts and climbed into bed.

It was after ten o'clock when he heard Kendra's Lincoln pull into the driveway. He lay awake, listening to her move around in the kitchen below, and then to the far away sound of running water. He'd just fallen asleep when he was awakened by a soft tap at his door. It opened just enough to admit her head and a stream of splintered light.

"Gray," she said softly. "Are y'all still awake?"

He sat and pulled the sheet around himself. "Yeah, I'm awake."

She took a step into the room. The burgundy satin of her robe gleamed in the soft light behind her and he saw that she carried a bottle of champagne and two glasses. "I didn't expect to be so late," she said. "I thought we might have a little drink together to celebrate your birthday." She moved unsteadily across the room, speaking each word with careful emphasis.

She hadn't been in his room since the first day he'd arrived, and Gray eyed her warily. "Alright."

She perched on the edge of his bed. Immediately he smelled the alcohol and the soft cloud of perfume that clung to her. She poured the glass too full and champagne sloshed onto the sheets when she handed it to him. Pouring another for herself, she set the bottle on the night table beside the bed. Her hand hovered above the radio for a moment before she turned it on.

When the sound of rock and roll blasted into the room she scowled and turned the dial to a soft rock station and sat back with a smile. She crossed her legs, exposing them up to the thigh, while she sipped her champagne. Gray stared at the wall, completely at a loss for what to think, let alone what to say. It was hard enough to talk to Kendra when she was fully dressed, let alone half naked.

"What's the matter, Gray?"

"Nothin'," he said, voice cracking.

He gulped his champagne, ignoring the sweetly sour bubbles that tickled his nose and the back of his throat. His glance darted to the door, and then across to the open window. Everywhere except to the long brown legs inches from his own. He downed the last of his drink and handed her the glass, hoping she would leave.

She didn't.

She reached across and refilled it, all the while talking in a faraway voice about birthdays, the passing of time, and growing old.

By the time he'd finished his third glass Gray felt lightheaded. She took it from his hand and set it on the table, then moved dangerously close to him. "Did I give y'all a nice birthday, Gray?"

He forced his eyes away from the outline of her breasts beneath her robe, so close they almost brushed against his arm.

"Yes Ma'am, Miz Kendra."

"I'm glad," she purred. "But we're not even close to done celebrating yet."

She ran her fingertips along his arm. When he tensed, she laughed, a deep, throaty, drunken laugh. "What's the matter, honey? Don't y'all like me touchin' you? Don't it feel good?"

He closed his eyes for a moment, confused by the champagne and her nearness and the sudden heat that filled the room. "I don't … No."

She laughed again, a wicked and musical sound that made him shudder. "You don't, or you don't know?"

"I …"

Her lips brushed his chin, and then slid to his neck while her hands glided over his chest. "I think you do," she whispered. "I think you like it a lot."

His heart hammered and his brain filled with a jumble of sensations as her tongue gently lapped at his arm pit. "Miz Kendra, I don't think we should be doin' this."

She sucked first one nipple and then the other. Electricity jolted through his body when she nipped at him with her tiny, sharp teeth.

"We're not doing anything wrong, darlin."

He tried to speak but his breath came out a ragged sigh as her hands slid down his waist. "You're a little honey-boy," she murmured. "I just want to hold you, honey-boy. Can't I hold you for a minute?"

She flattened her body against his. Her tongue made an agonizing journey to his ear while her hands slid over his buttocks.

"Oh, God … Stop."

"Why should I stop, Gray? Why should I stop if it makes you feel good?"

"'Cause I don't think Buddy would like it," he managed. "Fact I know he wouldn't."

This time her laughter was a rumble that started deep in her throat. "Buddy ain't here, darlin'. And I'm certainly not gonna tell him about it. Are you?"

"Miz Kendra. I think y'all are a little bit dru—"

"Kiss me, Gray, just once. If y'all don't like the way it feels, you just tell me and I'll go."

Before he could answer, she pressed her lips against his. He felt the sensation of her velvety tongue probing his mouth. A small moan escaped him. As if they were disconnected from his body, his will, his hands moved down her back, lost in the silky smoothness of her robe. Her eyes stared into his, strangely bright.

"Have you ever been with a woman, Gray?"

He shook his head.

"I didn't think so."

The confession seemed to excite her. In what seemed a liquid motion she was on top of him, straddling him with her thighs. She untied her sash and the robe slipped from her shoulders. Her breasts were large and firm and perfect and he couldn't keep from staring at them.

"Do you like what you see?" she teased.

His blood slammed through his veins, pounding so fiercely in his ears it drowned out his hoarse whisper. "Yes."

"Put your hands on them," she coaxed. "Feel how soft they are."

Gray was at war with himself; half hot, aching desire and the other half nagging conscience. He tore his eyes away from her. "I can't."

She took his hands and placed them firmly over her breasts, holding them fast. "There now, you see. It's not so bad, is it?"

Slowly, cautiously, he felt them, gently kneading until their centers stood out in stiff points against his palms. When he pinched them between his fingers she moaned and pulled his head closer. He sought her hungrily, yet carefully.

"Oh, that's so nice," she whispered. "That's so nice, honey-boy."

Finally she pulled away and took his face in her hands. "Know what I think, Gray Baldwin? I think y'all aren't as mean as you try to make out. I think you're just a lonely boy who hasn't had near enough lovin'." She kissed him gently, sinking her teeth into his lower lip. "Let me love you, Gray."

His breath came out in a series of sharp, painful gasps as she ground her hips against his aching arousal. She slowly moved down the length of his body, inching back the sheet with her fingers while her lips traced a path to his rib cage.

"Kendra, I'm begging you. Don't."

"Shhh." Her tongue darted in and out of his belly button before dipping beneath the waistband of his shorts. When it made contact with his hardened flesh he groaned and slammed his eyes shut.

"Mm. That's one beautiful piece of equipment y'all have there, honey-boy," she murmured.

A sound more animal than human rumbled from deep in his throat when she pulled back his shorts and took him into her mouth. All thoughts of right and wrong fled as she moved over him, working magic with her tongue. He grasped her head and pulled it tightly against him, rising to meet her as he felt more pleasure than he had ever, in his wildest fantasies, thought possible. He was helpless, at one with her mouth and her tongue and the throbbing beat of the music on the radio. She was a goddess. He loved her. And at the same time, he hated her.

When he awoke the next morning she was gone. Glancing around his room, he saw no wine, no glasses, no trace that she'd been there at all. Only the cold fingers of guilt that clutched his heart told him he hadn't dreamed it.

He put off going downstairs until he knew he'd be late for school if he put it off any longer. He walked into the kitchen. Relief pooled in his gut when he saw the note propped against the coffee maker:

Gray, I'll be volunteering at the Red Cross for most of the day. If I'm not home for dinner, order a pizza. Kendra.

Beside the note lay a crisp hundred-dollar bill. The sight of it sickened him. A hundred bucks for a lousy pizza? Or is it for something else? He shoved it away from him and slammed out the door.

Concentrating on anything that day was impossible. His moods swung from shame to elation and back again. Images of the previous night played out in his head like silent movies. How could he have let her do it? How could he not have?

He found himself looking at the girls around him with new respect, no different than they'd been the day before, and yet, completely changed now that he knew of their tantalizing powers.

He arrived home to find Kendra already there. She chattered all through dinner, telling him about her work at the Red Cross, and the donations she'd secured that day. She asked about his classes and his Sophomore Literary Group. She made no mention of the previous night and Gray began to wonder if he'd dreamed it after all.

He felt edgy, uneasy, unable to relax until her Lincoln pulled out of the driveway that evening. He opened his science book, closed it again, and turned on the television. He surfed through the channels, not seeing. The phone rang three times but he made no move to answer it. It was probably Buddy calling to check in, and he couldn't bear the thought of talking to him. He found himself thinking of Ace, wishing his friend was there to help him make sense of the damned thing.

He'd no sooner dropped into a fitful sleep when the headlights of Kendra's Lincoln swept across the walls of his bedroom. He heard Kendra enter the house and he tensed, following the sound of her movements downstairs.

When his bedroom door cracked open he slammed his eyes shut, pretending to be asleep. She moved across the room as silent as a shadow and slid into bed beside him. Her hands felt warm and soft as they moved along his back, encircled his waist and finally came to rest on his abdomen. A white-hot flame of longing leapt through his veins when she whispered his name. "Gray, are you awake?"

He kept his eyes closed, not answering, hoping she'd go away, knowing she wouldn't. She pressed her body tight against him. He moaned softly as her hand traveled along his thigh. Summoning every ounce of self control he possessed, he pushed it away. "Kendra, I ain't gonna do this. Buddy, he's been real good to me."

"Shh." She pressed her fingertips against his lips. "Don't think about it. Just think about how good I'm gonna make you feel." Her hand crept beneath the waistband of his shorts. "Don't you want to feel good, hm?"

"Kendra, it ain't right."

"Don't worry, baby. I'm gonna teach you everything you need to know." She loosened the sash on her robe and guided his hands inside. "Go ahead, honey. See how much I want you? I ache inside, just like you do."

She guided his hands down her body, bringing them to rest on the soft crop of hair between her thighs. He pulled away as if he'd been burned.

"Don't be afraid of it darlin'," she murmured, firmly guiding his hand back. "This is the best part of me."

Slowly, carefully, he pressed his fingers into the warm, velvety softness between her legs.

"Right here, darlin'." She guided his hand to a hot, throbbing knot of flesh. "Like this."

It was softer and warmer than anything he'd ever touched. He watched her face, almost drunk on knowing he was responsible for the fierce passion he saw there.

They explored each other for what seemed an agonizing forever, kissing and touching until he was certain he'd explode.

"All right, Gray," she finally whispered. "Do you feel how hot and wet I am now?"

He nodded and nervously wet his lips.

"That means I'm ready, sweetheart."

He stared into her eyes, terrified and wildly excited. "I ..." He swallowed. "I'm not sure I know what to do."

She laughed. "Oh, you are a sweet one, honey-boy. Come here."

She wrapped her legs around his waist and inched closer, arched her back, and suddenly, he was inside her. Warm and slippery soft, he felt her flesh tighten around him like a velvet hand. He rocked his body against hers, needing more, slowly, as she rose to meet him, and then faster.

He came almost instantly.

"Oh, God," he panted, turning his face away in shame.

"It's all right," she said, pulling his head to her breast. "It happens to everybody the first time." She laughed, a short, sharp bark. "Hell, it still happens to Buddy." Reaching for the pack of cigarettes she'd left on the night table, she lit one for each of them. "You'll get better. Just gonna take some practicing."

•

The following Thursday Buddy was home. Gray avoided him for three days, sick to his stomach and unable to look him in the eye. He knew if he looked him in the eye his guilt would be as obvious as an outright confession.

On Sunday, with no school and no place to hide, he walked downstairs and found Buddy waiting in the kitchen, a wide, Cheshire-cat grin on his face.

"Mornin' kid." He slapped Gray on the back, then lowered his voice. "You ready to get at that bike? She'll be going shopping, and if I know anything about my wife, that'll give us the whole day."

Gray managed a wan smile. *If y'all knew anything about your wife, you wouldn't be wanting to spend the day with me, I guarantee it.*

As they drove across town to Forrester Products, Gray found his sickness merging with anticipation. When Buddy unlocked the door to his workshop and flipped the switch, Gray's eyes moved anxiously to the corner. His relief was an audible sigh when he saw the Honda as they'd left it. Buddy rolled up his sleeves.

"Might as well start at the beginning."

He uncovered the motorcycle and moved it to the center of the room, then began to change the spark plugs. Gray stood in reverent silence as he removed the old, burned out plugs and screwed in the gleaming new ones. With that accomplished, Buddy smiled and took the key from Gray's hand.

"Be getting out of it damned easy if that's all it took." He turned the key and Gray listened to the silence with painful disappointment. Buddy smiled again. "Didn't think so."

He moved like a god, disconnecting the fuel line and checking the gas. Checking the battery. Cleaning and tightening the terminal connections and then checking it again. He reset the timing, disassembled the carburetor float, checked the gaskets and replaced the leaky seals. Gray all but got down on his knees. Hell, he'd have done a rain dance. Anything, anything to make the Honda run, but it didn't.

"Don't give up," Buddy said. "It could still be a lot of little things. He removed the carburetor and scanned the length of it. "What's the matter with you lately, Gray? You seem as nervous as a cat."

Gray's hand froze on the screw he was tightening. Not trusting his voice, he shrugged.

"Anything happen while I was gone?"

"No." He felt himself start to sweat. He turned away quickly, clipped an oil can with his elbow and sent it crashing to the floor. He bent to retrieve it, knowing as he did that it was over. Buddy knew. When he chanced a glance at the other man's face, he saw to his astonishment that Buddy was smiling.

"Only one thing I know of can make a man act like an ice cube on fire. Y'all got yourself a girl, don't ya?"

Gray's eyes crashed to the floor, his face darkening to a crimson Buddy mistook for embarrassment. He shrugged again. "Maybe."

Buddy reached across and took a bear paw swipe at Gray's head. "Maybe, nothing! Y'all got yourself a girl. Hey, I bet it's that pretty little darlin' from down at the supermarket, right? I don't suppose a skinny little punk like you could do much better'n that."

He inclined his face toward Gray, eager to be taken into sacred male confidence, and was visibly disappointed when Gray turned away. "All right, you don't have to tell me if you don't want to."

When Gray offered nothing further, Buddy turned back to his work. "Guess we'd better get this little darlin' moving, then. Man's gotta have a nice ride when he's got a pretty little girl to impress."

Chapter Thirteen
July, 1997

Lake Erie was everything Hope's father promised it would be.

The cabin was a small slice of heaven cradled between woods and water and even the fact she had to share a room with Jared could not spoil the good mood that had settled over her since they arrived. Sharing a room with her brother was a pain, but luckily Hope had barely seen the back side of the front door all week.

The first day they'd gone to Six Flags Theme Park, arriving when the gates opened and staying until they were blistered with walking and sunshine. They'd been to the Rock and Roll Hall of Fame and to the flea markets on Antiques Row.

One day her father took Jared out on a fishing boat and she and Dana spent the day strolling through Tremont, visiting the trendy boutiques. She thought of the awesome jewelry she'd bought and hugged herself. She'd wear the turquoise ankle bracelet with her white mini skirt, the shell earrings with her new gauze top. She smiled, thinking how jealous Morgan would be.

It seemed to Hope her parents were trying to make up for never taking a vacation by filling every inch of this one with activity. That morning they took off for Cleveland, even though it was raining. Looking out the window, she frowned. How could it rain and spoil the last day of their vacation?

She glanced longingly toward the lake, remembering the day she and dad went out in the rowboat, how she'd dipped the long net beneath the surface of the clean, clear water and gleaned a small fortune in brightly colored sea glass. She needed at least a dozen more pieces to finish the necklace she was making.

She scowled at the gray sky. It had been awesome out on the

lake and she'd waited all week for another chance at the beautiful glass. She needed a dozen more good-sized pieces, at least.

But it rained all last night and most of the morning and now the wind was slapping the waves clear up over the dock. Tomorrow they were leaving, heading back to dull, boring Mt. Bishop. Her scowl deepened as she thought of the necklace, lying half finished, at the bottom of her suitcase.

Moving away from the window, she pulled on her sneakers and grabbed the empty jar she used to collect her treasures in. As she walked past, Jared looked up from the video he was watching.

"Where do you think you're going?"

"I'm going for a walk down by the lake."

"No you're not."

She glared at him. "What's it to you?"

"You don't know how to swim and I don't feel like baby sitting you. And besides, dad told us not to go down there today. There's a big storm heading in and the lake is getting rough. I'll catch hell if you drown."

"I'm not going in the water, jackass, just beside it. And anyway, I'll be back way before mom and dad are."

He studied her for a moment, then turned back to his movie with a shrug. "Do whatever you want, Hope. You always do anyway."

She bit back a smile as she breezed from the cabin. She hadn't thought it would be so easy to get past him. He was sixteen, only four years older than her, but he acted like her warden whenever mom and dad were away.

She hummed a small tune as she picked her way down the steep embankment that led to the waterfront. It was raining harder than she'd thought, but no way was she going back for her windbreaker. She definitely wanted to be back inside when her parents returned, and besides, she might not get past Jared so easily next time.

She neared the water's edge cautiously. The lake was different today; wild and angry looking. There was a heaviness in the air, and thunder rumbled in the distance. She'd definitely have to hurry.

Holding tight to her jar, she waded into the water. It was much colder than the day before, and within moments her feet were numb. As she bent to pick up a smooth, green stone, a wave rose up and splashed her in the face, nearly knocking her off balance. Undaunted, she carefully put one foot in front of the other. The water was nearly up to her waist when she heard Jared's voice call sharply from the top of the embankment.

"Hope! You'd better get … ass … water! Dad …swim … rough…"

The wind whistled across the water, carrying his voice away from her. Ignoring him, she took another step, determined to find enough glass to finish her necklace. She scooped handfuls of sand and stone from the bottom of the lake and dumped them into her jar. She'd sort them out later.

When the jar was full, she turned back to see Jared climbing down the embankment. He looked mad and she knew he was going to tell dad she'd disobeyed.

She was inching her way back to the shore when she saw it; a flash of glittering white beneath the muddy waves, just inches from where she stood. Something dazzling and wonderful. The sea glass paled in comparison and she let go of the jar and stepped back out into the waves. She had to have it, whatever it was.

She held her breath, fighting back her fear as the waves tugged at her, beckoning her farther. If she could just edge her foot out a bit more without losing her balance, she could reach the prize.

Jared's voice called insistently but she couldn't make out his words above the sudden wailing wind and the sound of her own desire, telling her she must have the beautiful string of lights. One more step and it would be hers. Just one more—

All at once the lake floor sloped sharply, causing her to lose her footing. She thrashed as she went under, arms flailing as she groped wildly for her prize. She felt a rush of exhilaration as her fingers closed around it.

Pulling it close, she studied it and her triumph was swallowed up in disappointment. It was nothing but a Dollar Store trinket, a child's necklace, beads of tin and plastic dangling from a broken elastic band. With the realization that her coveted treasure was a piece of junk came a more terrifying one. She was in more danger than she'd ever been before.

The waves rushed over her, consuming her. Squatting on the lake floor, she jumped, shooting up from the water in what she thought was the direction of the shore. The swirling vortex caught her, pulling her back out into the lake. She screamed as once again the water closed in around her.

She surfaced, shrieking in panic, her hands crashing wildly around her as water filled her nose and mouth.

Suddenly Jared was beside her. His arms, small for a sixteen-year-old, pulled her head above the waves. She grasped hold of him, shouting above the wind as they both went under.

Jared kicked his legs, screamed at her not to fight, to hold his waist and let him guide her in. She couldn't hear him, couldn't make sense of his words through the hysteria that held her in its grasp.

The water was a relentless adversary, pulling them farther out into the center of its being. She spied a float several feet away and knew it was their only hope. She thrashed wildly, desperate to reach its safety as Lake Erie's icy hands pulled them downward, seeking to claim them for its own.

Oh, God … Oh, God … Daddy …

Wind and lightning and water and panic. Pulling. Pulling. Pulling. They were almost to the float when suddenly Jared stopped trying. She hadn't realized she was pulling him under until she released her hold on him and grasped the edge of the float. Her hands made contact, slipped down, made contact again.

From what seemed miles away she heard a voice screaming her name. Dazed, she looked around for Jared, then once again hurled herself against the side of the float. Weakened by the fight, she felt herself slip down into the water.

Two strong hands grasped hers, pulling her up to safety. A voice, deep and edged with fear demanded to know where her brother was. Through a haze of numbness she recognized it as the voice of her father.

"I don't know," she cried. "I don't know, I don't know …"

"Stay here!"

He surfaced and reappeared a dozen times while she lay inert on the float, struggling to breathe. Finally he surfaced for the last time, sobbing and shouting and praying out loud, as too late, he pulled Jared's body from beneath the float.

Heaving him over the edge, he knelt above him, alternately pushing on his chest and praying as he forced streams of muddy water from Jared's pale lips.

She watched in horror as water gushed from his mouth, his eyes staring blankly from his parchment face. Entangled in his hands she saw a string of white lights.

And then everything was black.

Chapter Fourteen
August, 1997

The Honda would never run. That was Gray's first, sickening thought when he woke up every morning, his last whispered prayer at night. *Please ... Let it run.*

He and Buddy had been working on it for weeks. They'd gone over the electrical system, rebuilt the engine, replaced everything replaceable, and still the motorcycle would not fire. Having exhausted his ability and his patience, Buddy asked his friend, Sammy, to look at it. Sixty-three and a retired builder of race car engines, Sammy was the master, or so Buddy said. If Sammy couldn't bring the machine to life, there just wasn't any life left in her.

On a muggy evening in August, Gray moved to the window for the dozenth time in an hour, peering down the street for a glimpse of Buddy's Chrysler.

"Why don't y'all give it up, Gray?" Kendra looked up from her magazine, her voice edged with irritation. "Seems to me for all the effort and time, not to mention the money y'all have put into that motorcycle you could have been drivin' a Cadillac by now." She turned back to her magazine. "What y'all want with that ol' broken down dinosaur anyway is beyond me."

Gray's anger flared. *What do you know about wantin', lady? Y'all ain't wanted for a damned thing your whole life.* Not trusting himself not to speak the angry thoughts, he stalked from the room. Upstairs, he stood at his bedroom window where he could keep up his vigil in private. Kendra's words echoed in the stillness of the air, mocking him from the empty street. The bike was worthless. A hunk of antique chrome and metal, bits of wires and hoses not worth the effort it had taken to repair them. Still … The Honda had come to represent something much larger to Gray, something as fitting as its name. A Dream. The bike needed him as much as he needed it, and needing was something a rich lady would never understand.

It was eight o'clock when Buddy finally pulled in the driveway. Gray's first impulse was to bolt downstairs and get it over with either way, but it seemed his feet were cemented to the floor. He stood there, stomach churning, chewing his fingernails until they bled. If Sammy hadn't been able to get the bike started, the dream was over. Gone. A done deal.

He heard Buddy's voice in the foyer, and then the clinking of silverware as Kendra set the table. He clutched the silver cross beneath his shirt and whispered a last prayer to the darkening sky. Finally Buddy's voice called to him from the living room. "Gray, come down here, boy."

He returned to the dining room, anxiously searching Buddy's face. When he didn't speak, Gray sank into his chair, allowing Kendra to heap his plate with food he knew he wouldn't eat. At last Buddy cleared his throat.

"I had Sammy go ahead and take the bike."

Gray nodded, his eyes trained on the flowery pattern in his China.

"Gonna need a nice paint job if she's gonna be fit to drive. If y'all still want her, that is."

Gray glanced up and saw his friend suppressed a smile.

"You got her running?"

"We got her running, all right. Damned near cost me my right eye." He indicated the angry red welt above his eyebrow. Reaching in his pocket, he pulled out a pile of broken pecan shells and spilled them on the table in front of Gray. "Some chipmunk built himself a nice little nest, padded her up with insulation and pecan shells. That damned exhaust pipe was clogged up tighter'n the queen's ass. Time we finally figured her out, she blew like the Fourth of July!"

Their laughter was so infectious even Kendra cracked a smile.

"Time I get back he'll have her painted up fit for a Duchess." He winked. "Then we'll see about getting you a license to drive her."

Gray's elation evaporated when he felt Kendra's foot caress his leg beneath the table. "Where you goin', Buddy?"

"Gotta run out to San Antonio for three days, then on to Dallas." Misunderstanding Gray's crestfallen look, he laughed. "Don't worry. She'll keep another five days."

It didn't surprise Gray when Kendra crept into his room the next night. He'd prepared for it, strengthened his resolve, promised himself this time he wouldn't touch her. But when she slid between the sheets, naked and damp from the shower, his resolve withered like a daisy in the sun …

•

By September the Honda was running like silk, the days were sunny and mild, and Kendra was getting braver. At first it was the whisper of her fingers on his leg beneath the table. Then a stolen kiss on the patio while Buddy dozed in front of the television. She started demanding sex in the afternoon, oblivious to the hell that would break loose if Buddy arrived home unexpectedly.

She started slipping into his room in the middle of the night and he'd lie beside her, sweating, listening. Every creak of the floorboards was Buddy coming to find her. Coming to kill him. He knew they wouldn't get away with it much longer. It was only a matter of time.

By October his stomach ached incessantly and his hands began to shake. He hated Kendra now. The thought of touching her made him want to throw up, but he didn't know how to stop. The more he backed away, the more demanding she became.

That this was the reason she'd taken him in in the first place was painfully obvious. If he refused her she would find a way to get rid of him, find herself a new play toy. And if Buddy ever found out. He shuddered. It was too awful to think about.

He was alert to Buddy's every mood, watching, listening, like a robin with its ear to the ground listens for changes and subtle movement beneath the surface. He lost ten pounds and became irritable and sullen. He spent his days praying Buddy wouldn't find out and his nights praying he would.

And then he did, and it all came apart.

At twelve noon on the first Sunday in October, Gray sat in his room, too depressed to do more than stare out the window at the autumn afternoon. He heard a knock at his door before Buddy pushed it open. He and Kendra had been out the night before and

Gray didn't expect to see either of them until suppertime. One look in Buddy's eyes told him the dull fire he saw had not been put there by alcohol. "Hey, Buddy," he said uncertainly.

Buddy walked over and stood before him. His eyes moved over Gray as if he were a stranger, not a trusted friend. He cleared his throat.

"I'm not a drinkin' man by habit, Gray, but I had a few tequilas last night. Kinda got to feelin' affectionate."

Gray's heart thudded. He saw the muscles in Buddy's jaw tense, and wet his lips with a tongue that was suddenly painfully dry.

"I brought my wife home and I made love to her for the first time in a month. And all the while she was cryin' out your name." His eyes collided with Gray's. "Now why do you suppose that was?"

Gray was struck dumb, unable to look away from the deadlock of Buddy's eyes.

"Y'all been as ornery as a hornet for weeks, and Kendra," his voice caught. "Kendra don't seem to want me touching her any more." He took a step closer. Gray flinched, but when he glanced again into Buddy's eyes he saw not violence, but sorrow.

"Buddy, I—"

"No, don't say nothin'. Ain't nothing you got to say I want to hear." He stared at him for a long moment, then reached in his pocket, pulled out a wad of bills, and threw them on the bed. "I'm going back to bed and I'm gonna try to sleep. When I wake up I want you to be gone, understand?"

Gray opened his mouth and then closed it again, knowing there was no excuse that would be good enough. "Yessir," he whispered.

"I'm gonna give you six hours, and then I'm gonna report that y'all ran off. If you're smart you'll be out of the state by then." His next words were spoken softly and full of contempt. "I don't expect they'll waste too much time on lookin' for you." He walked to the door. Without turning around, he said, "Take the bike."

"No," Gray said, finding his voice. "I don't want it."

"Take it! I don't want to have to look at the goddamned thing." Dropping his voice, he added, "Take the bike and go. And if I ever see you around my home or my wife again, I'll kill you, understood?"

Gray stuffed what clothes would fit into his back pack, then slid the money in his pocket and quietly left the Masons' home. He walked the bike for two blocks, then fired it up and headed for the expressway. After an hour's ride, he stopped to fill his tank. He didn't stop again until he crossed over the Georgia state line.

Chapter Fifteen

When Gray crossed into South Carolina it was dark and the Honda was skipping badly. Exiting at the first off-ramp, he stopped to fill his tank. Inside the gas mart, he eyed the potato chips and candy bars, finally deciding on a pair of rubbery hot dogs marked 2/$1.00. His stomach ached as he waited for the cashier to ring him out. He was edgy, unnerved, completely unaffected by her warm hazel eyes and easy smile as she slid his change across the counter.

He wolfed down the hot dogs on his way out the door. When his feet hit the parking lot, they cart wheeled in his stomach. A man squatted beside the Honda, his arms heavily muscled and tattooed where they protruded from his black leather vest. Gray stood rooted to the ground, watching. The last thing he needed was trouble. Summoning his courage, he squared his shoulders and crossed the lot.

The man glanced up as he approached. "This your bike?"

His voice was deep pitched and lazy, but something beneath the surface hinted at danger. When Gray nodded, he pointed to a puddle on the ground. "Looks like y'all leaking pretty good. Been runnin' her hard?"

Gray shrugged, his stomach knotting when the man's glance skimmed over his Alabama license plate.

"Might want to have them seals looked at. How far y'all goin'?"

"A ways," Gray answered.

His glance swept over the plate again. "Wouldn't run her too much farther, I was you. She's leakin' oil pretty bad." He removed the oil stick, wiped it on his pants, replaced it and then removed it again. "Might want to add one."

Gray squirmed beneath his steady gaze.

"I got a place up the road a ways. Be glad to take a look at her, if you want."

Gray was instantly suspicious. If there were two things he looked out for, they were cops and robbers, and this dude definitely wasn't a cop.

"What's it to you?"

The man laughed. "Hell, son, ain't nothin' to me. Y'all got a real nice machine here, a real rare beast and it looks like somebody put some work into her. If y'all wanna burn her up, it ain't a goddamned thing to me, you just keep right on goin'. I'll give you 'bout another twenty miles."

"You think?"

"Hell yes! Seems to me ownin' a nice bike like this here y'all would know how to take care of her. Unless you don't, in fact, own her." He leaned back on his heels and folded his arms across his chest, regarding Gray thoughtfully.

"I own her."

The man shrugged. "Ain't saying you do and I ain't saying you don't. From where I'm standin' it don't make a whole hell of a lot of difference." He spit out a stream of chewing tobacco. "If y'all want me to take a look at her, then say so. If not ..." He gestured toward the highway.

Ten minutes later Gray was following the man, who introduced himself as CJ, up a winding dirt road. CJ pulled his Harley into the driveway of a dilapidated double wide and parked it in a line with three others. Gray pulled in beside him and shut off the engine, his stomach knotting. Either CJ was over endowed with good old southern hospitality, or he was about to be bushwhacked. Either way, he had little choice but to follow him.

Inside, the trailer smelled of sweat and stale cigarette smoke. When Gray's eyes adjusted to the dim light he saw the owners of the other three bikes seated around a card table in the kitchen. There was also a girl, skinny with dark kinky hair, asleep on a sofa in the living room. As he followed CJ into the kitchen the other men glanced up, their eyes moving over him with the same lazy curiosity as CJ's.

"Y'all, this here's Gray," CJ said, setting the case of beer he'd bought on the counter. Ripping it open, he tossed a can to each of the men before handing one to Gray.

"Gray, these are Al, Jackie and Nicky."

Gray nodded in their general direction, popped open his can of beer and took a long swallow.

"He's got a Honda out there leakin' oil," CJ said. "Told him I'd have a look at her. It's coming from around the crank case, I'm guessin."

"Gonna have to wait until morning, Boss," said the one called Nicky, a scruffy, bearded Latino with eyes the color of midnight. "Now set your ass down here so I can win my money back."

"Oh, hell." CJ laughed easily and sank into the empty chair. Gray stood in the doorway, wondering if he'd just been invited to spend the night. His eyes moved over the filthy, smoke-yellowed room and the rough quartet at the table. It would beat sleeping under a bridge, but not by much.

When the card game finally broke up it was late and Gray's eyes felt like they were on fire. CJ shoved back his chair and stuffed his winnings in his pocket, then went to a drawer and pulled out a baggie. He shook its contents into a cigarette paper, licked it, fired it up, and passed it around.

When Al offered it to him, Gray inhaled deeply, choking as the hot, thick smoke burned down to his stomach. After his third hit he was feeling more relaxed than he had in weeks. CJ said something about squaring the bike away in the morning and the men scattered, leaving Gray alone in the kitchen.

He wandered into the living room and sank into a recliner opposite the girl. From somewhere in the trailer he heard a radio playing, or maybe it was a guitar, he was too disoriented to tell. He listened to the rise and fall of the music and concentrated on its patterns and its changing rhythms. Mostly, though, he concentrated on the girl.

She looked peaceful, pretty, despite the ugly purple bruises that colored her face and arms. He studied the subtle shadings, indigo to deep purple to gold, and idly wondered who had put them there.

He awoke hours later feeling stiff and cramped from sleeping in the chair. A stream dusty of light filtered in through the tattered curtains. He shifted and tried to focus his eyes. The girl sat on a stool before a cracked oval mirror, covering her bruises with makeup. She wore a wrinkled waitress uniform and a pair of scuffed white shoes. He caught her reflection in the mirror. Still pretty, he thought, but harder looking in the daylight.

She stood and he quickly closed his eyes. He felt her glance move over him as she walked past and down the hallway. He heard her knock softly at one of the bedroom doors. "CJ? Are y'all taking me to work this morning?"

Her voice was hesitant, almost fearful. Gray heard a muffled response come from the other side of the door. Moments later CJ followed the girl into the living room, cursing softly as he pulled on a pair of pants. They left the trailer and moments later the roar of the Harley shattered the morning quiet. Gray listened as it grew fainter and finally faded away.

When he woke again the room was filled with hazy sunlight and the smell of coffee and the hearty sounds of men eating breakfast. He wandered to the kitchen and stood in the doorway.

"Come on out, kid," CJ called from the table. "Help yourself."

Gray eyed the plates of sausage and scrambled eggs and was too hungry not to comply.

"Got your bike all squared away," CJ said through a mouthful of eggs. "Had ya a nice sized leak around the seal."

"I appreciate it," Gray said, reaching into his pocket. "What do I owe you?"

CJ paused for mere seconds, something in his manner making Gray strangely uneasy again. "Don't owe me nothing." His glance slid to the other two men and then back again. "Fact is we been talkin' her over. Got a job startin' tomorrow puttin' on a roof and vinyl sidin'. I could use another man if y'all wanna hang with us awhile."

When Gray didn't answer, he said, "Be worth two hundred bucks to ya. I'm figurin' the job'll take about a week, if y'all want in."

The other two men stared at him, awaiting his answer.

"I don't know nothing about roofing."

"Don't have to," CJ answered. "All you gotta know is keep your mouth shut and do as you're told." He bit into a link of sausage. "We don't ask no questions up here, but if y'all are afraid someone else might, I could hook you up with a Carolina plate for that beast out there."

Gray stared him with mixed emotions. Although he wasn't one-hundred percent sure of this big, ragged man, he didn't really have any reason to think CJ wasn't being straight with him. And the money would put more distance between himself and his latest screw-up.

"All right. I'm in."

CJ smiled. "Welcome aboard."

Gray had the impression that between jobs CJ and his crew did little more than play cards and get high. Later that afternoon when CJ took him out to his garage, he was surprised to find a well equipped workshop.

"Man's got a good pair of hands and is smart enough to use 'em, there's a man don't have to worry about where his next meal's gonna come from," CJ said, dismantling a carburetor.

Gray nodded and sat back to watch CJ work. Finally his curiosity got the better of him. "That girl that was here last night … She yours?"

"Who, Annie? Naw, not really."

"Whose is she?"

"Nobody's." And then with a smirk, he added, "Anybody's. Why, you want her?"

He shrugged. "I might."

CJ' shrugged and turned back to his work. "She's a good girl, I guess. Got a nice way of warmin' a man up, if y'all know what I mean. But you wanna be careful, you go sniffin' around Annie."

"Why's that?"

He grinned again, leaving the question unanswered.

Gray didn't talk to Annie when Nicky brought her back from town that night. He moved around the table with the others as she set out the boxes of carry-out food she'd brought, trying to seem disinterested as he watched her catlike movements.

When the smoke and the noise got to be too much, he took his plate outside and sat beneath a tree. The landscape was as perfect as if it had been painted in watercolors. The trailer seemed to squat against the hillside like an ugly brown sin against nature. He closed his eyes and breathed in the warm autumn air. When he opened them again Annie was sitting beside him. He gazed into her pretty, bruised face, and then down at his hands.

"Hey."

"Mind if I sit with you?"

"Nope."

She finished her meal and wiped her hands on the grass. "I don't know your name."

"Gray Baldwin."

"Anita Ramirez." She hugged her knees to her chest. "Y'all can call me Annie if you want to."

They sat in a silence that was as comfortable as the Carolina climate.

"Do y'all live here, Annie?" he finally asked.

"On and off. Nicky, he's my brother. Him and CJ own this place." A note of pride crept into her voice. "Are y'all gonna stay awhile?"

"Awhile."

"And then what?"

"I don't really have a plan." He leaned back against the tree and closed his eyes. "Not that havin' one's ever done me any good anyway."

"I don't have no plan either."

She pulled a joint from the pocket of her tee shirt and lit it, then passed it to Gray. Soon the warm, easy feeling returned and he found himself yearning to touch her. They talked until the sun began to set and he was acutely disappointed when she stood to leave.

"Are y'all gonna sleep out here tonight, Gray?"

"Yeah, I guess."

She turned and walked away, disappearing inside the trailer. He stretched out on the ground, all at once feeling miserable and frustrated. CJ made it sound like she could be had for a song. Maybe he should have been more aggressive. He closed his eyes and listened to the songs of the crickets, telling himself it was just as well. Tomorrow would be an early day.

He heard the trailer door close and then Annie returned, carrying two pillows and a blanket. Spreading the blanket over him, she set the pillows on the ground and lay down beside him. He pulled her close to him and traced the outline of her cheek with his fingers.

She smiled. "Y'all are a nice guy, ain't you?"

"No. I'm not."

"Yes, you are. You didn't come on strong with me, like most guys. Even though I could see how bad you wanted me."

Her frankness made him smile. "One thing I've learned, Annie, and that's wait 'till something's offered free and clear. It don't have near as much to do with bein' nice as it does with bein' careful."

"Hm."

He pushed his fingers gently through her hair and brought them to rest on the bruise above her eye. "Who did this to you?"

She didn't answer.

He brushed his lips against the bruise before moving them to her mouth. Her body melted against his and was gratified on a level that went beyond the physical. She wanted him. Not for the sake of a cheap thrill or to flex some sort of twisted female muscle, but to satisfy a hunger that was as basic as his own.

He moved his hands over her slowly, taking his time as he got to know the feel of her. She was different from Kendra, but at the same time, identical. He knew by the sound of her breathing and her soft moans of pleasure as he made love to her that Kendra had taught him well. Afterward, she wrapped her arms around him and rested her head against his chest. "Damn, Gray. Y'all surprised the hell outa me."

"Why?"

"I never dreamed y'all would be so experienced."

He laughed softly.

"Damn. I ain't never got off twice in the same night before. I ain't never been with nobody like you."

He stared at the bruises, and then into her dark eyes, all at once overcome with wanting. She wasn't anyone else's. Maybe she'd be his for awhile. "Why don't y'all stay with me then. For awhile."

She laughed. "Might as well be yours. I belonged to just about everybody else, one time or another."

"I ain't never belonged to nobody," he said softly. He lay in silence, looking up at the moon and feeling hollow. Finally he spoke again. "Back before the Civil War the landholders used to take a pretty girl for a slave if she didn't belong to nobody. They'd pierce a hole through her ear and put in their own stud. That way if she ever run off people would know who she belonged to." He removed the gold talon from his eyebrow and slid it into the hole in her earlobe. "Now you belong to me."

She laughed again. "Alright, Gray Baldwin. Now I belong to you."

His eyes burned into her face. "I'll be good to you, Annie. I'll never lift my hand to hurt you. That's a promise."

As she burrowed against him he felt a kinship, an acceptance so warm and so comforting his sixteen-year-old heart mistook it for love.

Two days later the skies opened up, drenching the Carolinas with rain. The resulting floods shut down entire cities and the job ended up taking three weeks longer than CJ had anticipated. When it was finished, there was another, and then another after that.

December arrived and Gray started to feel anxious, but whenever he mentioned leaving CJ urged him to stay, luring him with promises of more jobs, more money to be made. Gray might have stayed indefinitely if not for the bags.

On a chilly January evening he lay beside Annie in the small back bedroom they claimed for their own. "There's somethin' not right about them bags, Annie. I don't wanna carry them no more."

She yawned and propped herself up on her elbow. "What bags?"

"Them bags CJ has me takin' to the lumber yard every week. If it's money for supplies like he says it is, then why does he wrap it up in them brown paper bags? Why does he have me take it instead of takin' it himself?"

"'Cause he's busy. Seems to me y'all aught to be glad he's trustin' you with 'em."

"Well I ain't glad, and I ain't gonna carry them no more." He stared at her for a long moment and then his voice dropped to a whisper. "Annie, I don't feel right about this place. I'm thinkin' about moving along."

"To where?"

"West Virginia."

"Gray—"

"Come with me, Annie. This place ain't safe. You said yourself there ain't nothing keeping you here."

"I don't know."

"West Virginia's real nice," he urged, remembering a story Gladdy had read him years ago about mountains as blue as the sea and a way of life that was peaceful and easy. A place where a man could settle in, build a home. "Annie, please say you'll come with me."

"When would we go?"

His heart leapt. "Soon as we finish up this job I'll get another hundred dollars. That'll give me eight hundred."

Her eyes widened. "Y'all have saved up eight hundred dollars?"

"Hell yes. What'd you think I was doin' with it?"

"I don't know. I been working' at the truck stop since I was sixteen. Two years and all I got to my name up is about thirty bucks."

He stroked her hair. "With the money y'all are puttin' up your nose I ain't surprised."

She jerked from his grasp. "It's my own business."

"I know it is."

"It's my life and you ain't gonna tell me how to live it."

"I'm not telling' you how to live it, Annie. I'm just sayin' that with what y'all are spendin' for cocaine you coulda—"

"It's the only thing I got that makes my life bearable. You got no right to try and take it from me. And if that's the way y'all are gonna be, then you can just count me out!"

He silenced her torrent of words with a kiss. "I'm sorry I brought it up, all right?"

His apology was met with silence.

"Alright?"

"Alright," she said grudgingly.

He kissed her again, more gently this time.

"Gray?"

"What?"

"Where y'all got the eight hundred dollars hid?"

•

The money was all he and Annie talked about in the days that followed. Gray became increasingly tense, anxious to leave. He swore Annie to secrecy, knowing if he found out, CJ would try to stop them from going.

When the last job was finished, Gray took the Honda into town to be serviced. He packed his belongings into his backpack and was already in bed when Annie came in that night, carrying two glasses of wine.

"What's this for?" he asked.

"Just a little celebration." She lowered her voice. "On us gettin' out of this dump tomorrow."

He took the glasses from her hand and set them on the night table, then drew her close for a kiss. "I'm so glad y'all are coming with me, Annie. I'm gonna give you a good life, startin' right now."

She pulled from his embrace and handed him one of the glasses. "Let's relax a little."

After two swallows of wine her face was out of focus, and after a third he was having trouble making sense of her words.

"What kind of wine did you say this was?"

"Why?"

"It's potent stuff. I feel like I'm gonna—"

When he woke up Annie was gone. He climbed out of bed, gripping the edge of the dresser when a wave of dizziness came. He shook his head to try and clear away the cobwebs. Focusing on the room, he noticed Annie's make up and jewelry missing from the dresser. Alarmed, he tore open the drawers. Everything she owned was gone.

He sank back onto the bed as another wave of dizziness came, then gathering his equilibrium, pulled a chair to the edge of the closet. He reached behind the loose board in the back and pulled out the coffee can, knowing with a sick certainty it was empty. Pulling off the cover, he looked inside. The gold talon glinted up at him.

"You dog," he whispered. He hurled the can against the wall. "You stupid, back stabbing goddamned filthy dog!"

He took a dozen burning breaths to try and calm his rage, then grabbed his back pack and hurried from the house. He raced down the winding road, his thoughts traveling as fast as his motorcycle. Now he knew what CJ meant. Underneath those doe eyes of hers, Annie was nothing but a liar and a whore, just like all the rest of them.

They'd talked about West Virginia, but his instincts told him she'd gone south, to the only place she thought he wouldn't follow. If she left by bus, it would take her ten hours to get there. He planned to be there in eight. Betting his last twenty dollars on the hunch, he turned left onto the Interstate and thundered back toward Alabama.

Chapter Sixteen

It was easy this time. Annie sank back into the cool leather seat of the Greyhound bus and smiled with satisfaction. These boys CJ found were as good as money in the bank.

She watched the Carolina landscape roll past the window, her exhilaration turning to exhaustion. The wrinkle in her brow and the slight down turning of her lips had nothing to do with guilt. Anita Ramirez didn't believe in guilt any more. She'd lived too long in a world where there was no right or wrong, only survival. And if survival meant you had to cheat someone who trusted you, well, that was life. But this time she'd cheated CJ, too, and that was a dangerous thing to do. Gazing out at the morning sun, she wondered how long it would be before CJ realized she wasn't just laying low, that this time she wasn't coming back.

Her hand crept into her pocket and closed around the roll of bills, her ticket to a new life, one in which she wouldn't be the property of a man like CJ, with his matchstick temper and his dirty dealings. Or any other man. Alabama was as good a place as any to start over, and it was a place no one would think to look for her.

Her thoughts lingered on Gray. Underneath his soulful eyes and his slow, easy way of loving, he was the same cold mass of bone and muscle and temper as all the rest of them. Men wanted a girl only as long as it took to bleed out every last drop of loving and self respect, then they threw her away, as dried up and useless as a peach pit. Resting her head against the back of the seat, she closed her eyes.

She didn't open them again until the bus rolled into the terminal at Huntsville. Instantly awake, she collected her carry-on bag and stepped from the bus. She'd get a cup of strong, black coffee and then look for a place to spend the night. She'd buy herself some white magic to celebrate her freedom and then tomorrow she'd look for a job. She walked through the terminal and into the rest room, oblivious to the young man whose angry eyes followed her from feet away.

She used the toilet, splashed a handful of cool water on her face, reapplied her lipstick and stepped back out into the Alabama sunshine. With the speed of a jet liner, a pair of hands grabbed her and dragged her to the back of the building. Her yelp of fear was immediately stifled by a rough hand clapped over her mouth. When she saw a pair of steel gray eyes burning into her own, her breath released in a short, painful gasp.

"Gray."

"What's the matter, Annie?" he snarled, "Ain't ya happy to see me?"

Fear and surprise rendered her speechless.

"Lucky for you I'm in a hurry." He tightened his grip on her arm. "As states go this ain't one of my favorites, so I ain't gonna stay around and give you what you deserve. Now give me my money."

She worked furiously to clear her mind of the fear and anger that came with knowing she'd underestimated him. Taking a deep breath, she forced her voice into submission. "Alright. Let loose of me and I'll get it."

The moment his grip relaxed she thrust her knee between his legs, but not quickly enough. He blocked the kick with his arm and gave her another fierce shove. "Don't fuck with me, Annie." His eyes were savage, deadly. "There ain't a trick up your dirty little sleeve I ain't tried myself and right now y'all are about a stone's throw away from eating this goddamned wall." She stared at him, wide eyed and certain he would hit her

"Now give me my money!"

Her shoulders slumped in defeat. She pulled out the wad of bills and felt him tear them from her hand, like an autumn tree feels the loss of its foliage. Stuffing the money in his pocket, he turned and walked away.

As she watched him go, the icy hand of fear closed around her throat. Knowing she was broke and friendless in a strange city dissolved the last of her pride. "Gray?"

He didn't turn back.

"You ain't gonna leave me here with nothing, are you?"

His laughter sent a chill through her. "Way I see it I ain't leaving you no different than you left me."

Her mind worked quickly, knowing he was her only hope. Having used up all of his trust, she resorted to the only ammunition she had left.

"No, I guess you ain't. But before you go ..."

He folded his arms across his chest, his face still hard as granite.

"What I mean is, I know you must hate me. I deserve it, after what I did. But I can't let you go off forever without understandin' why I did it." She forced tears of repentance from her eyes. "Fact is, I ain't never had a reason to trust nobody. Not till you come along. I meant to go with you, Gray, I really did, it's just ..." Her tears streamed unchecked from her eyes. This boy wanted one thing out of life and that was love. She prayed to God he wanted it badly enough to believe her.

"What have you got to cry about, Annie? I'm the one got cheated and damned near poisoned, ain't I?"

"I'm sorry, Gray. I know I did you wrong." She swiped at her tears with her hand. "Y'all ain't mean enough to live the kind of life you'd have had with me. I'm nothing but a coke addict and a whore." She raised her eyes to meet his. "I wanted it to end with y'all hating me, to make it easier for you. But now you do and it only makes it worse."

"Why? Because I'm the one that ended up with the money?"

"No." She took careful aim at his heart, knowing it was her last shot. "Because I love you so much."

Bull's eye. She watched his face move through the changes. Doubt. Denial. Hunger. Not the sexual kind, but one that came straight from his soul.

"No you don't."

"I do, Gray. I swear it."

His face was ferocious in its anger. "No you don't. Nobody's ever love me my whole damned life. And if this is what love is, then you can keep it."

But he wanted to believe her, she could see it in his eyes. Running to him, she threw her arms around him. "I love you, Gray, and if you'll give me one more chance, I'll prove it to you."

He pushed her away. Glancing into his eyes, she saw a man at war. Finally he jerked his thumb toward the bike, his voice raw with emotions his eyes struggled to conceal. "Get on."

He strapped her carry-on bag to the bike and climbed on in front of her. She wrapped her arms tightly around his waist, not letting go until they were half way through the state of Tennessee.

Chapter Seventeen
August, 1998

Hope knew her mother would never forgive her for Jared's death. In the year that had passed there had never once been a softening of the angry line of Dana's lips, never a moment's reprieve from the silent accusation in her eyes. Did she think there would ever be a night in Hope's life when she would close her eyes and not dream of her brother's face and empty, staring eyes?

Hope shivered and wrapped her arms around herself, letting her cheek rest against the cool comfort of her pillow. So much had changed. Whereas mother's grief took the form of anger, and her father's, obsessive work, Hope dealt with her feelings by simply not allowing them. To an outsider it might seem as though she'd come through the tragedy unscathed. She laughed—too hard and too long and almost all the time, knowing if she ever stopped laughing she would cry forever. She was "Happy Hanwell" to the kids at school, a popular girl, the life of the party. But at home she was an object of hatred.

If the closeness mother and dad had shared a year before seemed like a threat, its evaporation was a dark, ominous cloud; a living, breathing danger that seemed to hang in the very air above the house. There was no more laughter, no flirting, no tenderness. They never even talked any more unless they were fighting.

She pressed her face in her pillow to try and drown out the angry words that seeped up from the floorboards.

"God help me, Dana, I can't live like this any more."

"… can't live at all … my son … can't get past … all I had."

"… a child, Dana. You can't go on blaming … or me."

Their voices dropped to furious whispers and then died away.

Hope told herself the thought of her parents divorcing didn't scare her. Divorce was as common in Mt. Bishop as the Saturday night meatloaf special at the diner. Morgan's mom was in the process of divorcing for the third time. In fact Hope's parents were only one of a handful of people she knew who weren't divorced or in the process. At least she didn't think it had gone that far.

Hearing the front door slam, she crossed the room and peeked out the window. If push really did come to shove she hoped they'd let her live with her father. As inside himself as he was now, at least he didn't treat her like a murderer.

She saw him stalk to his truck and wondered where he was going at ten o'clock at night. She saw the tired set of his shoulders and the defeated way he walked. For the first time, she thought of her father as old. Her eyes narrowed. It was Dana that was doing this to him.

"Let her go, Daddy," she whispered. "Who needs her anyway?"

Chapter Eighteen
August, 1998

There was little doubt in Gray's mind that Annie didn't really love him, but how could he make his heart believe it? Every time he got close enough to smell her unfaithfulness she changed again, became sweetness and light and a love he'd needed for so damned long he didn't know how not to want it anymore. She was making a fool of him and deep down he knew it.

He lay in the two AM darkness of the Hidden Mountain Trailer Park, waiting for her to come home. "Should have left her ass at that bus station," he muttered. "I'd have been half over her by now."

He rolled over and looked up at the moon, a thin white discus in the West Virginia sky. When he finally heard the front door open he closed his eyes and pretended to be asleep. She'd be stoned out of her mind by now, he knew, and he wasn't strong enough to listen to her lies tonight.

She stubbed her toe on the register vent at the foot of the bed and let loose a string of curses worthy of any of the men he worked with at the paper factory. She hated him, hated West Virginia, hated everything about her miserable life. He ground his teeth together against the angry reply that threatened to tumble from his mouth. *Go to hell, baby.* She slid into bed. He lay beside her, silent and frustrated as she fell into a drug-induced sleep.

She was still asleep the next afternoon when he left for his noon-to-midnight shift at the factory. The day would be endless, but the overtime pay would be good, and who knew? Next week there might not be any work at all.

He roared across town, enjoying the afternoon breeze and the scenery that rose like a blue mosaic behind the city streets. Most of the money he earned went to pay rent on the trailer and to satisfy Annie's steadily growing addiction. Not exactly the life he'd dreamed of, but a damned site better than some he'd lived. If only Annie would settle down and be happy, he knew he could be, too.

He clocked in with seconds to spare and took his place on the assembly line, where he'd work like just another piece of machinery. He pushed himself until his body ached with exhaustion and he was too tired to wonder where Annie was last night. If he confronted her, he'd have to listen to a bunch of shit about how he didn't own her, and then she'd withhold her body from him until he damned well knew it.

The arguments wore him out. In the end she'd have him convinced he was being stupid and insecure. But when he was alone again, the demons of doubt came creeping, whispering that he was being played for a fool. If he could catch her in the act he'd know for sure. And knowing would make him free.

When his shift ended, he drove home, torn between wanting to see her and hoping she wouldn't be there. He saw the truck before he pulled into their lot, a delft blue 4x4. He'd noticed it more than once parked in front of the diner where Annie worked. He climbed off his bike, glancing from the truck to the trailer, dark except for the soft glow of a lamp in the bedroom window. Opening the front door, he crept silently down the hallway. The smell of pot smoke and the sounds of muted laughter drifted to him from behind the bedroom door. Pulling in a breath, he opened it.

They were lying on the bed, laughing together as they shared a joint. A pizza box and a dozen empty beer cans littered the floor. Annie noticed him before the man did. She smiled. "Evenin', Gray."

His hurt immediately took the form of anger as a slow, searing fire licked at his insides. He glared at the man, who seemed perfectly at ease lying naked on Gray's bed. Then he glared at Annie. "What in the hell do you think you're doing?"

"Nothin' at all. Anymore."

Annie and the man laughed. Gray's anger ignited, a white hot ball of flames coursing through his bloodstream. He grabbed a fistful of Annie's hair and pulled her from the bed. "After all I've done for you, this is how you pay me back?"

"Stop it! Y'all are hurting me."

"How does it feel, Annie?"

Without warning Gray felt a swift punch to the kidneys and doubled over, losing his grip on Annie's hair. The next punch put him on the floor and he felt the pressure of the man's foot on his throat.

"Better behave yourself, little man. I got a good ten years and at least a hundred pounds on you and I could buy and sell you with what I carry around for pocket change."

Gray lay at the man's feet, consumed with humiliation and rage.

"This little darlin' ain't worth the trouble you're gonna be in if you don't simmer down and let me put my pants on."

With a swiftness born of fury Gray grabbed his foot and heaved upward, causing the man to lose his balance. Scrambling to his feet, he landed a quick, hard kick between the man's legs. Cursing, he lunged at Gray's throat.

In the confusion that erupted Gray heard the crashing of glass and the sound of the man's fist splitting his face open. Annie stood above him, naked and shrieking. Almost Herculean in his fury, Gray leapt at the man, striking blindly and fiercely until he heard the sound of crashing thunder and felt a searing pain in his shoulder. "Annie …"

He reached blindly toward the sound of her voice, then slumped to the floor as a rolling fog closed in around him.

•

He awoke two days later in a hospital bed. He was heavily bandaged and pieces of medical equipment seemed to be attached to every part of his body. A nurse stood at the foot of his bed. Seeing he was awake, she hurried from the room. He idly wondered what had happened to him and what caused her to look at him like she had.

Within moments a man entered the room. He wore rumpled khaki pants and a white cotton shirt. Focusing his eyes, Gray took a long, hard look at him. A social worker, no doubt.

The man pulled a chair to the side of the bed. "You're awake."

Gray tried to sit and felt a stabbing pain tear through his side.

"I'm Guy Timmons," the man said. "Your state-appointed attorney."

Gray stared at him in confusion. Whatever dope they had him on must be making him hallucinate. He almost thought the man said he was his attorney.

"Can you talk now or should I come back later?"

"I can talk," he rasped.

Guy Timmons studied him for a long moment. "You do realize you'll be tried as an adult?"

Gray struggled to organize his thoughts. "Tried for what?"

"That man you assaulted was an undercover police officer. You're being accused of attempted murder."

"What? I didn't assault no one."

"State's got a witness that says you did." He shuffled through the stack of papers he held. "A Miss Anita Ramirez."

"Oh, God."

"Miss Ramirez says the officer came by to check out a drug tip at the Hidden Mountain Trailer Park. You came home in a jealous rage. Knifed him in the leg before he got his gun and shot you in self defense."

Gray struggled to sit, but a wave of pain tore through his chest and he sank back into his pillows. "Get Annie in here. I wanna talk to her."

"Not possible. And I don't guess she'd want to talk to you even if it were. She's more black and blue than she is white, says it isn't the first time you've done her bodily harm."

Gray closed his eyes, wondering when the nightmare would end.

"I think our best bet would be to plea bargain."

Gray's eyes snapped open. "I ain't bargaining nothin'."

Guy Timmons' voice became rough, ringed with irritation. "Boy, I'm doin' you a hell of a favor even talking to you. I got your records from Alabama." He shuffled through his papers again. "In the past nine years you've been removed from twelve foster homes, in one of which you attacked a young man with a butcher knife."

"Oh, Christ," Gray said, burying his face in his hands.

"As recently as one year ago you had a damned nice placement in the home of a Mister Burdette Mason, from which you left voluntarily for reasons no one seems to want to talk about." He shuffled what seemed endless pages. "Your mama was a hooker, and your daddy's serving a life sentence for the cold blooded murder of an eighty-year-old woman. Now this pretty little girl says you stabbed a man for no reason other than talkin' to her." He looked at Gray pointedly. "If I put you in front of a jury I give you about a snowball's chance in hell. Maximum sentence is twenty years to life. If you cop to aggravated assault you'll be sentenced to ten and likely out in five. I suggest you think about it."

When he left Gray replayed the conversation in his head and tried to calm the fear that squeezed the breath from his lungs. He was innocent. At least as innocent as that lowlife cop. Surely a judge would see that. Surely they wouldn't send an innocent man to prison. Would they?

A month later he left the hospital in handcuffs.

Chapter Nineteen
October, 1998

The way Ace saw it he made two big mistakes. The first was getting close to Gray Baldwin. He never should have looked twice. God knew he didn't need any complications, and as far as white boys went he'd never liked 'em and damn sure never trusted 'em.

But there was something appealing about Gray. With his curly blond hair and spooky gray eyes, not to mention the hero worship he put on Ace. Who could resist that kind of temptation? After the chick rejected him and Ace held him in his arms there was no turning back, no more ignoring what he felt. He should have told Gray then. Maybe it would have made a difference. No, it wouldn't have. If he thought there was a chance in hell of getting Gray he'd be with him now, instead of in this shit hole prison.

He left the farm too soon, before he had his plan worked out, and that's where he made his second mistake: stealing the car. Who'd have thought those hillbilly cops would catch him?

He was doing all right, too. Odd jobs under the table, working long enough to get enough cash to move on again. He got nervous, paranoid. A black man wandering the streets was suspicious anywhere, but especially on this side of the Potomac. He'd made mistakes. Too many of them.

If he'd stayed at the farm another couple of months he'd of probably been able to save enough for a straight shot to Maine by bus instead of hitching rides, zigzagging like he had. But how could he stay, feeling the way he did?

He pushed his mop around the prison kitchen. Two years of his life for a busted up Honda Civic that barely run anyway. It didn't seem right.

Once started, thoughts of Gray Baldwin clung to him like a London fog. Two solid years of not being able to forget somebody was just about the worst kind of prison there was.

The doors clanked open and he glanced up to see a guard escort Brookie Marks into the kitchen. Ace grinned. He liked Brookie, though he'd never admit it. Doing fifteen years for assault with a deadly, Ace knew Brookie'd find a way to bust himself out, same as he'd done in Elmira, or so he said. He snorted. The brother had a line of BS as long as a man's arm. Still, Ace couldn't help but like him.

As the guard moved away Ace sidled up to his friend. "Where the hell y'all been, Brookie? I ain't seen your sorry ass pushin' no broom around here for a week."

"Been down the infirmary. Back trouble."

"Oh, hell."

Brookie grinned, revealing a mouthful of broken teeth. "Wait till you see the new boys just come in."

Ace leaned against his mop. "Anything good?"

"Couple of 'em. They's a real nice yellow-headed one."

"Y'all can keep them white boys, man. Been there, done that."

He resumed his mopping for a moment, and then reconsidered and asked the guard's permission to use the bathroom. Once inside he stood on the register and peered out the barred window. They'd have strip-searched them by now, then hauled them across the catwalk to start the dehumanization process. If there were only a couple, like Brookie said, it wouldn't take long.

He peered at the door at the end of the walkway. Within moments the door opened and the new inmates were marched outside. The first two were black, one lean and mean, with a swagger that said he wasn't about to take any shit from the big, heavily-muscled guard. "Guess again, homey," Ace muttered. As the last inmate was herded down the cat walk, Ace saw his golden hair and the unmistakable walk that spoke of fear beneath a veneer of toughness. He squinted hard, his heart leaping and sinking in the same moment. It wasn't possible.

"Gray Baldwin," he whispered. "Well I'll be damned."

Interlude
May, 2003

Five years is a long time for a man to live like a criminal if he isn't. On the fifth of May, Gray Baldwin walked out of the West Virginia State Penitentiary a free man, but more in bondage to anger and resentment than ever in his twenty-two years.

Though he had nowhere in particular to go, he walked fast, not looking back, breathing deeply of the magnolia-scented air. The dehumanization process had been thorough, starting the day they seized his clothes and handed him a blue, prison-issue jumpsuit. It felt strange to be walking wherever he wished, to be his own person again.

His alliance with Ace Javitz rendered him untouchable, and though he made it through his prison term unmolested, he hardly came through unscathed. He had nothing now, no one. He promised to look Ace up after his release—Ace, who still held fast to his dreams of Maine. Released eight months previously, Gray wondered whether he'd made it. With nowhere else to go, Maine seemed as good a plan as any.

In the weeks that followed, Gray inched his way north on foot. He bussed tables in a Morgantown diner, unloaded trucks at a warehouse in Harrisburg. Outside of Scranton he hooked up with a construction crew and hung drywall in a low-income housing project. The men were a hard working, hard drinking team and he hung on the periphery of their close-knit circle, studying their game, watching their eyes. On a rainy night in June he sat in on a card game and won two hundred dollars and the key to Max Trippley's bike—a 2000 Suzuki, and everything changed.

The crew became suspicious of him, subtly hostile. Gray tasted trouble in the air and trouble was one thing he didn't need. On a golden June afternoon he crossed the Pennsylvania line into New York State, not looking back.

Driving down the highway, he took in the gently sloping hillside; not the dramatic blue of the West Virginia mountains, but pleasing in its soft kaleidoscope of colors. By evening, feeling the pangs of hunger, he decided to stop for the night, find a cold beer, a hot meal, and a place to top off his gas tank. He'd left before pay day, and was getting short on cash. Maybe he'd find a place to work for a day or two.

Crossing into Stoddard County, he started seeing signs for food and lodging. As dusk fell, he exited the expressway and stopped at the first town he came to. A place called Mt. Bishop.

Book Two

Shadows

Chapter Twenty
June, 2003

"Where is this party, Hope?"

"It's at Jimmy's."

Sensing the ever-present anger behind their words, Ted looked up from his dinner plate, his glance moving from his wife to his daughter. *Please don't push her, Dana. Just once let's eat a meal in peace.*

"Who's going to be there?"

His glance shot back to his wife. *You sound like a drill sergeant, for God's sake.*

"Let's see ... the Clintons and the Gores for sure, and Queen Elizabeth said she'd try to stop in."

"I don't think there's any reason to be sarcastic, Hope."

"Sorry."

"No you're not."

Dana speared three carrots with a single, angry jab. Her pointed glance was not lost on Ted.

"Hope, tell your mother what adults are going to be at the party."

"Jimmy's sister Brenda and her husband. They're, like, thirty. I'll be home by one o'clock."

"Midnight," Dana corrected.

"Mother, I'm eighteen-years-old."

"All the more reason."

Hope's blue eyes flashed with anger. "What are you saying?"

The question was met with silence.

"What are you saying. Mother?"

Dana's gaze dropped to her plate. "Only that I don't want to see you throw away your future for a boy."

Ted cleared his throat, as if that would clear the sudden heaviness in the room. It was obvious Dana was referring to Hope's friend, Morgan Foster. He'd ignored the rumors that floated around Mt. Bishop for weeks, but finally saw the evidence of the girl's pregnancy for himself earlier that afternoon. Seventeen-years-old. Good God.

A silence as thick as the summer evening settled over the table until finally Hope pushed back her chair and stood.

"I'll see you later, Daddy." She bent and kissed his cheek, then strode from the room, leaving him to bear the brunt of Dana's anger. He carried his plate to the sink, watching from the window as his daughter strode down the sidewalk. He sighed. He supposed Morgan wouldn't be going to beauty school in the fall. He hoped to God that didn't mean Hope wouldn't be going.

Not that he didn't love his daughter, and not that he wouldn't miss her when she was gone, but the animosity between her and Dana was making his life miserable. Rinsing his plate, he turned to leave.

"Where are you going?"

"I've got some paperwork to catch up on."

"Of course you do."

His irritation flared and sheer force of will kept it from his voice. "Is there something wrong with that, Dana?"

"No."

He folded his arms across his chest and waited.

"Go ahead," she said, waving a dismissive hand at him.

"Why are you mad at me?"

She stood and carried her dishes to the sink. "I'm not mad at you."

"You seem it."

"I thought we might go for a walk together, that's all."

His glance moved longingly to the open window but his thoughts returned to his paperwork, the columns of figures he all but dreamt about at night, driving himself half crazy trying to find ways to cut expenses, to write the advertising miracle that would bring more bids to Hanwell Contracting. He considered the rigid set of Dana's shoulders.

"Maybe a short one."

"Don't bother."

He took a breath and mentally counted ten. "Dana, as much as I'd love to stroll through the daisies with you, I have paperwork that needs to be done. If you'll settle for a walk around the block, then fine. Let's go."

When she faced him again he saw she was near tears. "If you're going to make a chore out of it, Ted, then forget it. I'd rather go alone."

Her dishes forgotten, she covered her mouth with her hand and hurried from the room. There was a soft thud as the door closed behind her, and then the sound of absolute silence.

Chapter Twenty-One

The Mt. Bishop Diner was as tired and run-down as the town from which it took its name. The screen door turned sluggishly on its rusted hinges in the early morning heat, grudgingly opening to admit the regulars.

A dozen scarred formica tables were scattered around the dark paneled room, accommodating farmers in soiled work pants, old men in old smelling clothes, and women in dark skirts and blouses. The red upholstered chairs sagged beneath their weight, as weary of them as the waitresses who walked with fatigued steps in their soiled white shoes.

Gray took all of this in as he sat over his second cup of coffee, his back to the wall, eyes facing front. Watching. The table beneath his hands was slick with grease. The place was every inch a greasy spoon, the kind of place where Friday night's fish fry lingered in the air until Tuesday.

He curled his fingers around the chipped, white mug, taking comfort in its heat and ignoring the strawberry filling that oozed tantalizingly from the pastry in front of him. Rain spit against the dirty windows, making a streaky, watercolor painting of Main Street. He took another swallow of coffee and wondered how long the rain would last. Patience was a virtue. One of the many things he'd learned in prison.

A sign above the counter advertised: *Fresh, hot coffee, 75 cents. Free refills!* He wondered how long he could sit there before they considered him a nuisance. After spending a miserable night on a lumpy mattress at the Mt. Bishop Motel, he'd thought to head out early, get as far as the forty dollars in his pocket would take him. He'd hoped to make it to Buffalo, a little ways north, and find work. But the rain changed his mind.

He took another swallow of coffee and a bite of pastry and turned his attention back to the three farmers who sat in the booth ahead of him. One of them, a man in faded flannel with a weather-beaten face, took a swallow of coffee and drummed his fingertips on the unopened newspaper in front of him.

"I felt real bad about it. Ted Hanwell's done all my work for twenty years. But I had a deadline. What could I do?"

The second farmer, younger but no less weather-beaten, nodded. "I know what you mean. Smitty was telling how he waited six weeks for his addition, and even then it was done half-assed."

"It's a damned shame, though," the first man said, pounding his fist lightly on the table. "Used to be if the sign out front said Hanwell Contracting a man knew it'd be done right. And on time."

The third man spoke. "You gotta feel bad for Teddy, though. He ain't had it easy. Ain't been the same since he fished his boy outta that lake."

"Don't surprise me he's in trouble, though, working half a crew like he does. Smitty was telling how Ted can't keep no good men. The city gobbles 'em up as fast as he trains 'em. A man's only as good as his crew."

"Teddy, he's a good man, though. You gotta feel sorry for him."

"Like I said, I felt real bad giving the work to outsiders, but I had a deadline. What could I do?"

They paid their bill and walked from the diner and Gray turned back to his pastry until the waitress reappeared.

"More coffee?"

"Please."

Gray moved his cup closer to her pot, accidentally brushing her thigh with his hand. She stayed close, leaning forward just far enough that he could see down the front of her uniform. Instant fire spread through his groin and he quickly looked away. *Goddamn*, he thought. *I've been without a girl for too long.*

"Anything else I can get you today?" Her words were clipped and matter of fact, clearly saying it was time for him to leave.

"Actually, I'm looking' for a place called Hanwell Contractin'. Can y'all tell me where that is?"

She sized him up for a moment before gesturing down the tree-lined street. "Right around the corner, big gray building on Maple Avenue." She continued to stare at him as if he owed her some further explanation.

"Thank you."

She snapped up his coins and thrust them in her pocket, marching away without so much as a thank you kindly.

Outside, he went around to the back of the diner where the waitress said he'd find the men's room. It was dark and sour smelling and he was almost glad he'd done without breakfast. Pulling out his toothbrush and razor, he set them on the metal shelf above the sink. When he'd brushed his teeth, he splashed a handful of frigid water on his face, lathered with bar soap, and began to shave. He cursed when the razor gouged his chin and hurriedly stopped the flow of blood with a scrap of toilet paper. He would have liked a warm shower, but the water at the motel ran rusty with disuse.

He pulled a comb through his ragged curls and secured them in a loose ponytail, then frowned at his reflection in the mirror. He looked like a bum, but if what those fellas had said was true, it wouldn't matter. It didn't sound to him like Ted Hanwell was in a position to be choosy. He pulled the last of his cash from his pocket, counted it, and stuffed it back in. He sure hoped not, anyway.

Chapter Twenty-Two

Ted sat in his small, cluttered office, looking at his spread sheets and listening to the silent telephone with mounting despair. Even the bad times had never been this bad. Maybe it was time he faced it. There was just no miracle by which he could pull it together this time.

He heard the bell above the front door chime and fought the urge to hide. Another irate customer, no doubt, wanting to know what the hold-up was, or worse, withdrawing their contract. He couldn't say he blamed them.

He rubbed his tired, red-rimmed eyes. Glancing up again, he squinted with curiosity at the young man who stood in the doorway. His eyes took a quick walk over the man's frayed clothing and untidy mop of curls. Scruffy, but recently shaved, judging from the bloody scrap of toilet paper on his chin. "What can I do for you?"

"I'm lookin' for Ted Hanwell."

A Southerner. Surprisingly soft spoken, despite his rough appearance. What on earth could he want?

"I'm Ted."

"My name's Gray Baldwin." He gave Ted a quick, firm handshake. "I heard down at the coffee shop y'all were wantin' some men. Just so happens I'm lookin' for work."

Ted rested his index finger against his lips as he appraised the young stranger. Solid build. Good arms. A little on the short side, but rugged enough. "What sort of work have you done, Gray?"

"Roofin' and sidin', some drywall. Down south, mostly."

"Done any finishing work?"

"Yessir."

"Mhm." Ted thought about it, but not for long. His crew was

desperately short. If his back hadn't gone out again he'd be down at the site himself. The job was supposed to have been done a week ago. What did he have to lose? "Tell you what, son, you came on the right day. I've got a crew working two men short right now. Can you work today?"

"Yessir."

Ted scribbled an address on a sheet of notebook paper and tore it from the pad. "It's just off the highway, about three miles north. Tell them I sent you." He handed the paper across the desk. "Come back in the morning and we'll talk."

"Thank you, Sir. I will." He took the paper from Ted's hand and folded it into the pocket of his jeans.

The next morning when Ted pulled into the alley he was relieved to see Gray Baldwin waiting on the stoop. He'd been afraid the kid wouldn't show up. The crew was impressed with him, said he'd worked quietly and efficiently, not even stopping to eat lunch.

He stood when Ted climbed from the truck. "Mornin'."

"Good morning."

Ted unlocked the back door and ushered him inside. In his office, he walked to the coffee pot which he'd set to perk at seven AM. He watched Gray Baldwin from the corner of his eye. The kid seemed more at ease today, his nervousness betrayed only by the tapping of his fingertips against his thigh. "Have a seat. Gray, isn't it?"

"Yessir."

"Coffee?"

"Please."

Ted filled a Styrofoam cup and handed it to him, then poured another for himself and sat down at his desk. He took a swallow, then folded his hands in front of him. "My men said you did a good job for them yesterday. They seem to think I aught to take you on." Ted rummaged through the top drawer of his desk and pulled out an application form. "I'll have you fill one of these out. It's really just a formality, but I'm required to have one on file for every employee."

He handed it across the desk and immediately saw a change in Gray's eyes. What looked like relief only moments before now almost looked like despair. He ran his hand back through his curls, then tapped his fingers lightly against the form and gave it a small shove back in Ted's direction.

"Um, Mr. Hanwell ..."

"Call me Ted."

"Ted. I'd rather just let my work speak for itself, if that's alright." He gave Ted a level stare. "Fact is, there ain't nothin' I could write down on that piece of paper that would make y'all want to take me on."

Ted considered that for a moment. "Why do you say that?"

Gray cleared his throat, opened his mouth, then closed it again.

Ted chuckled. "Can't be that bad, can it? I mean, you weren't just released from prison or anything, were you?"

Gray's gaze was unflinching. "Yessir."

Ted's smile faded. "I see. May I ask what you did?"

He took an invisible breath and Ted could see he was deciding. "I was livin' in West Virginia at the time. It was a few years back."

"Mhm."

"I came home from workin' one night and found my girlfriend in bed with a cop. I guess you could say we had us a disagreement. He put a bullet in my shoulder and called it self defense. Told the judge I assaulted him."

"And did you?"

"No, Sir, I did not."

Ted studied him for a long moment before sliding the application back in the drawer. "I appreciate your honesty, Gray."

Gray watched him, looking as nervous as if he were in a courtroom awaiting a verdict.

"I have enough work lined up to take us through the fall. Are you planning to settle in Mt. Bishop?"

"I can't really say I have any definite plans right now, but I'd be willin' to stay on awhile if y'all need me."

"Where are you staying now?"

Gray chuckled. "I spent last night at a place called the Mt. Bishop Motel, but I'm sure not plannin' to make a habit outa that."

Ted smiled. The Mt. Bishop Motel was the eyesore of the village, as ugly in its reputation as it was its cracked, pink stucco.

"I wish I'd known that yesterday. I could have warned you." After a brief silence he continued. "Since you were honest with me, Gray, I'll be the same with you. I'm a little down on my luck myself.

At this stage of the game I could only pay you a fraction of what you're probably worth."

He paused, waiting for Gray's reaction.

"I have a little place a few miles outside of town. It's a hunting cabin, but it's got electricity and running water and it's quite comfortable." He paused, thinking of the property he'd bought years ago as a fishing retreat for himself and Jared. "I'd let you stay there rent free until winter as part of your wages."

"What happens in winter?" Gray asked.

Ted chuckled. "Have you ever spent a winter in New York State, Gray?"

"No, Sir."

"The cabin is on a seasonal road." He reached for his coffee and took a swallow. "One good snowfall and you could be stuck up there for days."

"Oh."

"Tell you what, why don't you come and have dinner with me tonight. Afterward we'll go up and take a look at it, see what you think."

"Thank you, Ted. I'll do that."

The words were spoken casually, but Ted saw what was unmistakably gratitude in the stranger's eyes.

Chapter Twenty-Three

Dana was dead set against it. Hope heard enough of her phone conversation with her father earlier that afternoon to pique her interest, and now sat in her bedroom with her ear pressed tightly against the register vent.

"... can't imagine why you'd invite him into our home, Ted. Lord knows ... trouble without ... ex-convict, no less!"

"He's a good worker, Dana. I want to give him a chance."

Hope knew they were talking about the hunky stranger who appeared in Mt. Bishop the day before. Everybody was talking about him. A southern man roaring into town on a black motorcycle wasn't exactly an every day occurrence in Mt. Bishop. And tonight, if she understood her mom and dad's heated argument correctly, he was actually coming to their house for dinner. That he was an ex-convict only sweetened the deal.

She smiled. If there were two things her mother hated they were southern men and criminals. Karma could be such a bitch! A delicious plan was taking shape in her mind. It would be payback for treating her like a baby, even though she was eighteen and would be leaving home in September. Three more months. She wished it was tomorrow.

She couldn't wait to get to Buffalo. And as soon as she had her cosmetology license under her belt she'd go someplace even cooler. New York City, maybe, or California. She'd be a makeup artist for models and movie stars.

She thought of her mother's newest fear. As if Hope would ever let herself end up like Morgan, stuck in Mt. Bishop forever with a baby and a loser like Jerry Plummer. Hope knew about birth control. She was going to lose her virginity before leaving for beauty school if it was the last thing she did, but she certainly wasn't going to be careless about it.

Padding to the bathroom, she rummaged in the cabinet and pulled out her White Musk shower gel and body mist. As she turned the shower on and slowly began to undress, her thoughts returned to the mysterious stranger and she smiled. She hoped he was as cute as everyone said he was.

At six, forty-five she heard the doorbell chime and shot a last, hurried glance into the mirror. She added another coat of lip gloss, blotted her lips on a square of toilet paper and sprinted downstairs.

She heard her mother's icy greet before she hit the bottom step. Stopping dead in her tracks, she listened, captivated by the slow, rhythmic patterns of his speech.

"Evenin' Miz Hanwell. I sure do appreciate y'all havin' me in to dinner tonight."

"You're welcome, I'm sure."

Her father spoke. "Gray, can I get you a beer, or a glass of wine?"

She heard the clinking of ice, and then her father asked, "Dana, did you call Hope?"

She moved to the open doorway and drank in the stranger's profile. His head was a tangle of honey colored curls, and his arms were bronzed and heavily muscled where they peeked from the sleeves of his tee shirt. Her breath caught. He was as gorgeous as she'd heard and then some.

"I'm here, Daddy," she said softly.

When he turned and looked at her, Hope's breath caught again. The first thought that came to her was that there must have been a mistake. Nobody with eyes that clear and that beautiful could have spent time in prison.

"Gray," her father said, "this is my daughter, Hope. Hope, meet my newest employee, Gray Baldwin."

She held her breath and waited to see if it was a go. His gray eyes moved over her. Instantly, almost imperceptibly, it appeared. The spark of approval, and then a look of hunger as primitive and as basic as man. Although he covered it up much more smoothly that the boys at school, it was unmistakable. He wanted her.

"Hello, Gray."

"Hey."

She gave him a bright smile and then negated it with her most practiced look of indifference. Only when he turned away did she allow herself another glimpse at his heavily muscled body, his honey colored curls. *My, my, my ...*

"Well then, shall we sit down?"

It was obvious from the stiffness in her voice and the thin, tight line of her lips that Mother, too, had seen the stark approval in Gray Baldwin's eyes. Hope smiled to herself as she took her place at the table. It would be a relief to have Mother's anger focused on someone else for a change.

All through dinner the two men talked shop, but Hope could feel tension radiating across the table. Twice she glanced up to see Gray's eyes on her and the message they conveyed made her tingle right down to her toes.

With the meal finished, her father and Gray lingered over coffee while she and Dana washed the dishes. Hope reached for a handful of silverware. "Gray seems nice."

"He's too old for you," Dana snapped, slamming a pile of plates into the sink. Hope bit back a smile and reached into the sink for a glass.

Moments later her father appeared in the doorway. "We're going up to take a look at the cabin now."

Dana's hand tightened on her dish cloth. "Alright."

He gave her a kiss on the cheek. "I shouldn't be too long."

Hope threw down her towel. "Daddy? Can you drop me off at Morgan's?"

Squeezed into the cab of her father's truck, Hope's knee brushed against Gray's. She felt the tension return, as subtle as a puff of air on glowing cinders. He spoke to her father as if she wasn't even there, but the rigid way he sat told her he was aware of her closeness. When they pulled up in front of the Foster's house he climbed out of the truck and stepped aside to let her pass. Once again she saw the smooth caress of appreciation in his eyes.

"Will you need a ride home later?" her father asked.

"I'll call if I do. See you later, Daddy." She turned to Gray. "Nice meeting you."

He nodded and gave her a small, tight smile.

It wasn't until later, as she recapped the evening blow by blow for Morgan that she realized he'd literally spoken no more than two words to her. But the subtle message behind his eyes told her all she needed to know.

Chapter Twenty-Four

The dog had been hanging around the cabin for three days. He was ugly as all get out, with heavy jowls and mismatched eyes. The first time Gray noticed him, he squatted and extended his open hand, speaking to the animal in a coaxing voice. The dog barred his teeth and snarled, his hair bristling along his spine.

"Damn." Gray withdrew his hand. "You Yanks don't trust nobody, do you?" He took in the torn left ear and crooked tail. "I understand, boy. Been kicked around some myself. Y'all wait right there."

He went into the cabin and returned with a bowl of water and another of leftover spaghetti. He set them at the edge of the driveway and backed away. "I hope y'all ain't fussy, 'cause that's all I got."

He turned and went inside, watching from the window as the dog took a hesitant step forward and then another. His glance moved warily to the cabin door as he devoured the food.

The next day Gray bought a bag of dog food and moved the dishes closer to the house, and the day after that, closer still. On the fourth day he returned home from work and found the dog waiting for him. "Evenin' Yankee," he said. "Y'all ready for your supper?"

The dog watched him intently, ears pricking at the now familiar word.

"Would you like to come inside and be my guest tonight, or do you prefer to dine on the patio?"

The dog cocked its head to the side and stared at him. Gray laughed. "Alright. Suit yourself."

He prepared the food and took it outside, leaving the cabin door open in case the dog changed its mind. Opening the boxes of carry-out he'd brought, he set them on the table, gazing across the hillside as he ate. The four rooms of the cabin were more than adequate, and he was grateful to Ted for taking a chance on him. The cabin was rustic, but more of a home than he'd known in years. "Peaceful," he murmured.

He frowned. Maybe a little too peaceful. There wasn't another house for miles and the cable service stopped at the end of the road. He could live without television, but another face would have been damned welcome.

One instantly came to mind.

Hope Hanwell was just about the prettiest girl he'd ever seen. He closed his eyes until her face was clear in his mind. She pretended to be as free and easy as the wind, but he knew what she really wanted was to be tamed. By him. It was in the way she looked at him, the way she smiled when she said his name.

But those kinds of thoughts would lead to nothing but trouble and he knew it. Underneath her pretty smile she was probably as lowdown as all the rest of them, playing men like checkers for what they could get and giving damned little back in return.

He finished eating, walked out onto the porch, and lit a cigarette. Maybe she wasn't playing him at all. Maybe he was just so damned lonely he'd seen flirtation in a simple smile. It didn't matter either way. He certainly wasn't so woman hungry he'd go after an eighteen-year-old kid. And Ted Hanwell's kid, no less.

It wasn't the four-year difference in their ages that made her untouchable, more the vast differences in how they'd spent those years. Face it, he was rotting in prison while she was dancing at the junior prom. They were coming from two different places, two different universes. The way Ted's wife acted, a body would think he'd shown up wearing a sign around his neck: *Convict and Cradle Robber.*

He sat down on the steps and leafed through a magazine he'd left there the day before. On Saturday he'd find the library and check out some books. Flipping through the advertisements, he paused when a striking blonde in a string bikini caught his eye. Maybe he'd go out one of these nights and check out the local talent. He turned the page. In any case, he'd make it a point to stay away from Ted Hanwell's daughter.

But that was easier said than done. In the days that followed it seemed Hope Hanwell turned up just about everywhere he went.

The diner. The supermarket. The public library. Given the size of Mt. Bishop, the encounters seemed neither strange nor orchestrated.

At the end of his second week at Hanwell Contracting he stood with the others and waited while Ted handed out the pay envelopes. When his was offered he tucked it in the pocket of his jeans.

"Thanks, Ted."

"You've more than earned it," Ted said with an easy smile. As he turned to leave, Ted said, "Hey, listen, we're having a little get-together on Sunday. A graduation party for Hope. Stop by if you don't have any plans."

Gray'd heard the other men talking about the party and spent the whole week half hoping for and half dreading an invitation.

He'd have to cash his check somewhere tonight, he decided, pick up something decent to wear. He couldn't very well show up in his work clothes. And there was the matter of a gift. What would a girl like Hope want, he wondered?

The clothes were easy. Black jeans, white shirt. But Gray found himself wandering through the mall, agonizing over what to buy her for a gift. He looked in every store window. Perfume? Too personal. Pen and pencil set? Too boring. He wandered into a jewelry store, remembering the gold chains around her neck and the rings she wore on each of her tiny fingers. He peered into a display case at the bracelets; bone china, hand painted with delicate flowers. Some had roses, some china lilies and butterflies, and one had a jade-colored strand of ivy.

"Can I show you something?"

The sales girl was lean and polished and spoke with the clipped confidence of a woman who was used to having men do what she wanted.

"Just lookin," he said.

"She'd love one of these little babies," she said. Unlocking the case, she removed three of the bracelets and placed them on the counter in front of him.

He picked up the one with the roses and felt the cool, paper thin glass beneath his fingers, the slim band of eighteen-karat gold that rimmed its edge. It was perfect. Beautiful and delicate, like Hope. He turned over the price tag and let out a low whistle. Fifty-nine bucks. Now that would be making a statement.

"Isn't she worth it?" The woman's smile was sultry, her voice a gentle caress.

"Every nickel, I'm sure." He set the bracelet back on the counter. "Maybe I'll look around a little more."

Compared to the bracelet everything else looked cheap. He wandered through the mall until closing time, when he found himself drawn back to the jewelry store. He glanced into the case. "Oh, hell," he muttered. "Why not?"

The girl walked over with a knowing smile. "You won't regret it," she said. "Which one?"

He pointed to the rose bracelet and watched as she placed it in a box and wrapped it with a burgundy ribbon. She winked. "I think you just bought some lucky girl's heart."

He tucked the box in the shopping bag with his new clothes and placed it in the saddlebag of his bike, hearing the echo of the woman's words.

They came back to him a dozen times the next day, and a dozen times they filled him with dread. He'd had no intention of trying to buy Hope's affection. It was just a gift, more a token of gratitude for her father's good will than anything else. She'd know that. Wouldn't she?

The party was in full swing when he arrived. A tent had been erected in the yard and it was packed full of balloons and streamers and people. He parked a block away and walked toward the gathering, a knot tightening in the pit of his stomach as he clutched the gold foil box. Just inside the tent he noticed a table piled with gifts. He shoved his inconspicuously near the back. He'd cut out before she opened it.

Looking around, he saw that the party was a mix of teenagers and middle-agers. He jammed his hands in his pockets and stood off to the side, knowing he looked every bit as out of place as he felt.

It seemed like hours that he stood there. When Hope finally glanced in his direction his heart hammered in his chest. *Cool off, Baldwin! She's just a kid.* But she looked more like an angel, wearing a white gauze skirt and a blouse as blue as her eyes, sheer enough that he could see the soft swell of her breasts beneath the fabric. Her hair was pulled up with a gold clip, but the strands that escaped framed her face in wispy ringlets. She walked toward him, smiling, two perfect dimples creasing the sides of her pretty pink mouth.

"Hi, Gray."

"Hey," he said softly. *Oh, baby, don't look at me like that. Please don't make me want you.* "Congratulations."

"Thanks."

It was hard standing so close to her. He reminded himself that she was a baby. But a baby with the body of a mannequin. He averted his gaze and concentrated on the food table; sliced ham, beef and turkey. A dozen kinds of salads but who could eat?

"Did you get something to eat yet?" she asked, clearly mistaking his hunger for hunger.

"Ahh, no. Not yet."

She smiled again and he felt twin lakes form beneath his armpits.

"We're having a band later. You have to promise to save me a dance."

The lakes became oceans. He cleared his throat, afraid if he opened his mouth his heart would jump through it. "Alright."

"Great. I'll catch up with you later, then."

He gave her a smile he hoped was halfway cool and watched her walk away. Damn, she had a nice little—

"Gray, glad you could make it."

He glanced up. Where had Ted come from?

"Did you fix yourself a plate?"

"No, not yet."

"Don't be shy. That's what it's here for."

After Ted left, Gray spoke with Chuck and Jimmy and their wives. Then a pregnant girl introduced herself, obviously looking for a daddy for her baby, judging from the way she looked at him. And then he was alone again. Alone, but ever conscious of the small town eyes that watched him with open curiosity. Alone, but ever conscious of the flash of blue and white, of white and gold and pink that glided across the tent, talking, laughing, filled with optimism and hope.

Hope …

He didn't know how long he stood there before Ted's wife announced that Hope was going to open her gifts. His eyes darted to the doorway of the tent but his feet moved with the other guests toward the table where Hope sat. She laughed, a sound as gentle and hypnotizing as wind chimes and he wondered what it would feel like to kiss her. *Stop it, Baldwin!*

She began to open her presents. A backpack. A hug for the lady in the red dress. A set of percale sheets. Hugs and kisses for the old couple in brown. A gift certificate. A cosmetic bag. A tee shirt with the words: *Hairdressers do it with style!* A touching moment. A hug for the pregnant girl. Envelopes full of money. Pen and pencil sets. Hugs. Kisses. More gift certificates. Three packages left. A crimping iron. A wristwatch. One more. A small gold box tied with a burgundy ribbon.

She read the card. Her eyes moved across the tent, seeking him. She tore the wrapping paper, opened the box, stared at the bracelet. And then a whisper. "Oh my God, Gray."

The sound of his name on her lips did strange and alarming things inside him.

"It's beautiful."

She stood. Tiny feet in white leather sandals walked toward him. Tiny arms wrapped around his waist. He smelled the tantalizing scent of white musk, felt her breath on his cheek and the whisper of a kiss. It was torture.

"Thanks, Gray."

He shoved her away more roughly than he'd meant to. "No problem."

He saw a question in her eyes, and then she was gone.

As the guests moved back into their circles Gray disappeared into the house. He wanted to use the bathroom, but mostly he wanted to recover from the kiss and to escape the eyes that watched him from over the tops of beer bottles and from behind cocktail napkins. Did they know about his past, he wondered, or did they treat every stranger that came to town like a criminal?

Passing through the kitchen and into the living room he couldn't resist walking over to check out the book case, but instead of the neat rows of books, his eyes were drawn to the photographs displayed beside them.

Most were of Hope and a boy with a shy smile and big green eyes. Ted's wife's eyes. Some of the pictures were of the boy and a younger Hope together, some with he and Ted, and some with Ted's wife. Dana had been slightly thinner then, and looked as if she had a reason to smile.

In each successive picture Hope grew older, but the boy stayed just the same. Who is he? Gray wondered. He vaguely remembered hearing one of the farmers at the diner say something about Ted pulling a boy from a lake. This boy? he wondered.

He picked up one of the pictures and stared into the freckled face. That would explain the weariness behind Ted's smile, the tired set of his shoulders and the indistinguishable element that made him seem old, though he couldn't be fifty—

"Did you need something, Gray?"

He turned at the sound of the voice, clipped and overly polite, and saw Ted's wife standing in the doorway. He quickly replaced the photo. "No, Ma'am. I was just wantin' to use your wash room."

"It's down there, first door on the left." She pointed down the hallway, her eyes never leaving his face.

"Yes, Ma'am."

He closed the door behind him and stared at his reflection in the mirror. All right, so she didn't want him looking at her pictures, didn't want him in her house at all, more than likely afraid he'd boost the silverware. She was probably out there counting it right now. To hell with it. He'd just say his goodbyes and take off.

When he returned to the tent the band was playing. His feet were irresistibly drawn to the platform where Hope was dancing. It was getting dark out, and the glow of the Japanese lanterns played against her white blonde hair. She swayed, a graceful blur of hips and hands and legs, swirling, gliding to the beat of the music.

Just look at all the men …

Boys, really. A different one for every song. Lines and lines of boys, all waiting for their turn. How many of them had she promised dances to, he wondered. How many of them had been between her pretty legs? The thought filled him with jealousy. Stuffing his hands in his pockets, he turned and strode from the tent. Driving up the road that lead to his cabin, he tried to tell himself he didn't care at all. She was just a kid. Ted's kid. He couldn't care less who she danced with.

Back home, the dog waited at the end of the driveway. He stood in the shadows, ears pricked and tail swaying when he saw that it was Gray.

"Evenin' Yankee." He walked past him, and then turned back. "I know y'all ain't real sure of me, but if you think you might wanna come inside for awhile, I wish you would." He left the front door open and went into his bedroom. When he'd changed into shorts he returned to the living room and saw the dog standing just inside the door.

"Come on in, boy. You know I won't hurt you, don't you? Fact is I'm needin' a friend tonight as much as y'all are."

The dog lowered its head and sniffed the floor before taking a cautious step inside. Gray grabbed a beer from the refrigerator and when he returned, the dog stood in the living room. He sank down in the recliner and twisted the top from his bottle. "I got a friend by the name of Ace," he said. "Used to have, anyhow. He was all the time telling' me how I should never let myself fall for a girl." He took a swallow from his bottle and wiped his mouth with the back of his hand. "I made that mistake once. Cost me five years of my life. I won't make it again."

He leaned his head back against the chair and closed his eyes. "Thing is, I got things I need and there ain't no other way of getting 'em." He opened his eyes and regarded the dog. "I know what y'all are thinking, but it ain't just that." He chuckled. "Nice as it would be."

He took another swallow from his bottle. "Can I tell you somethin', Yank? I ain't never told this to nobody so I'd appreciate it if you'd keep it to yourself. Two things I want that I ain't never had before and that's a home and a family." The dog lifted its tail in encouragement and Gray continued. "I been in the system my whole life, one way or another. Unless you count the years I spent with my mama, but that was pretty much hell, too, more I think about it. I never had nobody of my own. Nobody I could come home to at night and know for sure they'd be waitin' for me. Wantin' me. And I ain't talkin' about sex so much as … as about bein' wanted."

The dog rested his head on Gray's knee and Gray gently stroked his ears. "Somethin' about that little girl, Yank. Somethin' soft and pleasin'. I look at her and all I can think is I wanna scoop her up like a pretty butterfly, know what I mean? Thing is, I know I ain't near good enough. Ted, he'd have me run outa town on a split-rail. If I could even get her. Which I probably couldn't." He stroked the dog's head. "I'm depressin' you, ain't I? Hell, I'm depressin' myself." He stood. "I won't talk about it no more. Come on, let's go find something to eat."

The dog followed him to the kitchen where he opened a can of beef stew. When they'd eaten, they went outside and sat on the porch. Gray lit a cigarette and began to talk again. He spoke of loneliness and desire, and how those things led to foolish choices. He talked until midnight, and in the end, decided he'd be doing himself a favor to forget about Hope Hanwell.

Chapter Twenty-Five

Dana didn't trust Gray Baldwin. Even if he hadn't spent five years in prison and even if she hadn't had a distinct, well-founded aversion to southern men, she wouldn't have trusted him. Behind that soft, southern politeness lurked a dangerous man. She'd known it from the moment she saw the hunger smoldering in his eyes. His kind would stop at nothing to get what they wanted and Dana had no doubt that what he wanted was her daughter.

Bracing herself, she climbed the stairs, knowing how it would turn out even as she formed the words in her mind. From down the hallway she heard the sound of Hope's radio playing softly. She stopped just short of the bedroom door and bolstered her courage. Why couldn't Ted do the dirty work for once?

She sighed. As far as Ted was concerned, Gray Baldwin was a godsend, dependable and willing to work long hours for little pay. That was all Ted could see. Rehearsing her lines one last time, she raised her hand and knocked.

"Come in."

Hope sat in front of her mirror, putting on make up.

"Hope, can I talk to you for a minute?"

She ran a rose-colored pencil along her lower lip, then pulled a tissue from the box on her vanity and carefully blotted it. She rolled her eyes and expelled an exaggerated sigh. "I'm going to a party at Kim's with Morgan. Kim's parents will be there. I'll be home at one o'clock, if that's okay."

"That's fine, but that's not what I wanted to talk to you about."

As Hope combed her fingers through her hair, Dana's eyes went to the china bracelet on her wrist. "It's about Gray Baldwin."

"What about him?"

"I hope you'll have enough sense not to get involved with him."

Hope laughed. "Why would I?"

"I don't know that you would on your own. But I think he might have other ideas. I hope you'll put him in his place if he shows them."

She laughed again and Dana felt her blood pressure shoot up a notch.

"What on earth would make you think he would?"

"The answer to that is right there on your wrist. That's not the kind of gift a man gives to a girl he's not interested in." Hope made a face in the mirror and Dana bristled. She knew Hope would try and make her feel foolish. "With such a bright future to look forward to I hope you won't—"

"I'm not going to end up like Morgan, Mother!" She slammed the lid on her cosmetic case and turned from the mirror. "I have no intention of making a baby, with Gray Baldwin or anyone else, so will you please back off?"

"It's only that your father and I want what's best—"

"Don't you dare bring Daddy into this. He's the only one around here who doesn't treat me like I'm ten-years-old. He respects me as an adult. When are you going to do the same?"

"Maybe when you've proven to me that I can."

"I've never embarrassed you, have I? I've never given your precious town a damned thing to talk about. Have I?"

"No, you haven't," she answered, struggling to control her anger. "But you haven't always been honest about where you go, either. You've lied to us and don't think for a moment we didn't know it."

Hope jumped up and grabbed her purse. "I'm outa here."

"No, you're not. You're going to sit right here for once and listen to what I have to say!"

"Why?" Her eyes flashed with a hatred that almost made Dana cringe. "Because you've made such a huge success of your life? Because you got lucky enough that my mother died so you could snag my father? So now I've got to take lessons?"

"Hope, if you'd just listen to—"

"I'm done listening, Mother. I'm done, period."

"Honey, please calm down."

"Hang in there, Dana. In a couple of months I'll be gone and you won't have to put up with me any more."

"I wasn't saying that."

"Don't you get it? I don't care what you say. I'm just putting in my time here, and while I do, I'll go out whenever, wherever, and with whoever I damn well please!"

The words were hurled over her shoulder as she bolted down the stairs. Dana heard the front door slam and sank down onto the bed, too weary to fight her tears.

She was done, too. When she'd lost Jared she'd also let go of Hope, and yes, Ted. Everything she'd loved was lost to her forever and she was done trying to pretend otherwise.

Chapter Twenty-Six

Even as he stepped from the shower and wrapped a towel around his waist, Gray knew it was a bad idea. He went to his bedroom to dress, trying to convince himself otherwise. It was nice of Ted to throw a Fourth of July picnic for his crew, but even so …

He conjured up a mental image of his coworkers with their wives, girlfriends and children, and knew he'd feel like a spare part in an otherwise smooth-running machine.

Pulling on shorts and an old T-shirt he returned to the living room. Picking up a magazine, he flipped through its pages. Maybe he'd just hang out at home today, pick up a case of beer and get good and drunk.

He read an ad for motorcycle accessories, then set the magazine down and moved to the window. Who was he kidding? The thought of another day alone in the cabin made him want to throw up. Wandering back to the bedroom, he changed into a decent shirt. "I wish I could take you with me, Yank. It would give me someone to talk to."

The dog looked up from his blanket, then put his head back down on his paws and sighed.

"I know what you're thinkin' and you're wrong. I'm not going because of her." He ran a comb through his still-damp curls. "She probably won't even be there." The keen disappointment that came with the thought alarmed him and he shook his head. It wasn't good, his wanting to see her this bad. "I won't even talk to her," he muttered. "Won't even look at her. Much."

The town park was crowded when he arrived. He wandered through the picnic area and finally spotted Ted's crew at one of the pavilions. He walked toward them, unconsciously scanning the crowd for a glimpse of Hope. When he caught sight of her, his pulse quickened, only to plummet again when he discovered she wasn't alone. He cursed himself for being a fool. What made him think she would be?

He stood talking with his coworkers, unable to keep his eyes from traveling across the pavilion. Hope's boyfriend stood head and shoulders taller than her. *Plastic*, Gray thought bitterly. *Dude looks like he was made by Mattel.*

After an uncomfortable afternoon of keeping up his end of too many conversations he headed to the grill where Ted was cooking meat. He'd offer to help, he decided. Cooking would give him something to do besides standing around with his hands in his pockets and trying not to stare at Hope and Malibu Ken.

Relieving Ted of his duty, Gray laid out the steaks; lean, tender cuts of meat, and almost salivated when their scent filled the air. *Damn sure I'll eat this time before taking off.*

Before long Ted's guests began to queue at the grill. Glancing down the line Gray saw Hope and her boyfriend heading his way. He gripped the tongs until his knuckled ached. *Cool, Baldwin*, he reminded himself. *Keep it cool.*

Moments later Hope stood before him in a pair of cut off jeans and a red-checkered halter top revealing just enough of her breasts to make him ache. She smiled. "Hello, Gray."

"Hey."

"How are you?"

"I'm just fine, darlin'."

The boyfriend was staring at him, his eyes roving over him like a Mississippi mudslide. Gray saw approval in his eyes and quickly looked away. *Son of a gun.* His glance moved back to Hope and he wondered whether she knew her boyfriend was gay.

After a solitary meal beneath the shade of a red maple tree he wandered over to a baseball diamond where some of the picnickers had begun a game. Leaning against the bleachers, he watched. Hope stood in the outfield, looking cute as a bug in a backward baseball cap. He wouldn't embarrass himself by joining in, he decided. Sure as hell the minute he got downwind of her musk perfume he'd be all thumbs.

Hope's boyfriend was third man up to bat. Gray felt his entire body tense as he self-importantly swung a warm-up. When the pitcher sent the ball he swung, connected, and effortlessly sent it sailing out of the ball field. He ran the bases and then swept Hope up in his arms. Gray watched as he bowed her low and kissed her, every nerve inside him shrieking. His hands unconsciously doubled into fists and he shoved them in his pockets and walked away.

He walked, not knowing or caring where he was going until he saw signs pointing the way to something called the Indian Trail. Intrigued, he followed them.

The sun was warm on his back and a mild breeze blew the sound of crickets and birdsong along the winding path. He walked along, enjoying the flexing of his muscles as he pushed his body upward and into what seemed another world, into the sounds of water and wildlife and the beauty of the cut rock that surrounded him.

He walked until he was able to think rationally again. He should get out more, try to meet some girls. Girls older and wiser than Hope, who'd help him get her out of his blood and wouldn't make him huger for foolish ideals that didn't exist.

He paused to look over a stone railing and strained his eyes toward a pair of doves that soared across the gorge. He watched them fly together, perfectly in synch. They collected bits of nesting material then circled back and disappeared into a cleft of rock. He watched after them, thinking of the way they worked together and of warm, sheltering homes and of children.

"God, I'm lonely," he whispered.

"Want some company?"

He hadn't heard her approach and turned with a start at the sound of Hope's voice. Her eyes were smiling, like her mouth.

"I'm sorry. Did I scare you?"

"No. I was just lost in my own world for a minute."

She came closer and leaned over the railing. "Pretty, isn't it?"

"Yeah, it sure is."

"I've seen this gorge a hundred times but I never get used to it." She turned to face him. "You should see it at night when they light up the trails. It's so gorgeous it's almost spooky." She took a step back and held out her hand. "Walk with me to the top."

"What about your boyfriend?"

"He won't mind."

Gray folded his arms across his chest. "I would."

"He won't."

"Why? Because he's gay?"

He saw surprise register in her eyes, then it fell away and she gave him a dimpled grin that melted his heart. "Yes. Because he's gay."

He reached for her hand and they began to walk.

"How did you know about Jimmy?" she asked.

He chuckled. "Call it a second sense."

"Well nobody else knows. I hope you won't tell anyone."

He laughed. "Who'd listen to me?"

She gave him the dimpled grin again. "Probably nobody."

"Why do you play act with him?"

She stopped walking, shook a pebble from her shoe, and slipped it back on her foot. "It's a small town, Gray. We do what we have to to help each other survive."

His glance swept over her pale curls, her soft pink skin, already glistening with sweat and he suppressed a smile. What could this pretty baby possibly know about survival?

"It doesn't matter to me," she said with a shrug. "I'll be outa here soon enough."

"You will, huh."

"Yep. I'm going to Glamour International in September."

"Hmm. Sounds ... glamorous."

"It's a cosmetology school in Buffalo." Her voice betrayed a hint of irritation. "And when I finish there I'm gonna go to New York City and be a famous makeup artist."

"New York City, huh?" Once again he suppressed a smile. "Well I certainly hope y'all took a few extra lessons in survival."

"I can take care of myself."

Oh, baby girl. You're just too damned cute.

She went on to tell him about the apartment she'd lined up and the three roommates she'd met on the Internet. He listened, focusing on the soft lilt of her voice more than her words. She was happy. Chirpy. Like the little yellow parakeet Gladdy Parker used to keep in her sun room. God, he hadn't thought of that in years.

Finally they reached the top of the trail. Winded, they sat on a stone ledge and looked at the magnificent waterfall that seemed to tumble from the sky.

"Anyway," she said. "I'm doing all the talking."

"That's all right."

"No it's not. I want to hear your story."

"I don't have a story, Hope. Least not one I like to tell."

"Then tell me anything you want. I love the way you talk. I've never known anyone southern before."

"I'm just like anyone else."

"No you're not." Her eyes were shining. "You're mysterious."

He laughed softly. "Alright. I'm mysterious."

She smiled at him again. Her lips were palest pink, her hair fiery gold in the afternoon sunshine. He could almost see himself reflected in her clear blue eyes. *Don't make me want you, Yankee girl …*

Without warning she stood and jumped onto the ledge.

"What are you doin'?"

She held her arms out at her sides in a precarious balancing act as she walked, two hundred feet above the rocky floor. "I'm balancing."

"Hope, I really wish you wouldn't do that."

"I do it all the time. I'm practicing to be poised, and …" she imitated his drawl, "glamorous."

He jumped down from where he sat and opened his arms. "Well could you please do it sometime when I'm not here? Y'all are scaring the hell outa me."

Laughing, she jumped down into his arms. "I knew it."

"What did you know?"

"You act cold, but I knew you weren't really. Not deep down."

He reluctantly let go of her and they sat back down on the ledge.

"So where are you from, anyway?"

"Alabama, originally."

"I bet Alabama is a lot more interesting than here."

"Well, it's a lot warmer, that's for sure."

She laughed again. "You ain't seen nothing yet."

"So they say."

"Are you going to be here in the winter?"

"I dunno." He shrugged. "We'll see how it goes."

She asked a lot of questions and he kept his answers short and noncommittal until finally she was exasperated. "But what was it like growing up in the south? What do kids do for fun?" She gave him a sidelong glance. "I mean besides strumming on the old banjo and stuff."

He cracked a smile. "That's pretty much it."

She nudged him with her elbow. He nudged her back and they laughed. "Alright, you don't have to tell me anything if you don't want to."

"Thank you."

She squeezed his hand. "Jimmy thinks you're pretty cute." She added softly, "So do I."

He searched her eyes for her meaning. *Don't play with me, Yankee girl.*

She glanced at her watch and abruptly stood. "It's getting late. We'll have to hurry if we're going to make it to the stadium."

"What stadium?"

"Mt. Bishop High School's football stadium. Best fireworks in the county, believe it or not. Come on."

He hesitated. No way would Ted and his wife be all right with the idea. "I don't think I can make it."

"Oh, Gray. You have to go."

He smiled. "Why do I have to go?"

"Because, well, I guess you don't have to, but I wish you would. I was hoping we could go together." Her lips gathered into a gentle pout. "I've never ridden on a motorcycle before."

When they arrived back at the picnic area a hazy twilight had begun to fall. Ted and his wife were busy packing up the cooler and Gray knew by the sudden silence and the rigid line of Dana's back that he had been the topic of their conversation. Ted glanced at them. To Gray's relief, he smiled. "Well there you are. We were starting to think you two had fallen into the gorge."

"Nope," Hope said breezily. "Just enjoying the scenery. And the company."

Dana threw a handful of plastic silverware into the cooler and slammed the lid down.

Ted averted his gaze. "Well then, I guess we're ready to call it a day."

"If you don't mind, Daddy, I'm going to ride back with Gray."

Dana's lips became a thin, tight line as she glared at Gray.

"Alright."

Hope kissed her father's cheek. "We'll see you at the stadium."

"We're not going," Dana said.

"All right then, we won't see you at the stadium." Hope's voice took on the brittle timbre of cracking twigs. Gray stared at the ground.

"Don't stay out too late," Ted said, and then to Gray, "I'll see you in the morning."

As they walked to the parking lot Gray let out his breath in a low whistle. "Man. Your mama hates me, don't she?"

Hope shrugged. "Don't worry about it."

"I ain't particularly worried about it. Just be a whole lot nicer if she didn't, that's all."

Hope stopped walking and faced him. "In the first place she's not my mother, she's my father's wife. And second, don't take it personally. She hates all southern men."

He looked at her in surprise. "Why?"

"Her first husband was a southerner. He took her for all she had and then some, I guess."

"Hmm," he said, beginning to understand. "She don't want to see you make the same mistake."

She unwrapped her sweatshirt from around her waist and pulled it over her head. "She doesn't have to worry about me. I told you, I can take care of myself." Reaching for the extra helmet that hung from his bike, she said, "Is this mine?"

He fastened the strap beneath her chin. "Y'all are gonna have to tell me where this stadium is."

"Well actually, by the time we get there it will be mobbed. Why don't we just watch from the top of Begger's Hill?"

He climbed on in front of her and started up the bike. When her arms went around his waist he felt his blood turn to fire and sternly reminded himself that she was Ted's daughter.

They drove to the top of a hill that looked out over the village, then climbed off the bike and settled themselves on the ground. His thoughts returned to Dana.

"Your mama," he began. Seeing her look of annoyance, he corrected, "Your daddy's wife. Did she already have a boy when she married him?"

Hope's eye's narrowed. "How do you know about that?"

"I don't, really. I saw his pictures on the book case. Is he your brother?"

"Was. He's dead now."

"What happened to him?"

"I don't want to talk about it."

"Alright."

They sat quietly for a moment and Gray found himself unable to stop thinking about the boy. "What was his name?"

"His name was Jared and I don't talk about him. Ever."

"Why not?" he asked softly.

"Same reason you don't talk about your past. It hurts too much."

She turned away and didn't speak again. Soon bright fireworks began to light up the sky. Gray stole quick glances at her profile. He saw her jaw set in anger and was sorry he'd asked about her brother. He reached for her hand, and chancing another glance, saw that the angry line of her face had softened. They sat in the mild July darkness, not speaking. When the last of the fireworks died, she stood and brushed off her legs.

"I'll make you a deal," she said. "From now on there's no past for either of us. There's just you and me and today. Okay?"

"Okay," he said softly. He reached for a strand of her hair and ran it through his fingers, his eyes fixed intently on hers. *And what about tomorrow, Yankee girl?*

"Gray?"

"Yeah."

"Why are you staring at me like that?"

"I don't know."

"Are you going to kiss me?"

"I might."

"You can if you want to."

He wanted to. And once he started he couldn't stop. He kissed her, gently and urgently, his mind a mixed bag of emotions. Musk and peppermint and guilt and desire. His tongue probed her mouth while his hands roamed over her, pulling her closer to the core of his need. Musk and peppermint and guilt. Desire. She pressed her body close, wanting him as much as he wanted her.

He slid his hands up the back of her sweatshirt. Her skin felt soft as rabbit's fur. How could anything feel so soft? He reached for the bow of her halter and slowly pulled it free.

"Gray?"

"Hmm?"

"I said you could kiss me. I didn't say anything about taking off my clothes."

But she wanted him. She wanted him just as sure as he was standing there. He knew it. He pulled away from her. Slowly, like a band aid pulled from an unhealed wound. She wanted it. And if she'd been anyone but Ted Hanwell's daughter he'd have taken down his pants and given it to her. Every hard, aching inch of it.

Chapter Twenty-Seven

By August Hope's goody two shoes image was shattered, Dana was sufficiently pissed off, Gray Baldwin was falling in love, and still Hope did not quit. The fact was, she was having too much fun.

She loved the blood-chilling rides on his motorcycle, hair flying in the wind and arms wrapped around him for dear life. She loved the parties and concerts, other girls watching, their jealousy showing like a neon sign. She and Gray were complete opposites. He was Tolstoy to her tabloids. Pearl Jam to her Alanis Morisette. He was willing to try everything, and nothing at all like anyone she'd ever known.

She shivered, thinking of his kisses, hotter lately and more demanding. This was no frustrated boy fumbling in the back seat of his father's car. This was a man, an experienced lover whose touch left her aching with desire. She knew it was only a matter of time before Gray's patience ran out and it scared her how much she wanted him to take her across the line.

A frown creased her brow. If Gray wanted more than a summer fling, well, that wasn't her problem. Anyway, as soon as she left for beauty school there would be a line of girls three deep stretching from the bakery to the back door of Hanwell Contracting to take her place. The thought made her furious.

"What are you scowling about?" Morgan lay stretched out on the chaise recliner in her mother's living room, looking more enormous and uncomfortable by the day.

"Nothing." Hope sighed. "I just wish you were going with me to Glamour."

"You and me both."

"Have you heard anything from Jerry lately?"

"No."

Hope sipped her iced tea as she flipped through a hair styling magazine. "When's he done with boot camp, anyway?"

"I don't know. And if you want the truth I don't think I care."

Hope glanced up from her magazine in surprise. "I thought you loved him."

"Well I don't. Not if he doesn't love me." She rubbed her bulging stomach. "Hope, I'm getting scared."

Hope crossed the room and hugged her friend, allowing her hands to rest on Morgan's hard, stretched belly. "It's so hard to believe there's a person in there."

"I know."

"Morgan, can I ask you something?"

"You know you can."

"Was it worth it?"

"I don't know any more." She massaged her stomach. "I bet Gray would be worth it. I bet he's phenomenal in bed, isn't he?"

"I don't know."

"Come on, Hope. I've always told you everything, and now you're trying to tell me you and Gray haven't done it yet?"

"We haven't, Morgan."

"That's not what they're saying around town."

Hope smiled. "I don't give a damn what they're saying."

"Hope?"

"Yeah?"

"What's gonna happen between you and Gray when you leave?"

"I don't know." She shrugged. "He'll find someone else, I guess."

"Not if you don't want him to, though."

"I don't care what he does, Morgan. I'm going to be a famous cosmetician. I'm going to live in Soho and hang out with movie stars and—" Seeing Morgan's crestfallen expression, she said, "Oh, Morgan, I'm sorry. I didn't mean to rub it in."

"Don't be sorry. I messed it up for myself."

"But you don't have to marry Jerry. You could give the baby up for adoption and go to school next year. We could still get a place together."

"I don't want to give the baby up," she said, clutching her middle. "I thought I did, but I don't." They sat in silence for a moment, then, "That's why I was thinking if Jerry doesn't come back, I mean, if you're not gonna want Gray any more, then maybe I could try to get him."

Hope looked into her scared, swollen face with mixed emotions. Then she shrugged again. "I don't care."

Morgan's eyes were suddenly wide. "They say Gray shot a cop."

"No way."

"But it's true he was in jail. You said so yourself."

"It was a mistake. No way Gray shot someone. He's too gentle."

"Hope, are you sure you don't want him? I mean, the way you talk about him you get all weird, like you're in love with him."

"I am not in love with Gray. He's just a way to pass the time."

Chapter Twenty-Eight

"I wish you'd have a talk with him, Ted."

"I happen to like him, Dana. He's a good man."

"That's my point, Ted. He's a grown man. And Hope's just a girl."

"She's out of school, my dear. Next month she'll be out on her own." He bent to remove his boots. "And anyway, I'd rather see her spending time with Gray than the last one. At least Gray's got some maturity, some common sense."

"Can't you please take my side for once?" Dana's voice rose as she followed him to the refrigerator. "He's getting serious about her. I can see it in the way he looks at her. I'd hate to see her jeopardize her future over him. Lord knows she won't listen to a thing I have to say."

She hovered beside him as he opened a can of beer. "Ted, please."

He sighed. "Alright. I'll caution him."

"Thank you."

"But I'd appreciate it if you'd bend a little, too. Try and be a little more tolerant of him for all our sakes."

"I'll make an effort."

He walked out to the patio and sank wearily into a chair. Gray's adoration for his daughter was not as lost on him as Dana seemed to think. He'd noticed the longing looks, the outright fear on his face whenever she mentioned leaving. Gray's obsession with Hope was just one more thing to come between he and Dana, one more bone of contention. He tipped back his can and took a long swallow. They'd been happy together once, but that seemed like a long, long time ago.

The next morning Ted stopped Gray as he was leaving for his

job site.

"Can I talk to you for a minute, Gray?"

Gray followed him to his office. "What's up?"

Sensing his apprehension, Ted smiled. "We haven't seen much of Hope this summer. I'd like ... that is, my wife and I would like to take the two of you out to dinner on Saturday."

Gray's eyebrows shot up in surprise. "Alright."

"Gray, I'll be honest with you. My wife and I are a little bit concerned." He saw the apprehension reappear and quickly added, "It's not that we dislike you—"

"Ted, I know your wife don't like me. I guess she's got her reasons for that, but I swear to you, I'd never do anything to hurt your daughter."

"I know that, Gray. I just ... We just..." *Oh, Christ, Ted, spit it out!* "I hope you won't get her into any sort of trouble."

Gray's embarrassment started at his neck and spread to the roots of his hair. He stared at his shoes, then back into Ted's eyes. "No, Sir. I won't."

"Good."

He stood, clapped his hand on Gray's shoulder, and breathed a sigh of relief. Thank God that's over.

He watched Gray climb into the waiting truck, knowing that if anyone was going to get into trouble it wouldn't be his daughter.

Chapter Twenty-Nine

Fifteen minutes into the evening Gray knew it was going to be a disaster. The restaurant was the kind with crystal bud vases and white linen napkins, the kind Gray hated. Hope sat sullen and angry beside him, and silent Ted wasn't helping matters either.

Dana was playing the diplomat, trying to draw him out. He squirmed beneath her gaze, drinking glassful after glassful of water he didn't want just to put off answering her questions, to give his mind minutes to formulate answers that for anyone else would have taken seconds.

"So Gray, do you have any family back home in Alabama?"

Actually, Ma'am, I never knew my daddy. He slit an old woman's throat for the six dollars and change in her pocketbook and was rotting in jail before I was walkin'. And my mama, she never had no more children because you see, she didn't even particularly want me, but that's a whole other story ...

"No, Ma'am."

"Have you always been a contractor by trade, like Ted?"

I ain't ever been nothing, Ma'am. I was plenty smart enough to go to college, though. Had me a good friend who could've gotten me into the best school in Alabama. Then he found out I'd been with his wife. I never even finished high school after that ...

"No, Ma'am."

"Have you got any hobbies?"

I like to play poker and drink beer and ride around on my motorcycle.

"No, Ma'am, not really."

She took his evasiveness for rudeness and sank into an uncomfortable silence. Gray pushed a forkful of potatoes around on his plate, wishing someone would say something, anything to break up the tension.

He cleared his throat. "I do like to read, if y'all would call that a hobby."

"Do you?" She looked at him with interest. "What sort of things do you read, Gray?"

"Most anything. I like Stephen King and James Patterson. I like the older works too, Faulkner, Steinbeck, Hemmingway."

"Really?"

Good God, she was smiling at him. Not the cold, tight façade she normally used to conceal her disapproval, but a real, honest to God smile. By some miracle he'd stumbled onto common ground with her and now her attitude was so warm he could almost feel its heat.

"Dana used to teach English," Ted commented. "Literature is her great love. Besides me," he added jokingly.

Everyone laughed except Hope. The ice seemed to be broken, but instead of being glad she seemed more sullen than ever and Gray couldn't fathom why.

At nine o'clock they left the restaurant with a collective sigh of relief, Ted and Dana to the comfort of home and marriage, and Gray and Hope to a bonfire at the park. The last one of the summer, Hope said, and Gray was glad to hear it. The state of perpetual motion she seemed to thrive on was getting old.

She climbed on the bike behind him and wrapped her arms around his waist. He felt instant heat and reminded himself of his promise to Ted.

The bonfire was already blazing and the beer, flowing, when they arrived. It seemed to Gray the energy level was at a fever pitch. Hope's friends were laughing too hard, talking too loud and too long about pre-med school in Boston, a degree in aeronautics from Washington State, the study of rocks and minerals in New Hampshire. It seemed to Gray they were all eager and excited and at the same time scared to death of the future.

Hope flitted from one group of friends to the next, drinking, hugging, kissing, ignoring him. Obviously punishing him, but for what?

When she returned to the keg for the sixth time he walked up behind her and rested his hands on her shoulders. "Why don't y'all slow down on that a little bit, darlin'? I don't want to take you home drunk."

She turned, giving him a sultry pout while her eyes traveled the length of his body. "I'm starting to think you don't want to take me home at all, Gray."

He gazed into her eyes, uncertain of her meaning. His lips formed a half smile that barely concealed his surprise. *Don't tempt me, Yankee girl ...*

And then she flitted away, leaving him to trail behind like a lost pup. He watched as she wrapped herself around a mountain of a boy in shorts and a wife-beater shirt. She gave him a squeeze before moving on to another boy. Remember the time ... remember the game ... remember when? His hands balled into fists in his pockets at her blatant flirtation.

He put up with it for as long as he could, but when she started in with her talk about New York City and movie stars she pushed him over the edge. Fear rose violently in his gut and he converted it to anger. When she caught his eye from behind the shoulder of her wife-beater prince, he shot her a dagger stare and walked away. He was halfway up the Indian Trail before she caught up to him. "Gray, slow down!" She yanked on his T-shirt. "Hey, I'm talking to you!"

"Well ain't that a surprise," he muttered. "Finally my turn?"

"What's the matter with you?"

He shoved his hands deeper in his pockets and stared at the ground. "Can't wait to get out of here, can you?"

"What?"

"Can't wait to leave us poor slobs behind and start your goddamned glamorous new life. Can you?"

"You're mad because I'm going away to school?"

"No, I ain't mad because you're going to school."

She moved closer to him, her voice a caress in the darkness. "Then tell me what you're mad about."

"I ain't mad, Hope. I'm just—" *It's a big ol' world out there, Yankee girl, and it's full of better men than me. Men who could give you things I could only promise. But none who'll love you more than I do...* "I'm gonna miss you."

She smiled and slid her arms around him. "It's not like I'm leaving tomorrow. We have two whole weeks."

"I know." He cupped her face in his hands and kissed her, long and hard and like he was kissing her for the last time. His need for her had never been more fierce. She pressed herself tightly against it and a low moan came from deep within him. "I can't stand it, Hope," he whispered.

"Gray …"

He silenced her with another kiss, his conscience battling with his need as his body blended with hers, almost one. Almost.

"Gray …"

He kissed her again. Musk and peppermint and skin as soft as rabbit's fur. She wanted him. He knew it. Wanted him as much as—

"I want you to take me to a motel room," she whispered.

He pulled away from her. "What did you say?"

"I said I want you to take me to a motel."

He laughed softly. "A motel? Darlin', why would I wanna—"

"The Mt. Bishop Motel."

"Oh my God." He laughed again, but a glance at her face told him she was serious. "Hope, you can't mean it."

"Yes, I do. I've never been to a motel with a man before."

"I would hope not."

"Please, Gray. It would be so sexy."

"It would be kind of obvious. And kind of sleazy. Why don't we just go back to my cabin?"

"Because I want to go to a motel," she pouted. "It wouldn't be sleazy, it would be sensuous, and besides, who would ever know?"

"Anybody who drove past and saw my bike in the lot."

"Gray, please."

And then she was kissing him, teasing him, her tongue making subtle promises he couldn't begin to withstand. He groaned. "Baby, are you sure that's what you want?"

"Positive."

But when they stepped inside the cramped, musty room twenty minutes later she seemed anything but sure. "Wow. It's so …"

"Sleazy?"

"Yeah."

"We don't have to stay."

"I want to stay."

He drew her close and kissed her, gently, reassuringly. The kiss went deeper, hotter. Hotter and hotter until his body ached with knowing that at last he would have her. He slid her shirt up and over her head, alternately kissing her and whispering her name. His hands glided to her back and unhooked the clasp of her bra.

Her breasts were warm and firm. He covered them first with his hands, and then his mouth, his excitement growing unbearable as she moaned and clamped her hands behind his neck. She arched toward him, offering more, but when he nudged her shorts down over her hips and slid his hands inside her panties, she pulled away from him. "Gray, no."

He ground his teeth together against the obscenity that threatened to spill from his lips. She was teasing him. But when he looked into her eyes he saw not a coquette, but a frightened child. "What's the matter, baby?"

"Nothing. I need to use the bathroom, that's all."

He released her, watching as she grabbed up her purse and disappeared into the bathroom. He lay on the bed to wait, still thinking of the expression on her face. It hurt him. Surely after all this time she wasn't afraid of him? Surely she didn't think him the dangerous criminal her mother did? He stayed fully clothed, not sure now which way it would go.

She finally returned to him, wrapped in a towel. She lay down beside him and he caressed her gently, knowing he was back at square one. He moved his hands over her, caressing, kissing, forcing himself to take his time. She went rigid as he unwrapped the towel. He ran his fingers over the satiny smoothness of her panties, lowering his head to kiss the insides of her thighs, and finally, the mound of hair, as soft as corn silk, that lay between them. "No, Gray." She pulled his head away. "Don't."

He cursed and raked his fingers through his hair. Did she always put up this much of a fight, or was she just trying to drive him insane?

"Don't play with me, Hope. Y'all were the one who wanted to come here in the first place." Seeing the fear returned to her eyes, he softened his tone. "I know you want me, baby. You don't have to pretend. It ain't a turn on, believe me."

"I'm not pretending."

"Then what's the problem?"

"I'm afraid."

"Of what? Of me?"

"I don't have any birth control. I bought a sponge but I don't know how to put it in." She blinked back tears, suddenly angry. "You're the one who should have taken care of it."

"I did take care of it, Hope." Reaching in his pocket, he removed a condom from his wallet and showed it to her. "Okay?"

She gave him a small smile. "Okay."

He pulled her head to his chest and stroked her hair. "You're safe with me, baby. I'm not gonna get you pregnant and I'm sure as hell not gonna be down at the coffee shop in the morning' braggin' about this." He paused. "I don't know what kind of men y'all have been with, and I'm not askin'. But there ain't a man alive who's ever wanted you more than I do right now." He traced her cheek with his fingertips. "So if y'all have any more reasons why we shouldn't make love tonight, I wish you'd tell me what they are."

"I don't," she said, snuggling against him.

"Good."

He pulled off his shirt and then his pants. Her eyes moved over him, staring, curious, looking at him as if she'd never seen a man's body before.

She placed her fingers on the angry scar on his shoulder, then brushed her lips against it. He eased himself down beside her and let her move her hands over him. Her touch was whisper soft and he closed his eyes against the waves of pleasure and pain it brought him. When she discovered the hard, bulging mass between his legs, she jerked her hand away.

"Touch me, Hope," he said, guiding her hand back. "I want you to feel how much I want you."

With trembling fingers, she began to stroke him, softly kissing his lips at the same time. It was agony.

"Hope," he groaned. "Baby, are you ready for me?"

"I don't know," she whispered.

He parted her thighs and slowly moved his fingers inside her, then maneuvered himself between her legs and lapped at her soft, female-scented flesh with his tongue. She shuddered and cried his name. Inflamed, he rolled the condom over his throbbing flesh and eased himself on top of her.

"How do you like it, baby?" he said hoarsely, nudging himself inside her. "Like this?"

"I don't … care. Any way you like it."

"Wrap your legs around me. Here, up high. I want to get as

much of you as I can."

He thrust himself inside her and groaned with relief. She was a warm, wet glove, encircling him, grasping him as he pushed himself harder, deeper inside her. She cried out and he felt her body go rigid beneath him. Damn, she was tight. How could a woman be so tight? It was almost as if she'd never … Oh, God.

He peered into her face. Her eyes were clamped shut, her teeth ground together in pain.

Oh, God. Oh, God…

He withdrew, then began to rock against her, more gently. He held himself in check until it was sheer torture, knowing he was taking a virgin but no more able to stop himself than to stop a speeding train. Slowly, carefully, gently, until she started making low, moaning sounds and whispering his name. Not in fear, or a plea to make him stop, but in pleasure as he awakened her untouched womanhood.

"Do you love it, baby?" he asked hoarsely. "Tell me you love it."

She moaned.

"Tell me, baby. Tell me you love it."

"Gray …"

"Tell me …" He felt her body shudder beneath him and felt his own release near. "Tell me you love it."

"I—"

"Hope, tell me you love me."

"I love you!"

His release was explosive, more intense than anything he'd experienced before. Spent and sweating, he couldn't move except to pull her body closer. Closer and closer, knowing now that he'd never let go.

He watched her face for a long time. When she finally opened her eyes he reached out to her, moved his fingers through her hair.

"Y'all were a virgin," he said. "Weren't you?"

She lowered her eyes. "You could tell?"

He lifted her chin, forcing her to look him in the eye. "Why didn't you tell me?"

"I thought …" She tried to turn away but he held fast. "I was afraid you wouldn't make love to me if you knew. Because my dad's your boss. I wanted my first time to be with you."

"Why?"

"Because."

"Because why?"

"Because I love you."

The confession hit him with the force of another bullet. It knocked the breath from his lungs and brought sudden, unexpected tears to his eyes.

"Do you mean it, Hope?" he choked.

"I proved it, didn't I?"

He buried his face in her neck, all at once overwhelmed by the enormity of what she'd given him. And because he wanted to, because he needed to, and because he loved her too much not to, he believed her.

Chapter Thirty

He believed her, and now there was no way to take it back. Hope sat on her bed, chewing her fingernails and trying to think. What she meant was that she loved the way he looked, all tanned skin and muscle lying beside her, and the incredible things he made her feel. She hadn't meant that she loved him, exactly. At least not in the way he thought. But she said it. And it had changed him.

The minute the words left her lips she saw the transformation. He was suddenly a little boy, naked and wearing his need for it to be true all over his face. The confession unshackled him, made him reckless, like a deer rushing headlong toward the Interstate, unaware he was about to be crushed.

She should have clarified it there and then, but there was something about the way he looked at her. She never knew a girl could have that kind of power over a man. It was as intoxicating as the alcohol she drank to get up the nerve to go through with it.

She bit her nail down to the cuticle and winced. She thought for sure when her father found out Gray took her to the Mt. Bishop Motel he would send him packing. Evidently he hadn't heard about it. Just her luck the grapevine would dry up when she needed it most. Or maybe Daddy had heard about it and he liked Gray too much to believe it. Hell, even Dana liked him now. God. What was she going to do? How was she going to get herself out of this m—

"Hope?" Dana's voice called up the staircase, shattering her thoughts. "Gray's here!"

"Of course he is," she muttered, making her way down the stairs. In the living room, Dana stood at the window. "It looks like he has a surprise."

Oh, God, what now? She walked to the window and peered out. Gray and her father stood in the driveway, talking as they looked over a red Jeep Cherokee. "What on earth ..."

Dana smiled. "Looks like he got rid of that awful motorcycle."

"Oh my God!" Hope hurried out the front door. "Gray?"

The men stopped talking and turned in her direction.

"Hey," Gray drew her close and kissed her as if her father wasn't even there. "Here you are."

"Where's the bike?"

He glanced at Ted, then turned back to her with a smile. "I traded it in." He patted the side of the Jeep. "What do you think?"

Hope's stomach knotted. "Why did you get rid of it?"

"Because this is four wheel drive, darlin'. It'll be a whole lot more practical for winter. Not to mention a lot warmer."

Her heart sank to her toes. "You're staying, then?"

He dropped his arm around her shoulder. "Of course I'm stayin'."

"I'm certainly glad to hear that," her father said.

"Come on," Gray said, grabbing her hand. "I want you to have the first ride."

She stared out the window, barely listening as he talked. He pulled up in front of the cabin and laughed when his mutt rushed at the Jeep, snarling and barking until he saw that it was Gray.

"What do you think, Yank? Should we keep it?" he said, rubbing the dog's ears. When the dog had been thoroughly scuffed, Gray walked over to Hope, slid his arms around her, and kissed her. "Mmm. I've been waitin' for that all day."

She gave him a grudging smile, hating that his kiss could turn her to jelly.

"I've got somethin' I've been wanting to talk over with you, Hope."

She tensed. "You do?"

"I've been thinkin' about buying this property from your daddy."

For a terrifying moment she couldn't breathe. "You have?"

"I've been thinkin' about knocking down this cabin and buildin' something better." He studied the small house and she knew he was envisioning a newer, bigger property. A home. "I could do most of the work myself. With what I'd save in labor alone we could afford to build somethin' real nice."

We.

"I don't know, Gray. Isn't it sort of isolated?"

His lips whispered down her neck in a string of kisses. "That's alright, ain't it?"

"Oh, Gray."

His hands traveled to her bottom. "Let's go inside and talk it over."

Lying beside him in his bed an hour later, her thoughts raced like Nascars. An idea had occurred to her, a possible way out. Morgan wanted Gray so badly she could taste it. If Hope could somehow interest Gray in her best friend it would make it easier for everyone. It would be perfect, really. Morgan would have a father for her baby and Gray would have the home and family he craved. But how to make him see that?

"My friend, Morgan," she began, "she's gonna be so lonely when I'm gone."

"She ain't the only one." He kissed her and quickly changed the subject. "I could probably lay the foundation in the spring. Have it done by fall if nothin' goes wrong."

"We're a lot alike, me and Morgan. More alike than most sisters."

"I'd have to hire the electrical work done, and most of the plumbing. But if I worked right along I could probably have it done in a year."

"Gray, are you listening to me?"

"Sure I'm listening."

"I'm still going away to school. The fact that we sleep together doesn't change that."

"I know that, Hope." He was quiet for a moment. "That's something else I've been thinkin' about. This career of yours."

She propped herself on her elbow and looked eagerly into his face.

"Ain't but one or two beauty shops in this whole town. Way I see it, y'all could open up a salon of your own. Classy lady like yourself, I bet y'all would make a killin'."

Her hopes plummeted. Perfect. A salon in downtown Dullsville, where she'd waste her life doing the same old boring hairstyles and applying blue rinses to a bunch of old ladies' heads. Oh, God. What was she going to do?

"Gray, can we not talk about this right now?"

"What's wrong, baby?"

"It's just a lot to think about all at once." She gave him a weak smile and rolled over, hoping she didn't look as sick as she felt.

•

"I have to admit it, Ted. I was wrong about Gray."

He smiled. "I won't say I told you so."

Dana moved closer to him, lifting her shoulders as he slid his arm beneath them. "He really seems to care about her, and I must say she seems more settled down."

"Mhm."

"Maybe now she'll give up on the idea of going to New York City and come home when she finishes her training, settle in Mt. Bishop."

"That would make Gray Baldwin a miracle worker." He massaged her shoulders. "I hate to jinx it, but maybe things are looking up."

"Lord, I hope so." She snuggled against him. "Business is better, then?"

"I'm cautiously optimistic. I have to admit, Gray's really had a positive effect on the team."

"Who'd have thought we'd be saved by a southerner?"

He laughed softly. "I don't know if I'd go quite that far."

She sighed. "I just hope …"

"What?"

"Well, Hope does have a way of manipulating people. I'd hate to see either one of them get hurt."

She felt Ted's body tense beside her. "Dana, please. Don't borrow trouble. Let's give her the benefit of the doubt."

"You're right. I'm sorry." She pushed her gloomy thoughts from her mind, not completely convinced, but not wanting to rock the boat now that it seemed to be docked in peaceful waters.

Chapter Thirty-One

She was made for him. She satisfied his body as completely as she filled his heart and sated the twenty-two-year-old hunger in his soul. Gray watched her sleep, hating that he'd have to wake her soon and take her home. He traced the line of her cheek, wishing she would stay with him. Not just for a few hours, but forever.

His eyes moved to the calendar above the bed and he felt a fist clench in his gut. Tomorrow. An aching emptiness spread through him, one he knew would remain until she finished school in May. Nine whole months. How could he let her go? "I'm gonna miss you, Yankee Girl."

He didn't realize he'd spoken his thoughts until she opened her eyes and smiled at him. "I'll miss you, too."

"Can't I take you up there tomorrow, Hope? I'd like to meet your roommates and have a look at where y'all will be stayin'."

"No."

"Please?"

"My parents have their hearts set on taking me. And besides, if you're there it'll only make it harder."

He moved his fingers through her hair. "When did you say your first break was?"

"Thanksgiving."

"Damn."

Silence.

"I could come up and visit you before then, if y'all get feeling homesick."

"We'll see how it goes."

"Thanksgiving's two months away."

"I know."

"I just thought maybe y'all would like—"

"Gray." She covered his mouth with her fingers. "If you start coming up every weekend I'll never get used to being there."

The words hurt. It almost sounded like she didn't want him hanging around her, messing up her new life. "Hope, I got a bad feelin' about this."

"It'll be alright."

"Call me when y'all get settled in and give me your phone number, okay?"

"I will."

"You know you can call me any time, right? Day or night."

"I know."

"And if it turns out it ain't what you expected, if you don't like it after all, you know I'll come and get you."

"I know."

Silence.

"Gray, will you do me a favor?"

"Name it, babe."

"Will you call Morgan sometimes? Take her someplace once in awhile?"

"Oh, Hope ... I'd really rather not."

"Please? For me? She doesn't have anyone to talk to, and since Jerry broke up with her she's lonely. And her mother's being a royal bitch. So please?"

He sighed. "Alright."

She smiled and kissed his cheek, melting his heart. "Thanks."

Riding home, Gray's hand resting possessively on her thigh, Hope shot a glance at his profile and felt a stab of regret. What if she changed her mind, decided she did want him after all? She bit her lip. That would mean a life sentence in Mt. Bishop, being tied down, never having had a chance to live. *Oh, Gray, please don't make me hurt you ...*

As if he read her thoughts he squeezed her hand, and in that moment, his thoughts were transparent. *Please, Hope. Don't go ...*

•

She called him every day the first week. Her classes were hard. She hadn't known she'd have to learn bone structure and pressure points. Her roommates were cold. She hated them all. Had he called Morgan yet?

The second week she called half as much. She'd learned her first hair style, applied for a part-time job as a shampoo girl at a classy salon downtown. Her roommates weren't so bad after all.

By her third week gone there was a chill in the air and the hillside around Gray's cabin had erupted in color. He stared out the window, barely seeing the beauty, unable to get warm because she'd only called him once all week.

He turned back to the book of house plans that lay open on the table. "What do you think of this one, Yank? I kind of like the split logs." He turned the page. "Maybe she'd like somethin' a little more contemporary."

The dog waved his tail sleepily and closed his eyes, not moving from his place by the stove. "Damn. I wonder what she's doin' right now." He considered the possibilities, then scraped his chair back from the table. "Ain't but one way to find out, I guess."

He dialed her number and listened to the hollow ringing on the other end of the line. Each unanswered ring made him feel lonelier and more disconnected from her than the last.

"Maybe she's out workin'," he said, replacing the phone in its cradle. "I'll try again in a little while."

He called every half hour until midnight, then fell into a troubled sleep and dreamed he'd been shot in the heart.

Chapter Thirty-Two

She was head over heels in love with the city. Hurrying through the crowded streets at ten o'clock on a chilly November evening, Hope paused to take in the city lights and the falling snow. She felt the movement and the heartbeat of the city beneath her feet and hugged herself, shivering more with excitement than cold.

She dashed to the bus stop and climbed aboard, giving the eye to a man with a long, black ponytail who reminded her of Drake. He winked and she rewarded him with a smile. Swinging down into an empty seat, she crossed her legs. *Alive*, she thought. *I'm eighteen and alive in a city that still has a pulse at ten o'clock at night.* And to think she'd almost given up and gone running back to Mt. Bishop. What a colossal mistake that would have been.

She caught her reflection in a store window as the bus rolled past and smiled. Dana would have a fit. Running her hand over the fiery red bristles, she grinned in defiance at the rebuttal she could only too well imagine. Oh, yes, Dana would have a fit, and let her. Hope didn't answer to Dana anymore. Or anyone else.

Her smile faded with a glance at her watch. She'd busted her butt to get out of work early. She hoped she wouldn't miss Drake if he called. Drake Sloan was the kind of guy who didn't give second chances.

When the bus groaned to a stop she got off and sprinted the three blocks to her apartment, another thing Dana was having fits about. She hurried past the derelict row houses and the drunks on the corner, breathing a sigh of relief when the front door of her building closed behind her. All right, so it wasn't the greatest neighborhood. What did her parents expect for the lousy two hundred bucks a month they gave her?

She took the narrow steps two at a time and breathlessly flung herself through the door marked 4B. Inside, Penny sprawled on the sofa, painting her toenails. She gave Hope a breezy, electric blue wave.

"My God is it getting cold out," Hope exclaimed, throwing down her tote bag.

"So put a little padding on yourself for chrissakes," Penny replied.

Savannah's voice called out from the kitchenette, "I'm ordering pizza. Who's in?"

"I am!" Hope shrugged out of her coat and leafed through the stack of mail on the table. All junk. Throwing it back down, she turned to Penny. "Anybody call for me?"

"If you mean Drake, then no. But some guy named Ray's called here, like, sixty times. He wants you to call him back."

"Gray," Hope absently corrected as she rummaged in her bag for her cigarettes.

"Hey, if he's as hot as he sounds, I'll call him."

"He's okay." She felt a pang of guilt and brushed it aside. She didn't owe Gray Baldwin a damned thing. Plopping herself down in a chair, she straightened out a wrinkled cigarette and pulled out her lighter. She wished Savannah would get the hell off the phone.

She lit her cigarette and took a deep pull. Drake Sloan was everything Gray Baldwin wasn't. Hope could hardly believe such a classy and gorgeous guy was her cosmetology instructor. At thirty Drake had already been to Europe twice, and if Hope had her way, when he left for France this summer, she'd be going with him.

He'd invited her out for coffee twice. Not to some dull, rundown diner, but to a real coffee house with poetry readings and deep, soulful music. But she wasn't kidding herself. Getting Drake Sloan would take a lot more finesse than getting Gray Baldwin had.

She walked down the hallway to the bedroom she shared with Penny and pulled off her boots and tights. She'd put them on again if Drake wanted to go out, but after four straight hours on her feet shampooing heads, her legs were killing her. The ringing of the phone sent her racing back to the living room. She lunged for it and snapped it up.

"Hello?"

"Hope?"

Damn! "Yeah."

"I been tryin' to get ahold of you all night."

"And here I am." *Damn and double damn!*

"Where y'all been, baby?"

She rolled her eyes and Penny laughed from the sofa. "Work."

"Oh."

Silence.

"How's everything goin'?"

"All right."

"I sure do miss you."

"How's my dad?"

"He's good."

"Have you seen Morgan lately?"

"I took her to the movies last night, like you asked me to."

"How was it?"

"It was all right, if you like James Bond."

"I mean how was being out with Morgan?"

"I'd have rather been out with you."

Silence.

"Hope, I been wantin' to talk to y'all about next week."

She braced herself. "Next week?"

"Thanksgiving." His voice dropped. "Baby, I cant wait to see you. What day will y'all be done? I told your daddy I'd come up and get you."

Oh, God. "Gray, the thing is …"

"What?"

"Turns out I can only get Thursday and Friday off from work. I don't know if it would be worth it to come home for just two days."

Dead silence.

"Gray?"

"Sure it would."

"I was thinking maybe I'd just stay here."

"Then I'll come up. I've got the whole weekend off."

"I'll be studying most of the time. Let's just wait until Christmas."

She could hear the tension in his silence, feel his disappointment radiating from the phone line. "Hope, I can't wait until Christmas. It's damned near killing me to wait until Thanksgiving. I need to be with you."

Her guilt flared to anger and she felt the overwhelming need to be rid of him, to hurt him if that's what it took. "Is it really me you miss, Gray, or is it the sex? I mean, can't you get that anywhere else?"

It was a long moment before he answered. "Thanks."

"Gray, I'm sorry. I didn't mean to—"

"I'm doin' the best I can not to bother you, Hope, but it's hard for me, all right? I miss seein' you every day and tellin' you things. And yeah, right now I'm damned near crazy to be inside you. What's wrong with that?"

"Nothing," she said softly.

"So what day should I come and get you?"

"I don't know. I'll call you back."

"When?"

"Tomorrow."

"Will you?"

"I said I would, didn't I?"

"Hope, I love you, baby. I love you so much it's killin' me."

"Look, I've gotta go. I'll call you tomorrow."

She didn't.

Chapter Thirty-Three

If Gray didn't know the truth it was because he couldn't bear to. He spent Thanksgiving Day alone with his dog and a microwave dinner he was too sick to eat. He'd called Hope every hour since ten that morning but she wouldn't answer the phone.

By four o'clock his fear was a serpent, winding its way through his body, squeezing, sucking his heart out a little at a time. He watched the falling snow and for once didn't see its beauty, only its coldness. He was losing her.

He dumped his dinner in the garbage and resumed his silent vigil at the window. Did she find someone else, or did she just misplace her love for him?

He dialed her number until midnight and then dropped, mentally exhausted, into bed. He tossed and turned until the moon gave way to the sun's pale light. The only thing he knew for certain was that something was terribly, horribly wrong. At five AM he stepped from the shower and pulled on a pair of jeans and a sweatshirt. Something was wrong. He'd set it right or die trying.

He drove toward Buffalo, unaware of the music that played on the radio and the other cars on the highway. Nothing existed but the questions he needed to ask her. Nothing but the serpent that tightened around his body, hissing a truth he couldn't face.

At eleven o'clock he pulled up in front of a line of row houses and squinted at their faded numbers. He stared at the sagging porches and then at the corner where a group of drug dealers congregated. Everything inside him wanted to throw her in the truck and take her home.

He got out of the Jeep and strode toward the house. Opening the front door, he was assaulted by the sour stench of neglect. He covered his nose with his hand. God Almighty.

He stood outside unit 4B, bracing himself. He knocked, and his heart hammered in rhythm with every beat of his fist. When it opened, he drew back and stared, open-mouthed, at the girl who stood before him. She was skinny and punkish, sporting a fiery red crew cut and matching body suit, a diamond stud glittering from her nose.

"Hope?"

The color drained from her face. "Gray."

"My God. What have you done to yourself?" He reached out and touched the stiff bristles on her head.

"What are you doing here?" she demanded, jerking away. He continued to stare in disbelief. "Other than staring at my new hair style?"

"Style!"

Her chin tilted in defiance. "You don't like it?"

"I hate it."

"Thanks."

"It makes you look like a goddamned dyke for chrissakes."

She tried to slam the door but his hand shot out and caught it. *Be cool, Baldwin,* he warned himself. *Don't blow this.*

"I'm sorry, baby." He did his best to smooth the edge from his voice. "I just wasn't expectin' … It's gonna take some getting' used to, is all."

She glared at him, her eyes murderous.

"I'm sorry, all right?"

"You should be."

"I am, Hope. Really." They stood in uncomfortable silence. "How are you, baby?"

"I told you I was fine, didn't I?"

"Yeah, I guess you did." *Don't be cold, baby. Don't shut me out.* He cleared his throat. "Can I come in?"

She shot a glance over her shoulder into the room.

"I'm not gonna embarrass you in front of your friends, Hope. I just wanna talk to you."

"There's nobody else here," she said, grudgingly stepping aside.

The room he stepped into was only slightly less decrepit than the rest of the building. Its walls and ceiling were yellowed with cigarette smoke, its burnt orange carpet dirty and frayed. Neon beer signs shouted from the windows. He glanced around at the disorder, total except for the table in the corner, set for two with flowered dishes and two ivory candles flickering in pewter candlesticks. The serpent tightened around his chest. "Expectin' company?"

"No."

He put his hands on her waist, gently drawing her close. She turned her face from his kiss. The serpent hissed, sucked the air from his lungs.

"Hope," he whispered. "My God, baby. What's happening?"

"Nothing's happening."

He swallowed, willing his voice to perform. "Then why can't I kiss you?"

She reluctantly turned her face back to his and he brought his lips down to meet hers.

"Gray, don't. I ..."

"You what?"

"I ..."

His glance flickered back to the table. He tightened his grip on her as he felt the room begin to sway. His voice cracked despite his effort to control it. "Found somebody else, didn't you?"

She stared at the floor. "No, I didn't."

"Don't lie to me, Hope. Just ..." He raked his fingers through his hair. "Just tell me the truth."

She stared at him, mute except for the guilt in her eyes. He drew a ragged breath. "Seems to me if y'all loved somebody y'all would be happy to see 'em after two months. Seems you'd wanna be with 'em."

"Gray—"

"Seems to me you'd at least return their goddamned phone calls!" He was losing control. Fear and rage and pain gripped him, causing his entire body to tremble. "Course if it was no longer true that you loved 'em, well, that would be a whole other set of circumstances. It would explain a lot." His eyes bore into hers as he awaited her answer. "Hope?"

She bit her lip.

"Hope?"

"I don't," she whispered.

The sound that came from his throat was half jagged breath and half moan. He pressed his hands to his ears, as if that would block out her words. He gazed into her eyes and saw everything he'd ever lost. "Two months…" His voice caught. "Two months ago it was true and now you say it ain't. How is that possible?"

"I don't know."

"No!" He grasped her arms and gave her a small shove, then buried his face in her neck. "I want you to tell me how that's possible."

"Gray, I'm sorry."

He was crying, rocking her back and forth, pleading. "You loved me, I know you did." Trembling, face buried in her neck, heart crushed. Bleeding. "Please." *Please make it be true again. Please don't hurt me. Oh God in heaven, please…*

His tears spilled down her neck, wetting the front of her clothes. He knew he was making himself needy and pathetic but he couldn't stop. He was a child, terrified of the sudden darkness and desperate for reassurance, for light. And she wouldn't give it.

"Gray, my God. Please don't."

He pulled in a last ragged breath and released her. She despised him. He could see it in her eyes. He looked away from her, wiping away his tears with the back of his hand. She didn't want him any more. It was over. "All right, baby," he said. "That's all I came to find out."

He looked into her eyes one last time, then turned and forced his legs to walk away.

Outside at the curb he knelt and vomited into the gutter. He didn't see the two men who poked each other and laughed as they passed him by, didn't notice them open the door he'd just come through, or notice the camera or the bottles of wine they held. He didn't notice anything at all. He was empty inside. Hollow. Dead.

Chapter Thirty-Four

Moments after Gray left there was another knock at the door. Hope stood in the living room, steeling herself against another onslaught of pain. She knew it would be bad when the end came, but she hadn't known it would kill him.

The knock became more insistent and she pressed her hands against her ears. *Go away, Gray. Please don't make me hurt you any more.*

"Hope! Come on, babe, open up. We're damned near turning to icicles out here."

Drake! Wiping away her tears, she hurried to the mirror. Oh, God, she looked a mess. She hadn't even finished putting on her makeup.

"Just a sec!"

She dabbed her face with foundation, then spritzed herself with the Opium perfume he loved. As narcotic as the real thing, or so he'd said.

When she opened the door, Drake stood in the hallway wearing a black wool coat, his hair and beard sparkling with snow.

"Hello, beautiful." He pulled her to him and kissed her, swatting her behind before pushing his way inside. "I brought a buddy. This is Kent. Hope you don't mind."

She forced a smile. "Hi, Kent."

He was huge, black as midnight and built like a steam engine. His eyes moved over her in unabashed appraisal, photographing her tightly clad figure as precisely as the expensive camera that hung from a strap around his neck. She hated him immediately.

"Hey, I'm starved. Why don't you call Ling-Ling's and order something," Drake said, turning on the television.

"Alright." She picked up the phone and angrily punched in the number of his favorite Chinese restaurant. How could he be so dense? When she'd found out her roommates were all going away for the weekend she thought it would be perfect—candles, music, wine. She might as well have gone home herself, for as romantic as this was going to be.

She ordered three combo platters and sat down on the couch beside Drake, only slightly pacified when he dropped his arm around her shoulders. Within moments he and Kent were engrossed in a football game and she sat, fuming, until she thought she'd explode. Finally she stood.

"Where are you going?" Drake asked.

"I have studying to do."

He pulled her back down beside him. "You don't have to study, you'll do fine. Stay."

Despite her annoyance, she obeyed. When the food arrived she picked at it in miserable silence, shooting murderous glances at Kent. Drake refilled her wine glass and dropped his arm around her again. After three glasses, the drone of their voices and the noise of the football game lulled her to sleep.

What seemed moments later Drake shook her awake. He switched off the TV and threw the remote aside, then slid his hand to her knee. "Now that that's out of the way we can all get acquainted." He kissed her, plunging his tongue deep into her mouth. His hands roved over her body, pushing her back onto the sofa. Confused by the wine, she yielded to the pleasure.

"That's right, baby," he murmured. "Were you afraid I didn't know why you invited me here? Were you afraid you weren't going to get it?"

Something in his eyes made her uneasy and she gave him an uncertain smile.

"Come on, babe. You should know that Drake Sloan would never disappoint a lady."

All at once he was pulling at her clothes, his hands moving roughly over her exposed breasts. "Mm, nice," he murmured, covering one with his mouth. When she saw Kent stand and load his camera, the sobering realization of what was happening hit her and she pushed Drake away.

"Stop!"

He laughed. "Don't worry about him. He's just here to capture the moment on film."

His mouth came down on her breast again, his teeth raking her nipples until they stood out in painful points. She grasped his ponytail and yanked him away. "I said stop."

She heard the click of the shutter the same moment she felt the sudden, blinding pain of Drake's fist connecting with her face.

"Don't ever do that!" Catching her wrists in his hand, he shoved her back into the cushions. "We can do this either way, Hope," he snarled. "To tell you the truth I rather like a fight. It turns me on."

He jerked her pants down over her knees and plunged his fingers inside her, nearly tearing her apart with the force. Seconds later he unzipped his pants and thrust himself inside her. The pain was unbearable. She clamped her teeth together in agony, nearly choking on her terror as he described in graphic detail what he would do to her if she told anyone.

Tears streamed down her face as she remembered Gray's gentle touch and whispered words of love. *Oh, Gray, help me ... Gray ...*

When Drake was finished he stood and pulled his pants on. "You disappoint me, babe. I thought you'd be better."

She pressed her face into the cushions and waited for him to leave. To her horror she felt another set of larger hands pulling at her body. She glanced up into Kent's twisted face and knew the nightmare wasn't over.

He pulled her roughly from the sofa. "How do you want it?"

She stared at him in terror, unable to speak except to cry out when he thrust his hand between her legs.

"What's the matter, huh? You sore?"

"Yes," she sobbed.

His breath was sour with wine, his fingers wet with blood when he withdrew them. He slid them back in and then over her anus. "How 'bout this one? Feels nice and tight."

"No! Please. Take me the other way if you want to, just please ... not that."

He laughed, a low, growling sound that drove the color from her face.

"You hear that?" he said to Drake. "She's begging for it. This bitch can't get enough."

He shoved her across the room to the table and bent her over a chair.

"All right, slut. Now you're gonna find out the meaning of the word."

Time seemed suspended. Hope swirled in a fog of unreality as he unzipped his pants. She felt a searing, gut twisting pain as he drove himself inside her. He was huge. He groaned, squeezing her hips as he forced his way deeper inside. She cried without shame, knowing her was killing her. Oh, God, would he ever stop?

Oh, God ... Daddy ... Gray ... Don't let him kill me.

Finally he was finished. She clung to the chair until the sound of their laughter faded. When she heard their footsteps retreating down the hallway she raced to the door and slammed it shut. With the last of her strength she slid the deadbolt into place.

Chapter Thirty-Five

It was early, not even nine o'clock, but Ted Hanwell wasn't a man to lie in bed once the sun came up. Not even on Sunday. He hefted the strings of Christmas lights up the ladder and carefully strung them on the hooks he'd installed years before. Snow pelted his face. Good Lord, could Dana have chosen a colder day for decorating?

Inching along the eaves, he noticed the troughs needed to be cleaned and tightened down. And Christ, would you look at the gunk around the chimney. He sighed. What was that old saying about everyone having shoes except the cobbler's kids?

He saw Gray's Jeep pull in the driveway and glanced at his watch. What would bring him on a Sunday morning? Snugging the string of lights in place, he climbed back down the ladder. One look at Gray's face told him it wasn't a social visit. Something was terribly wrong. He could see it in the dark shadows that lined Gray's eyes, and the red-rimmed suggestion of alcohol. "Morning, Gray."

He drew closer, stopping just short of where Ted stood. "Y'all got a minute, Ted?"

"What's the matter? Are you sick?"

"No." He stuffed his hands in his pockets, shivering with cold. "I just wanted to give y'all a heads up. I'm thinkin' it's time I moved along."

"Moved along? You don't mean for good?"

"Yessir."

Ted's heart plummeted. "I don't know what to say."

Gray stared at his shoes, saying nothing.

"We're in the middle of a project. I can't finish it a man short. Not on time."

"I'll stay another week, get her finished up before I go."

Ted sighed and ran a hand back through his hair. "I could pay you more. We're in good shape now."

He raised hollow eyes to meet Ted's. "It ain't about money, Ted. Y'all have been more than fair and I appreciate you takin' a chance on me like you did. Meant a lot to me." His gaze dropped. "There just ain't anything here for me."

Ted heard the raw pain in his voice and suddenly understood. "Give her time, son. She just needs a little breathing room. She'll come back."

"To you, maybe. Not to me."

He took in the dejected slump of Gray's shoulders, the quality of emptiness that spoke of a man with nothing left to lose or gain.

"There's nothing I can do to change your mind?"

"No, Sir."

"You'll finish the job, though?"

"Yessir."

Ted watched him turn and walk back across the yard, his mind reaching for a solution even as his heart told him none existed.

At noon the heavenly scent of Dana's chicken and biscuits lured him to the kitchen. She stood at the oven stirring gravy and turned when he came in. "Was that Gray I saw outside earlier?"

"Yeah."

"What's going on?"

"I'm not really sure. He says he wants to move along."

She paused, spoon in mid-air. "Oh, no."

"I hate like hell to lose him."

"Do you think he and Hope had a falling out?"

"If anybody fell out, it wasn't Gray. The kid's a mess."

"I was afraid of this."

Dana set the meal on the table. They'd just filled their plates when the phone rang. Dana answered it, and when her voice rose in alarm, Ted stood.

"It's Hope," she said, handing him the phone.

He cradled it on his shoulder. "Hope?"

"Daddy?"

"What's wrong, honey?"

"Daddy." She choked on a sob. "Can you come and get me?"

"You mean today?"

"Yeah. Right now. I don't …" Her voice broke off abruptly as she succumbed to tears.

"Hope, what's wrong?"

"I don't want to be here anymore."

His stomach did a two-step, but for his daughter's sake he kept his voice calm. "All right, sweetheart, sit tight. I'm on my way."

He hung up the phone and reached for his coat.

"What is it, Ted?"

"I don't know. But I don't think it's good."

"She's coming home?"

"Evidently."

"I'm coming with you," Dana said, grabbing up her coat.

Ted laid a hand on her arm. "I don't know what I'm going to find when I get up there, Dana. I think maybe I'd better go alone this time."

An hour and a half later Ted knocked on the door to his daughter's apartment. When it opened he found himself face to face with a cadaver of a girl, colorless except for her bright blue fingernails and jet black hair. She eyed him with open hostility. "What do you need?"

If it hadn't been for the sick churning in his gut he would have found it humorous, being kept at bay by this anorexic little bull dog.

"I'm looking for my daughter, Hope Hanwell."

"Oh." Her look immediately softened and she moved aside to give him entry. Hope's suitcases were piled in the center of the room. He fidgeted, looking around at the feminine chaos while the other girl went to find Hope. When she appeared in the doorway he was more shocked by the angry bruises on her face than the bright red crew cut.

"Hope? Honey?"

"Daddy." She crossed the room and flung herself into his arms. He cradled her, stroking what was left of her hair. She crumbled against him, all at once his little girl again. He held her, speaking gently until her tears subsided to a faint sniffling, then wiped them from her cheeks with his fingers. "What happened, sweetheart?"

She drew a shaky breath. "I got mugged."

"Mugged? Where?"

She sniffled. "I was on my way home from work yesterday. These two guys ... they beat me up and took my purse."

"Oh, baby." He pulled her to his chest again, burning with anger.

Why had he ever allowed her to come and live in the bowels of the city? "We've got to call the police, file a report."

"I don't want to, Daddy," she said, eyes brimming again. "I just want to go home."

He loaded her suitcases into the back of the truck, then slid inside and took her hand in his. "Hope, did they do … anything else?"

She shook her head and turned her face to the window. He laid a gentle hand on her back. "You can tell me if they did."

She shuddered, and said in a whisper, "They just took my purse. That's all."

He looked at her pale, bruised face. Unconvinced, he gave her hand a squeeze and turned the truck toward home.

Chapter Thirty-Six

She'd been home for more than a week but it didn't have anything to do with him. Gray heard the whispers at the Laundromat, the diner, even Speedy's Gas Garage. Whispers as subtle as tumbleweeds blowing around the town of Mt. Bishop saying something terrible happened to Hope in Buffalo.

He worked long and silent hours, his mind burning with questions he had too much pride to ask. He worked as though driven by demons, aloof, withdrawn, his bastion of solitude once again intact. But under cover of night, he'd drive into town, park his truck across the street from her house and gaze up at her bedroom window. He'd see the soft glow of light behind her curtains and wonder, did she fall asleep with the light on again, or was she lying awake, tormented, just like him? *Did you love me at all, Yankee girl?*

Sometimes he sat for an hour and sometimes for the entire night, clutching the silver cross beneath his shirt and trying to believe there was a reason for his existence before driving away as silently as he'd come.

On the tenth of December the last job was finished. Gray went home and filled a bowl with dog food for Yankee, then pulled a microwavable dinner from the freezer. He sat at the table and looked around the cabin. His cabin. The closest he'd come to having a real home. He gazed at the ever changing hillside and thought of all the hopes and dreams that were born here only to die again, unless …

He picked up the phone and dialed her number. He'd be leaving tomorrow forever. He should at least call and say good bye.

Before the phone rang he lost his nerve and hung up. She'd have heard by now that he was leaving and obviously didn't care. She didn't want him anymore. He had to get that through his head.

The thought kept him feverish and sweating, turning in his bed late into the night. Feverish and sweating, until finally he gave up the fight and pulled on his clothes. He'd go out and get some air to clear his head.

A half hour later he was sitting in front of her house, gazing at the soft light behind her curtain, aching for a glimpse of her, if only a shadow on the wall. Feverish, sweating, aching with need. *Yankee girl, did you love me at all?*

When morning came he was too undone to eat breakfast. His mind was made up. He'd been her lover, her very first. There had to be a goodbye in there somewhere, didn't there? He packed his possessions into boxes and set them beside the door. The dog lay curled up on his blanket in the kitchen and he gave Gray a nervous flip of his tail.

"I'll be back soon, boy," Gray said, stroking his ears. "Then we're outa here."

His stomach turned over as he pulled into Ted's driveway. Climbing out of the Jeep, he strode to the front door and knocked. Moments later Dana stood before him, eyes wide with surprise. "Gray, my goodness, I thought you'd left town."

"Mrs. Hanwell, I'd like to talk to Hope. Is she here?"

"Well, yes, she is," she hedged. "But she's not feeling well. I don't know if she's up to company."

He dug in his heels. "Mrs. Hanwell, please. I won't stay long. I just want to say goodbye."

She hesitated. "Let me go and ask her."

Hope's voice came softly from the living room. "It's alright, Mom. I'll talk to him."

He swallowed a breath and stepped inside. The girl who stood before him looked like a child lost in one of her father's old sweatshirts. Her lip was split and her face covered with the remains of bruises. But more alarming was the dullness behind her eyes, the hollow looking sockets that had once sparkled with life. It was an expression he knew well, one he'd worn for most of his life. *Who hurt you, baby? Tell me who it was and I'll kill him.*

He cleared his throat. "Hello, Hope."

"Hi, Gray."

Dana said something about milk and gas for the car, and then the front door closed and they were alone. He moistened his lips. "I was just wantin' to come by and see y'all before I leave."

"Where are you going?" she asked, her face expressionless.

"I'm not sure, exactly. New England, maybe. Maine."

She nodded and slipped back into silence.

He shifted his weight and raked his fingers through his hair, utterly stripped of pride. Everything inside of him ached to hold her, to crush her against him and beg her to take him back. "Hope … Baby, are you all right?"

She dropped her gaze to the floor and shook her head, her voice barely a whisper. "No."

He jammed his hands into his pockets, knowing she wasn't his to touch. Not anymore. "Is there anything I can do?—"

She shook her head again and choked back a sob.

Her tears were too much for him. He went to her. His hand hovered before coming to rest on her cheek. "Baby," he said softly, "let me help."

She looked into his eyes, her face twisted with pain. "Why do you even care anymore?"

He sucked in his lower lip and blinked back tears. He knew he was leaving himself wide open, but if there was one chance in a million it wasn't over … "Because I love you, Hope."

Her eyes filled with tears. "How could you?"

"Because you're my girl." His voice cracked. "And I know that ain't true no more, but I can't let go of it, Hope. I can't stop feelin' it and I— I can't— Oh, Christ—" He lost control. Sorrow welled up like a river deep inside him, stealing his breath. And then she was in his arms, clinging to him, needing him as much as he needed her. "Hope, please give me another chance."

"I can't," she whispered.

"You loved me before. If y'all will give me just one more chance I know I can make you love me again."

She raised her tear-stained face to his. "I don't know how to love. I could tell you I would love you, but in the end I'd only destroy you."

"Shh. Don't say that."

"It's the truth! Loving me has already killed two people. Don't let me kill you, too. Just go, Gray. Just leave."

"What are you talkin' about? You're all mixed up, baby, let

me—"

"I killed my mother and my brother," she wailed.

He locked his arms around her and stroked her hair, whispering softly to try and calm her.

"My mother was only twenty-three when she got pregnant. I was her first baby, her only one. Three months into her pregnancy she got cancer. It came down to her or me."

"Hope, you can't think that was your fault."

She continued as if he hadn't spoken. "I grew into a stupid, selfish little girl. Stupid enough to go into a stormy lake knowing I couldn't swim. Jared told me to come out. He kept calling to me, 'Hope, come back!' but I didn't. He wasted his life trying to save me, just like my mother." She convulsed, her entire body trembling. "As long as I live I'll see his face when my father pulled him out of the water."

"Hey." He took her face in his hands and forced her to meet his gaze. "There's things that happen in life, Hope. Ain't nobody's fault and there ain't no reason for 'em. Just all kinds of bad shit happenin' every day. You didn't kill your mama or your brother. You ain't mean enough for killin'."

She rested her cheek against his chest and he held her fast, cradling her until at last she spoke again. "I can't believe you still love me, after—"

"I'm never gonna be done lovin' you, baby. As long as I'm alive I'm gonna be your man. I'll live every day of my life to make you happy, if—"

"If what?"

He drew her closer, every nerve in his body on fire, every breath in his lungs a prayer. "If you'll be my wife."

He held on, straining to hear her thoughts above the silence.

"Would you keep me safe?" she whispered.

"I swear to God. If you stay with me I'll never let anybody hurt you."

All of eternity stretched out before him as he waited. Yes or no. He stared into her eyes, knowing it could go either way. "Hope?"

"Yes," she whispered.

"You …" The word knocked the breath from his lungs. "You will?"

She nodded and he crushed her against him. She'd returned to him, and he'd never let her leave again. "I want it all, Hope. The ring and the house and the babies. We'll have it all, right?"

"Yes, Gray. We'll have it all."

Pure, undiluted joy coursed through him. "We'll have it all, but first I want the rest of the story, includin' what happened up there."

She pulled in a jagged breath. "I can't tell you about it."

"Yes, you can. I want you to tell it to me now. All of it. And then I'm gonna tell you about me." He ran his fingers lovingly across her cheek. "And then there ain't gonna be no more secrets or no more past. There's just gonna be you and me and our future."

Interlude
May, 2004

Before he pressed his fingers against her cold, white skin, Ace knew he wouldn't find a pulse. He stood to his feet, staring into the lifeless eyes, the blood red mouth that sneered at him even in death. She'd goddamned well deserved it. Trying to cheat him out of his share of the score had been her first mistake. Laughing at him had been her last.

He walked into the bathroom and splashed a handful of cold water on his face, trying to clear his head. Though she was less than the scum that overflowed the Boston gutters, he knew taking her life would cost him his freedom.

After filling the bathtub with water, he returned to the bedroom and retrieved her naked body. After setting her down in the tub, he took a towel from the hamper and meticulously wiped down the shabby apartment. By the time anyone missed her all traces of him would be gone. He looked at her with disgust. Just another dead hooker. Maybe no one would even care. Maybe they'd just assume she fell in the tub and broke her stupid little neck and let it go at that.

When he was satisfied everything he'd touched was wiped clean he returned to the bedroom and rummaged through the dresser. Finding nothing, he slid his hand beneath the mattress. Nothing. She was smarter than he'd thought.

After a thorough check of the living room he moved on to the kitchen. He spied the rows of canisters on the counter. One of them was newer than the others and depicted a polar bear drinking a bottle of soda. Though he'd never learned to read, Ace recognized the emblem and knew the letters spelled the word Coke. He lifted off the lid, peered inside and smiled.

Dumb bitch.

Counting the bills, he cursed her for her stupidity. The coke had a street value of over two grand and she'd gotten six hundred. He stuffed the bills in his pocket. Split two ways it would have been three hundred each. She'd died for three hundred lousy bucks.

He walked to the window and looked down into the deserted alley. His best bet would be to use the fire escape, and from there …? No way he could stay in Boston. Sooner or later someone would ask questions. Hadn't they seen him with her at Stokey's? Hadn't he talked to her in the back room at Sizzler's the night she died?

No, even Boston wouldn't be big enough to hide him if someone got nosy. What he needed was a big town, a town as cold and as heartless as he was. A town like New York. With this decided, he climbed out the window and down the fire escape and disappeared into the alley, just another black shadow in the Massachusetts darkness.

Book Three

Flight

Chapter Thirty-Seven

June, 2004

"Are you sure you don't mind, Hope?"

"I'm sure."

"Absolutely, positively sure?"

"Yes, Morgan, I'm absolutely, positively sure I don't mind watching Quincy tonight."

"Will Gray mind?"

"He'll mind even less than I do. Not that I do, at all."

"I feel funny, though. You guys are still newlyweds. You probably had a romantic evening planned."

Hope frowned at the phone. "We're living with my parents, Morgan, how romantic do you think it gets?"

Morgan laughed. "When will your house be done?"

She sighed. "They finished laying the foundation, but it's still gonna take forever."

"Hope, I'm so happy for you."

"Thanks."

"I can't believe you got married. Can you believe you actually got married?"

"About as much as I can believe you're waitressing at the Mt. Bishop Diner."

"It's Sherry's Restaurant now."

"Oh yeah. I forgot."

They giggled.

"So I'll drop him off at four, then?"

"Four it is."

"And you're sure you don't mind?"

"I'm hanging up now, Morgan." She hung up the phone, thinking of Quincy's soft little hands and his toothless grin. Six months old and twenty-seven pounds of baby fat and cuddles. It surprised her how much she liked having him around.

Not that she was in a hurry to start having babies of her own. She could see how tired and how tied down Morgan was. Babies were so final. She frowned, thinking how Gray would spend the entire evening playing with him. He'd feed him and rock him, even change his diapers. And then he'd start in again about having a baby of their own. They'd gotten married in February. It was only June. What was the rush?

Later that night Hope and Gray lay in bed, talking over the day. Gray told her about the porch he was putting on a house on Water Street, about the progress he was making on their own house, and that her father was going to help him start putting up the shell soon. He asked whether she'd been out at all that day, suggested some fresh air might do her good.

She listened to the sound of his voice as she drifted off to sleep. She felt his arms slide around her, resting on her middle, and braced herself for the question she'd known all evening he would ask.

"Hope?"

"Hm?"

"When can we start tryin'?"

"I don't know, Gray. Don't you think we should wait until the house is finished?"

"If we started tryin' now, though, the house would be finished by the time—"

"I think we should wait awhile."

"Why?"

"Because I'm only going to be nineteen once."

Silence.

"You still want to have kids with me though, right?"

She heard the insecurity in his voice and knew it would take months, maybe years to undo the damage she'd done to his trust. "Of course I do," she said, snuggling against him. "I just want to have you all to myself a little while longer."

He smiled, pacified for the time being. He kissed her, and she succumbed to the pleasure of his hands, his tongue, his body. She loved that he always fell asleep holding her and that the last word on his lips at the end of the day was her name. Any doubts she had in the daytime that marrying him had been the right thing to do were laid to rest at night, lying in the safety of his arms.

Chapter Thirty-Eight

Gray had never known life could be so good. His days were so much more meaningful and his nights so much sweeter now that he had Hope. He cherished every day of their lives, and Sundays most of all.

On Sundays, Hope came up to the property to keep him company while he worked. She'd read to him from her tabloids while he pounded nails and measured fittings, still not quite able to believe it was his own house he was building, his own beautiful wife perched on the ladder.

She was quieter than usual today, and he knew she had something on her mind. His gaze wandered to where she sat, staring into space and he wondered what she might be thinking, wondered if it was a good time to bring up the subject of children again. Now that he'd come this far, he was impatient for the rest of it. If only she'd stop putting him off his happiness would be complete.

He thought of Quincy and dreamed of the day he'd have a boy of his own, an extension of himself he could love and share things with. Or a girl, blue eyed and petite like Hope, that he could cuddle and give all the things he'd never had.

He reminded himself Hope was only nineteen. He'd dreamed of having a family all his life, but to her it was still a new concept. He lifted a beam from the pile and fit it squarely into the groove he'd routed. He wouldn't push her anymore. She'd get used to the idea sooner or later, come to want it as much as he did. Wouldn't she?

Without warning his fear came rushing back. What if she didn't? She was feeling better every day, stronger. What if once the nightmares stopped and she felt safe again she decided she didn't need him anymore?

The thought was painful and he quickly rejected it. She married him, didn't she? If that didn't prove her love nothing would.

"Gray, let's take a break."

He turned at the sound of her voice and saw that she'd poured him a cup of coffee from the thermos Dana sent. They sat together on the floor of what would one day be their kitchen, talking about color schemes, tile, and wallpaper. The sparkle in her eyes eased his mind. The house would give her an outlet for her creative energy. And once the house was finished …

"Hope?"

"Hm?"

"Do y'all think three bedrooms are gonna be enough?"

"That's what we decided, isn't it?"

"Yeah, but I been thinkin', if we decide we want three or four kids—"

"We're only having one."

He stared at her, momentarily stunned. "Who decided that?"

"I did. One's enough nowadays." She picked up her magazine and casually flipped through it.

"Excuse me … I don't have a say in this?"

"My body. My decision."

"This is unbelievable."

"I don't want to talk about it right now, Gray."

"Maybe I do."

She continued to flip through her magazine, ignoring him. His anger flared and he cautioned himself to be cool, to let it go for now. He sat for a moment, trying to calm himself but he couldn't. Her nonchalance pissed him off. He tore the magazine from her hands and flung it across the room.

"What do you think you're doing?" She stood to go after it and he grabbed her arm and pulled her back down beside him. "I wanna talk about it, Hope. Right now."

"Of course you do. That's all you ever want to talk about and I'm getting sick of it."

"Well excuse me for thinking' you'd follow through with what you promised." His voice rose in anger and he struggled to control it.

"What's that supposed to mean?"

"Forget it."

"No, I won't forget it."

"You said you wanted your own house and security and I'm doin' my best to give it to you. When are you gonna give me what I want?"

"You wanted to get married and I married you."

"It ain't like nobody forced you!"

"I know that."

"Then why are you makin' out like it was some big, goddamned sacrifice?"

"I'm not!"

"Well it sure sounds like it from where I'm sittin."

"Maybe I didn't know being married meant I was done having fun!"

They were shouting. He knew if they kept up it wouldn't turn out good, but he was too angry and hurt to back down. "Fun! I'm workin' sixty hours a week, not to mention the hours I'm puttin' in up here. Y'all will have to forgive me if I don't have any energy left to go out and trip the light fantastic."

"Whatever that means."

"It means why don't y'all grow up?"

She glared at him. "I'm your wife, not your property. I have a right to go out and enjoy myself whether you like it or not."

"I ain't never tried to keep you from havin' fun." He drew a deep breath, nearly shaking with the effort to control his temper. "Hope, I don't wanna do this."

"As a matter of fact, I'm going out this weekend."

"Goin' out where?"

She faced him in defiance. "Some friends of mine are home from college. There's a party on Friday night and I'm going."

"Without me."

"That's right."

"The hell you are."

"The hell I'm not."

"No way, Hope. It ain't happenin."

"And why not?"

"Because it ain't right, that's why not."

"All right then, come with me. But I didn't think you felt comfortable around my friends."

"I'm a hell of a lot more comfortable around your friends than I am with you runnin' around at night without me."

"You don't trust me?"

He stared at her, hesitating just long enough that she knew it was true. Her eyes filled with tears. "I made a mistake, Gray, how long do I have to pay for it?"

When he didn't answer she jumped up and hurried from the room.

They drove home without speaking.

That night as he lay awake in the dark, Gray was unable to keep up his silence. He was scared and miserable and too weak to fight off the demons of doubt that tortured him any longer. "Hope?"

"What?"

"Are you sorry you married me?"

"No."

"'Cause if you are, I mean, if y'all are thinking' maybe you made a mistake, it ain't too late to say so."

"Oh, Gray." She pulled him close and smoothed back his hair as if he were a child. "Don't think that. We had a fight, that's all. It's no big deal."

"But if y'all ain't havin' any fun ..."

"I didn't mean it. I don't even want to go to the stupid party."

"Yes, you do."

"No, I don't."

"Y'all ain't been out since ... I want you to go to the party and have a good time."

"You do?"

"Yes. I do." She wrapped her arms around him and rested her head against his chest. "You just gotta understand somethin', baby. I never got to be a nineteen-year-old. This time in your life when y'all are wantin' to get out and kick up your heels, I don't know what that is. I spent those years tryin' to survive."

"I'm sorry, Gray."

"Ain't nothin' for you to be sorry about. We're just coming from two different places. But I'm gonna try and understand where y'all are at. I won't stop you from seein' your friends. And I won't bring up havin' a baby no more either. Whenever y'all feel like you're ready, you just let me know."

"All right."

He rolled over and kissed her. "I love you, Hope."

"I love you, too."

"Promise you'll never leave me, all right? No matter what."

"I won't leave you, Gray. Not ever."

She said it with confidence, believing every word.

Chapter Thirty-Nine

Life sucked and then you died. Ace drew up the collar of his shirt and crouched in the doorway of an abandoned storefront as a torrent of rain made muddy rivers of the streets. New York City was no haven of anonymity. It was just another prison. Concrete and asphalt and not one damned place to go to get out of the rain. And the people... Damn. He thought New Englanders were cold.

Every face he met seemed to mirror his own, savage eyes, pieces of lost humanity, each one competition for sleeping space in the subway station or the scraps of linguini and bread in the dumpsters of the Italian restaurants two streets over. For every job he might have got, a thousand faces wanted it just as bad, faces that said they'd kill for it.

When the rain let up he shoved his hands in his pockets and slunk from the doorway. He fingered the empty package in his pocket. Damn. Not one smoke left in his pack. He glanced at the puddles that ran along Severn Street. There was a time he'd have thought himself above scouring the streets for a cigarette butt, a time it'd have taken a hell of a lot more than a smoke to make him risk disease. Not anymore.

He looked up at the buildings—cold, concrete fingers that choked out the sky. Then he looked at the faces. Armies of lost soldiers marching in circles, going nowhere, just like him. He'd have been better off staying in Alabama. He turned into the alley he loosely thought of as home and stretched out on the ground beneath the stairwell of an abandoned bakery. At least the tattered awning had left the ground partially dry. He looked past the filth and thought of sailing ships and pristine coastlines, of lighthouses and seagulls.

If he hadn't let himself get sucked in by the promise of easy money he might have made it. Now he never would. But heading back to Alabama with his tail between his legs would be too much like quitting.

He'd heard about another place with forests thick as apple butter and logging jobs a dozen to the dime. Canada. Resting his head against his arms, he drifted off to sleep.

He slept until the sun was a crimson promise stretched out across the Manhattan skyline, then walked to a public rest room and washed with a grimy bar of soap. Half refreshed, he searched a nearby garbage can and found a slice of cold pizza, barely touched. He stuffed it in his mouth and wiped his face with the back of his hand. There was a time he'd have thought himself above it.

At six-fifteen he ambled toward the Interstate. He'd walk if he had to. He was getting out.

He was two miles outside Jersey City, dog tired and too hot to take another step when a tractor trailer pulled to the side of the highway. Summoning his last ounce of energy, he ran up to the window, careful to keep his good side to the driver, young and buck-toothed, wearing a baseball cap and a grin as wide as New Jersey.

"Where ya headed, brah?"

Ace grimaced. He hated these extra-white white boys who called every brother they met "brah." It was worse than being called a nigger. But ridin' with Smilin' Joe here would sure beat walking. "Canada," he said.

The driver smiled more widely, which Ace wouldn't have thought possible. "Climb in. I can take you as far as Buffalo."

They hadn't gone a mile before Ace was ready to open the door and jump. He kept his face to the window, his head resting against the back of the frayed seat while the driver talked his BS.

He'd saved two years to buy his rig. This was his first over-the-road run, hauling produce from New Jersey to Western New York. He had a sweet wife and a kid named Oscar. Ace tuned him out, oblivious to the chatter until he realized the man had asked him a question.

"What happened to your face, anyhow?"

"'Scuse me?"

"Your face. You get in a knife fight or something?"

Ace gave him a cold, hard stare. Dumb bastard.

"Got hit by lightnin."

The man's face registered shock. "No shit?"

Ace closed his eyes again, idly wondering how much money dude had on him. Soon the drone of his voice and the slow, steady motion of the truck lulled him to sleep. He woke again when he felt the semi roll to a stop. He looked at the half dozen small factories and the tired old houses. He'd thought Buffalo would be bigger. "We there?"

"Not yet. I got fifty cases to dump off at a supermarket here first." He grinned. "Help me offload 'em and I'll buy you lunch."

Ace's stomach knotted in hunger. He shrugged. "Maybe."

"Bound to be a diner here somewhere." He poked Ace in the ribs and wiggled his eyebrows. "Cute waitresses, tight uniforms."

For the sake of his stomach Ace hid his disgust. He looked out at the shabby houses, made drearier by the overcast skies. "What is this place, anyway?"

"This?" He stifled a yawn. "This dump is called Mt. Bishop."

Chapter Forty

Gray was feeling good. The job went smoothly and he'd finished up early for once. He'd stop and pick up his paycheck, he decided, then spend the rest of the afternoon working on the house. Hanging drywall wasn't one of his favorite jobs, but he had to admit, seeing the house morph from a skeleton into a real home was worth every ounce of blood and sweat he invested.

He whistled as he walked through the doors of Hanwell Contracting on that early August afternoon. He'd work no later than six, then he'd take Hope out for dinner. Someplace nice. The thought filled him with longing. He hadn't seen nearly enough of her lately.

Ted was in his office on the phone. When he signaled him to wait, Gray paused in the doorway.

"Uh-huh. Today, then, for sure? All right. Yes, I'll hold." He sighed and shifted the phone to his other shoulder. "You on your way out?" he asked Gray.

"Yeah."

"Can you do me a favor?"

"Sure."

"I can't get away and I'm damn near starving. Can you run down to the diner and get me a sandwich?"

"No problem. What do y'all want?"

Ted reached in his pocket with his free hand. "Ham and Swiss on rye. Extra mayo."

Gray waved away his money and walked from the building. His stomach churned as he walked toward the diner. The clock on the bank said 2:15. He hadn't eaten since breakfast. Maybe he'd get something, too.

Stepping into the diner, he was once again taken back by the sunny yellow countertops and spanking white floor. Even the same old lunch crowd looked shiny and new. When the diner was been auctioned off for back taxes three months before, Sherry Englert, a retired school teacher with a passion for culinary arts, bought the aged landmark and breathed new life into it. Her potato egg bake oozing with cheddar cheese was fast becoming a town phenomenon, and she made an apple crisp that would melt in a man's mouth. He walked up to the counter and scanned the board advertising the day's specials.

"Be right with you, Gray," Morgan called from behind the counter.

"Take your time, darlin'."

He shoved his hands in his pockets and rocked back on his heels, eyeing the board until Morgan returned, pink cheeked and breathless.

"What can I get you?" she asked.

"Ham and Swiss on rye, extra mayo, and a large order of potato skins, and … ah hell, make it two."

She jotted the order on a pad and passed it through the window, then turned back to him and rested her elbows on the counter. "Where's your wife been hiding? I've barely seen her all week."

"Makes two of us."

"Is she still working at LaDonna's?"

He winked at her. "Was this morning', but you know how she goes through 'em."

She laughed. "Well anyway, it looks like I'll have a sitter tonight so I can go to the party after all. Hope said I could catch a ride with her." Seeing the storm clouds that rolled across his face, she added, "With you guys, I mean. If that's okay?"

With a sentence his good mood evaporated. He hadn't known she was going out again tonight. "I'm not goin', but I'm sure she won't mind."

"Oh, okay then. Well, I'll call her later."

"Do that. And y'all can tell her I won't be home until late."

Two men approached the register and Morgan hurried over to cash them out. Gray's gaze returned to the board, though his appetite was gone. Was Hope ever going to settle down? He was trying to be patient, but damn it he was getting sick of her running around. And why couldn't she stick to a job? The latest, selling overpriced underwear to women as vain and bored as herself, was her third job in a month. When was she gonna grow up?

He was so intent on his thoughts he wasn't aware of the men at the register until he heard one of them speak.

"Have a nice day," Morgan said.

"Yes, Ma'am."

Recognizing the southern accent, he turned. As the man walked from the diner Gray had a fleeting impression—a flash of silver against skin as dark as pine pitch, a square jaw beneath a proud, prominent nose. He squinted out the window as the man walked away, studying the sturdy shoulders, the broad back. *It can't be ...*

"All set. Gray?"

His glance moved to Morgan's face and then back to the parking lot as the two men walked toward an eighteen-wheeler. It just can't be ...

"Just a second, darlin'."

They were almost to the truck when Gray opened the door. He hesitated for only a second then cupped his hands around his mouth.

"Ace!"

He stopped walking and turned back. He was older, harder looking and thinner than Gray remembered, but he would have known the coal black eyes and jagged scar anywhere. He walked toward him. "It's you, isn't it?"

He ran the last half dozen steps and threw his arms around his friend with a whoop. "Ace Javitz! Well I'll be damned."

He held him at arm's length and saw that Ace was smiling. It was the slow, lazy, smirk he knew so well.

"Gray Baldwin. If y'all ain't a sight for sorry eyes I don't know what. How the hell you been, Boy?"

An hour later they stood looking at Gray's house.

"Damn, son. You mean to tell me y'all own all of this?"

Gray couldn't hide his pride. "Built it myself."

"Damn. Somebody gone and got you civilized, ain't they?"

"Yep." He laughed, feeling fifteen-years-old again. "Ace, I can't wait for y'all to meet my wife. You won't believe how pretty she is."

Ace's eyes hardened. "Marriage ain't nothin' but just another kind of prison. The worst kind they is. I thought I taught y'all that."

"Maybe for some people, but not for me. She's the best thing ever happened to me my whole goddamned life."

"Hmph." Ace spit a stream of chewing tobacco on the ground and stared at the house. "Must be doin' somethin' right, be able to afford this."

"Well Ted, that's her daddy, he gave us the land for a weddin' present and loaned us half the money. He comes up to help me work on it some. He's the best damned contractor y'all ever seen."

Ace shook his head.

"What?"

"Nothin'."

"No, come on. What?"

"Ain't nothin' comes without a price tag. Ain't y'all learned that yet?"

"What do you mean?"

"He give you a piece of property and his daughter, now he own you."

"He ain't like that, Ace."

"She own you, though. I can see it on your face."

"Hey," Gray said, uncomfortable with the turn the conversation had taken, "Ted's lookin' for another man right now. I know he'd take y'all on if you wanna stay awhile."

"I dunno."

"I could ask him, if you want me to."

Ace shrugged and spat another stream of tobacco. "You can ask him."

Ace and Gray worked on the house until dark and then returned to the diner with a spirit of renewed brotherhood. Gray recapped his past few years with honesty and humor. As usual, Ace was tight-lipped.

"So y'all never made it up to Maine after all."

"Nope."

"Where'd you say you been? Massachusetts?"

Ace downed the last of his coffee. "Any place in this town a man can get a real drink?"

Gray paid the bill and they walked two blocks to Mario's, a small bar that sat between a pawn shop and a set of railroad tracks. They started talking again and before Gray knew it the bar was closing and he was drunk. He dropped Ace at the Mt. Bishop Motel with enough money to stay the night and headed home.

When he crept into their room, Hope shot up in bed and turned on the light. "Where have you been?"

He made his unsteady way toward her, shedding his clothes as he went. "Hope, y'all wouldn't believe it if I told you. I ran into an old, old—"

"You reek. How much have you had to drink?"

"I don't know, couple beers." He sat on the edge of the bed and pulled off his shoes. "Anyhow, your daddy sent me down to the diner this afternoon and I—"

"Gray, you can barely talk. Where have you been all night?"

"That's what I been tryin' to tell you. I ran into an old, old friend of mine from way back—"

"I know, Morgan told me. Some big black guy."

"His name's Ace."

"You still haven't told me where you were all night. I went up to the house looking for you."

"Went someplace called … hell, I don't remember. Little beer place out beyond the tracks."

"Mario's?"

"Yeah, that's what it was."

"You went to a bar?"

"You ain't letting' me tell—"

"You went to a bar without me?"

"Yes, I did," he said, suddenly remembering he was angry with her. "And by the way, where the hell did you go off to tonight?"

"You never bothered to come home and find out!"

"Would it have mattered?"

"Yes, it would have!"

"If I'd come home and asked y'all not to go out, you wouldn't of, 'izzat what ya'll are sayin'?"

"That's what I'm saying."

"Bull shit."

"It's not bull shit. You're bull shit."

He shook his head. "I don't know about you, Hope."

"I don't know about you, either!"

"Keep it down 'fore y'all wake up your daddy and Dana."

"I can't believe you went out without me."

"Well I did. How does it feel?" He pulled off his pants and slid into bed. "I like to go out and have a good time too, Hope. Ever think of that?"

"You could have gone with me to any one of those—"

"Oh, bull shit I coulda. Y'all wanted me at them parties of yours about as bad as a goddamned hooker wants the Pope."

"You are such an asshole!" Grabbing her pillow, she jumped out of bed.

He grabbed her arm. "Where are you goin'?"

"To sleep on the couch."

"Get back here."

She jerked free. "No."

"Hope for Christ's sakes get back in bed."

"You don't own me, Gray Baldwin!"

Suddenly Ace's words came back to him. *She own you, though. I can see it in your face* ...

He rolled over, angry and not sure why. "To hell with you, then."

"Oh, that's real nice, Gray." Her voice betrayed hurt, and as the door closed behind her his first impulse was to go after her. But when he tried to sit the room began to spin. He sank back into his pillows and closed his eyes.

"To hell with you," he muttered.

Chapter Forty-One

That Ace hated Hope Baldwin was a given, a general fact established in his mind the moment he learned of her existence. Not just because she was a woman and he hated all women. Because she was Gray's woman. The more specific hatred that came with knowing she didn't love or deserve him came after he met her. And it came with a vengeance.

But he was cool, careful not to betray the jealousy and white-hot anger that burned beneath his surface. Not yet. Not until he'd had a chance to work it all out. A chance to work on Gray. Gray ...

Older now, not the skinny, vulnerable kid he had to step in and protect so many times. But still naïve enough to risk his damned fool neck on anything that looked like love. Gray. Still needing him, but this time not knowing it. Not yet, anyway.

Setting his thoughts aside, Ace rolled out of bed and into his clothes. Gray would be coming to pick him up for work soon, though Ace wasn't sure why. Hanwell's wasn't but a few blocks from the motel and from there he'd ride to the site with Chuck.

Chuck ... His lip curled. *Out to make trouble, just as sure as I'm standin' here.* So he missed a couple of days, left early a couple times, so what? It wasn't like he was being chipped down to fit in Ted Hanwell's shoes, like Gray.

His thoughts were interrupted by a quick tap at his door. He opened it to find Gray standing beneath the rusty awning, his hair and clothes dripping with rain. "All set?" he asked.

"Lemme grab my hat." Ace picked his way through the clutter, pushing a handful of carryout boxes from the top of his dresser. He shook the crumbs from his baseball cap and shoved it on his head.

They dashed to Gray's Jeep and climbed inside. Ace could tell by his sidelong glances and silence Gray had something on his mind. He sat beside him, feeling edgy, wishing he'd come out with it.

"S'up, man?"

"Nothin'."

"Come on."

"I just wish y'all wouldn't say nothin' to Chuck today, that's all."

"'Bout what?"

"'Bout anything. Just do your work and stay clear of him, all right?"

"My work is to stand around and hold his damned nails for him," he muttered.

"I think he's givin' Ted the idea y'all are a troublemaker. I wish you wouldn't give him a reason to think it, Ace."

"I ain't give that son of a bitch no reason to think nothin'."

"Well don't, all right? Just be cool." He pulled into the alley behind Hanwell's. "Are y'all coming up to help me tonight? I think between the two of us we could get that counter top laid in."

Ace shrugged. "I guess."

"Why don't y'all eat dinner with us tonight."

"Hell. I'd rather eat outta a dumpster than sit across the table from that old bitch again. Lookin' at me the whole time like I was a army of ants dropped in on her picnic."

"Dana ain't so bad."

"Hmph. I'm feelin' sorry for you, son. Y'all farther gone than I thought you was."

"I wish you'd try to get along with people, Ace. It'd make it a whole lot easier on everybody."

Ace's anger flared and died again with a look into the smoky gray eyes. They walked in the back door where Chuck's crew waited. Gray slapped his arm. "I'll see you after work."

For Gray's sake, he tried. He worked in silence, ignoring the other men's subtle put-downs. And later that night he sat at the table, as quiet as a shadow while Dana Hanwell glared at him like he was the devil in the flesh. He heaved a sigh of relief when it was over, eyeing the half full platters as they were carried from the table. Damn. He would have liked to fill his pockets with some of those biscuits.

Gray announced they were going up to work on the house and

Ace's heart sank when Hope grabbed a bag of flower bulbs and a trowel and followed them to the Jeep.

He sat beside her, gagged by her perfume and the way her hand rested on Gray's thigh. He stared out the window, ignoring her attempts at conversation.

"So Ace, Gray tells me you spent some time in Boston."

Damn it all... When had he let that slip? "S'right."

"I went there on my senior trip."

He closed his eyes and tuned her out.

"... Back Bay district ... Copley Square ... cappuccino and biscotti..."

"Hmph."

"Did you ever go to the Hard Rock Café?"

"Nope."

"Oh."

Gray cleared his throat. From the corner of his eye Ace saw him give Hope's hand a squeeze. "I bet it was a big change for you, after Alabama." She laughed. "Gray couldn't get used to the cold. Never took off his long underwear until June."

He turned and looked out the window again.

When they reached Gray's property Hope took the trowel and plants and carried them to the end of the driveway. Gray was quiet, speaking only of the counter top and measurements. When they'd trimmed it to size and fitted it in place, Ace finally confronted him. "S'matter, Gray?"

"Nothin." He ran a bead of caulk along a seam, smoothed it, and wiped away the excess. "You could have been a little nicer to her."

"Why? She don't like me any more than her mama does. If it wasn't for y'all she wouldn't even give me the time of day. I guarantee it."

"She's tryin' to get to know you, Ace. They all are. I wish y'all would lighten up and give people a chance."

Ace felt his calm veneer begin to crack. "First y'all want me to keep quiet, then you want me to talk. From now on maybe I oughta ask you first before I take a piss, how'd that be?"

"Knock it off."

"What else can I do to keep from embarrassin' you, man? Change the color of my skin?"

"This ain't about the color of nobody's skin."

"The hell it ain't. Got a whole town full of people lookin' at me like I was a gorilla come to town in the damned circus."

"They did that to me, too, at first."

"Yeah, but good ole Gray, he found a way to fit hisself in. Made hisself into a prince and got him a princess in the deal. Well I don't live in no fairy tale world like y'all do."

Gray's jaw muscle tensed. "What are you tryin' to say?"

"Maybe y'all wanna take a good, hard look at your little princess."

"What are you tryin' to say, Ace?"

"Hell." Ace looked away.

"I asked you what are you tryin' to say to me here?"

"What the hell you think she doin' while you out workin' every day, huh? Just sittin' around waitin' for y'all to come home?"

"She works."

Ace snorted. "She don't work but three morning's a week. Seems to me that leaves her with a whole lot of time on her hands."

"Y'all are talkin' about my wife." Gray's voice was tight with anger, but there was no mistaking the doubt that flickered across his face.

"Don't look it to me. Or to a lot of other people neither, if what they sayin's true. What the hell she doin' runnin' around every night, if she's your wife?"

"I trust her."

"Wake up, boy! Didn't that nasty little mess down in Virginia teach you nothin'? She's makin' a damn fool outa you."

Gray's eyes flashed from anger to surprise. Ace turned to see Hope standing in the doorway.

"Gray, can we go?"

Gray sighed and ran his hand back through his hair. "Sure, baby."

Ace helped pack up the tools, avoiding Hope's icy stare. When he finally looked at her he saw that their hatred was mutual.

Good, he thought. *Now they both knew where they stood.*

Chapter Forty-Two

"I hate him."

Morgan rolled up a dirty diaper, swiped at Quincy's bottom with a wet wipe, and slid a clean diaper beneath him. "Why do you hate him?"

"Because he hates me. For no reason. And because he's trying to turn Gray against me. We've done nothing but fight since he showed up."

"What's new? You've done nothing but fight since the day you met."

"I'm serious, Morgan. He gives me the creeps."

"Why, because he's black?"

"No, not because he's black. Because he's evil."

Morgan laughed. "Come on, Hope. He's not evil."

"Why are you taking his side?"

"I'm not taking his side." She lifted Quincy to her shoulder and bounced him. "I don't even know him."

"I wish I didn't."

"I don't think he'll stay long. I can't see a guy like Ace hanging around Mt. Bishop. But for Gray's sake you should try to get along with him."

"I can't. I hate him."

Morgan patted Quincy's back, still bouncing him. "He's been in the diner a few times. He doesn't seem all that bad."

"Well he is, believe me. I mean, they say they go up to work on the house but I think half the time all they do is drink. He's even got Gray going to bars without me."

"You're not old enough to get into bars."

"That's beside the point!"

"If you were old enough to go to bars, you'd go to them. With or without Gray. Admit it."

"I would not."

She carried Quincy down the hall and soon reappeared, rubbing her shoulders. "That kid weighs a ton."

"And that's another thing. He doesn't even stay home on Wednesdays anymore, and you know how much he used to like helping with Quincy."

"Maybe it hurts him too much."

"What do you mean?"

Morgan shrugged. "You said yourself he's crazy to have kids. Maybe Quincy reminds him of what he's missing."

Hope considered that for a moment, then shook her head. "No, I don't think so. He hasn't brought that up in a long time."

"Maybe he's waiting for you to."

Hope sighed.

"It seems to me this marriage of yours is a little bit one-sided."

"Why?"

"You want to go out with your friends but you don't want Gray to go out with his. You don't want kids, so he can't have them either."

"I want kids, Morgan, just not right now."

"Maybe he's tired of waiting."

"What are you saying?"

"Only that if it was me I wouldn't be leaving a hottie like Gray home alone at night. And neither would a lot of other people."

"Like who?"

"Like half the girls in this town who'd love to give him what he wants, that's who."

"Including you, Morgan?"

She looked away. "I didn't say that."

"You didn't have to. And by the way, if that was supposed to be a threat it didn't scare me."

"I'm hardly a threat to you, Hope. Gray made that clear when you were in Buffalo."

"But if he hadn't, you'd have been all over it."

Morgan gave her a scalding glance. "You didn't want him, but when it came right down to it you didn't want me to have him either. That's the problem with you, Hope, you're selfish. You always have been."

Hope stared at her. "Excuse me?"

Quincy's voice came from down the hallway, howling with rage.

"Perfect." Morgan stood. "Look, I don't want to fight with you about this. All I'm saying is that if you're smart you'll realize what you've got and take care of it. Believe me, it's way more than a lot of girls have."

When she disappeared down the hallway Hope got up and left. She drove toward the mall, thinking of all the things she wished she'd said. Who was Morgan to tell her what to do? Like Morgan had any sage advice on how to keep a man.

When she reached the mall she found she wasn't taking her usual pleasure in looking at the clothes and jewelry. A threat nagged at the back of her mind, a terrifying threat whose face looked a lot like Ace Javitz's. He was trying to get between her and Gray, Hope just knew it.

As she strolled through the mall it seemed everyone around her was either pregnant or pushing a stroller. She watched couples with their children, imagining they were her and Gray. What if Morgan was right? What if Gray was tired of waiting? Now that Ace planted doubt in Gray's mind, what if he decided to dump her and look for someone else?

Her heart started to pound as irrational fears consumed her. She hurried from the mall, trying to remember where Gray said he'd be working. She saw his surprise the moment she pulled up to the job site. He set down his drill and hurried over to her. "What's wrong, baby?"

"Nothing's wrong. I just missed you."

He gave her an uncertain smile. "I'd have been home in an hour."

She wrapped her arms around his neck and kissed him. "Maybe I didn't want to wait."

He drew back and gazed into her eyes. "What's gotten into y'all today, Hope?"

"Nothing. Yet."

He nuzzled her neck. "Well, we'll have to do something' about that real soon, won't we?"

She felt his arousal and laughed, then became serious again. "Gray?"

"What, baby?"

"Can you not go up and work on the house tonight?"

"Oh, Hope. Any other night I wouldn't. I got a guy comin' out to help me finish up the plummin' then me and Ace are gonna finish the bathroom."

"How about if just you and me go? I'll help you finish the bathroom."

He laughed softly. "Darlin', that tub weighs five times what you do. For this job I need a man." Seeing tears spring to her eyes, he laid a hand on her cheek. "Hey ..."

"Gray, please don't let him come up tonight. Can't I be alone with you?"

He pulled her close and smoothed back her hair. "All right. If it means that much to you."

"It does. I feel like we're losing each other."

"I know, baby, but as soon as we get the house finished we'll be on our own again. That's why I been spendin' so much time workin' on it."

"Gray?"

"What?"

"I want to start trying. Tonight."

His arms tensed around her. "What?"

"Tonight. Up at our own house. After the plumber leaves. I want to start trying."

"Baby, do you mean it?"

She nodded.

"Oh, Hope." He pulled her to him. "But what about your pills? I thought y'all had to wait awhile before—"

"I flushed them down the toilet two weeks ago," she lied.

He held her like she was a piece of Steuben glass. She smiled, knowing she'd found the shard that would cut his ties with Ace Javitz forever.

That night while Gray and the plumber worked, Hope filled their bedroom with candles and rolled out a sleeping bag. When she heard the plumber's truck rumble from the driveway, she slipped into the silk camisole she'd bought that afternoon and lay down to wait. At last Gray came and lay down beside her, his eyes glittering in the candlelight as they moved over her.

"Hope, are you sure you're ready? 'Cause I don't want you to feel like you were pushed into anything."

"I'm sure."

He kissed her. "My God," he whispered. "I didn't think a man could hold this much love. I feel like I'm goin' to explode."

He made love to her as tenderly as if it had been the first time. She watched his face with a pang of guilt and knew he was dreaming of the child he thought they were creating.

Chapter Forty-Three

By October Gray's house nestled against the flaming hillside, a haven of warmth and fulfilled dreams. Most of his dreams, anyway.

On a Friday afternoon, he checked the calendar, optimistic but cautious. She was two days late. They'd been making love morning, noon and night for almost two months. Maybe they'd finally connected.

He picked up his book on reproductive cycles and reread the chapter on ovulation. He checked the calendar again. This would be her fertile time, wouldn't it?

When he heard her car pull in the driveway he shoved the book under the sofa cushion. His calculating annoyed her, took all the fun out of trying, or so she said. She came through the door carrying two buckets of paint and he took them from her hands. "Got it, huh?"

"Yep." She smiled and kissed his cheek.

He scanned the label on the can, then looked at her in surprise. "This says China rose."

"I know."

"I thought we decided on beige."

"We did, but when I got to the paint store beige seemed so boring."

"So what y'all are telling me is I'm gonna be sleepin' in a pink bedroom."

She moved her lips to his neck. "Yeah, but pink makes me feel sexy."

He slid his arms around her waist. "Well in that case let's get busy."

"I thought we'd start tomorrow morning," she said, pulling

away.

He held her fast. "Why not right now?"

"Gray ..."

His lips touched down on hers as his hands roved over her. "What?"

"Don't."

"Why not?"

"Because I want to go out tonight."

His hands glided over her bottom. "It won't take all night."

"Are we talking about painting the bedroom, or something else?"

He pulled her hips closer to his. "I'll give y'all one big, fat guess."

Placing her hands on his chest, she gave him a shove. "Do you want me, or do you just want to make a baby?"

His hands fell away. "What kind of question is that?"

"Lately I get the feeling you think of me as a baby factory. You used to make me feel irresistible."

"You are irresistible."

She drew her lips into a pout. "Really?"

"Absolutely."

"And we can still go out? Afterwards?"

He sighed. God, he was tired. The manic pace of the past few months was catching up with him. All he wanted was a quiet evening at home. "Sure we can. Where do y'all want to go?"

"Well the thing is, Jen's having a party tonight and—"

"Oh, Hope. I don't want to go to a party tonight."

"We haven't been out in so long."

"We could go and see a movie."

"Boring!"

"Y'all shouldn't be drinkin' anyway."

"Neither should you."

"I mean since we're tryin'. What if you're pregnant?"

"I'm not."

With two words his world shattered. "You don't know that for sure."

"I got my period last night."

He stared at her in dismay. "Why didn't you tell me?"

"Because you get so disappointed."

"So you just let me keep on thinkin' there was a chance?"

"There is a chance. Just not this month. So can we go?"

He turned away. "You can go if you want to."

"Now you're mad."

"I ain't mad."

"This is what I'm talking about. You're all bummed out now."

"I can't help it."

She hugged him again. "Let's go out and have a good time. We'll forget about it for tonight."

"Hope I ain't goin' to none of your stupid parties tonight. I hate 'em."

"Fine."

"I'll just stay here and paint the goddamned bedroom. Maybe Ace'll come up and help me."

"I'm sure he will," she said icily. "Why don't you call him right now?" Throwing the phone at him, she turned and marched from the room.

He carried the cans of paint to the bedroom and pried one of them open, fighting the impulse to join her in the shower, to tell her he was sorry. He fought the urge, laying down tarps instead, fought it when she pulled on her jeans and the sheer, white sweater he loved. He stirred the paint, wordless. *Let her apologize to me for once.*

She put on her makeup, dried her hair, put in a call to Jen. She called Morgan. He poured the paint into a pan and ran his roller through it.

Let her come to me.

She breezed from the house, put her car in gear and pulled from the driveway, leaving him standing at the window, alone with his pride.

He kicked the wall, then returned to the bedroom, sank down to the floor and rested his head in his hands. The last thing he wanted was to be alone tonight. Why had he let it happen?

•

The phone rang a half dozen times before Ace answered. "Yeah?"

"What were you doin'?"

Ace's voice was strangely quiet. "Just getting' my shit together, man."

"What's the matter?"

"Didn' you hear?"

"I didn't hear nothin'."

"Your old man give me my walkin' papers."

"What?"

"That's right."

"What happened?"

"Ain't nothing' happened, man. Just give me my paycheck and told me to shove off."

"I'll go and talk to him."

"Won't do no good."

"Just stay where you are. I'll be there."

Twenty minutes later Gray stood in Ted's study. Ted laid down his pencil and closed the ledger he'd been writing in. "Sit down, Gray."

"Ace says y'all fired him today."

"That's right. Please sit down."

When Gray was seated across from him Ted sighed and folded his hands in front of him. "Maybe I should have talked to you about it first, but it wouldn't have changed anything. I gave him a chance as a favor to you, but it just wasn't working out."

Gray searched his mind for an excuse for his friend, knowing there was none.

"He's got a hair trigger temper. He's belligerent to everyone but you. Half the time he doesn't show up for work, and the other half he shows up drunk. Frankly, I don't need that kind of help. If it was anyone else, I'd have let him go a month ago."

Gray nodded.

"I also know he's been causing friction between you and Hope. Old friendships aside, maybe it's best to let him go his way."

•

Gray found Ace's motel room littered with beer cans. He stood in the doorway and watched as Ace threw his clothes into a bag.

"Were you gonna tell me this time before you took off?"

Ace stopped his work and turned to face Gray. "I was gonna tell you."

Gray stepped into the room. "It's gettin' late. Why don't y'all stay until mornin'. We'll get some beer, talk things over."

"She gonna be there?"

Gray laughed bitterly. "I doubt it."

Ace threw his bag in the corner and gave Gray a grudging smile. "What the hell, then. For old time's sake, huh?"

Two hours later Gray sat in his living room, half wasted and sprawled out on an easy chair.

"So where she take herself off to tonight?" Ace asked, reaching for another beer.

"Party."

He shook his head. "Figures."

Gray rested his head against the back of the chair, feeling deflated. "Y'all never liked her, did ya?"

"Nope."

Gray nodded, neither angry nor defensive. "Why not?"

"'Cause I think you bein' cheated." Ace took a swallow from his can. "And I think she just like all the rest of 'em. Don't give a damn about nobody but herself."

Gray sat in silence, drinking his beer and wallowing in his misery.

"Do you really need her shit, Gray? Is she worth it?"

"I love her, man," he said softly.

"Even if she don't love you?"

"She loves me."

"She don't love you. Wake up, man! If she love you she be here."

Gray rubbed his eyes, feeling tired and confused. "I don't know what to think no more."

"All they good for is to get a man feelin' low down and dirty."

"I do feel low down. Way low down."

"I can fix you up." Ace reached in his pocket and pulled out a small pill wrapped in plastic. "Here, take this."

Gray held the pill in the palm of his hand and studied it. "What is it?"

"Just somethin' to take the edge off."

Gray handed it back. "I don't want it."

"Come on, man, eat it. It'll take that low down dirty feelin' away and send y'all right straight to heaven."

Gray studied the pill again. What the hell. He popped it into his mouth and washed it down with a slug of beer.

Within moments the room became a kaleidoscope of color,

swaying in and out of focus. "Damn. What did y'all tell me that pill was?"

"Just a little helpin' hand." Ace moved closer to the chair. "Little peace a mind. How y'all feel now?"

"I don't know. Sorta …"

Ace extended his hand. "Come on down here."

Gray stood. The room spun out of control and he stumbled. Ace caught him and guided him to the floor. "Easy now. Just let it do it's magic." He pulled Gray to his chest and began to rub his shoulders, speaking softly in his ear. "How you feel, Gray?"

"This is really strange, Ace. I feel so …"

"Just let yourself feel good, Gray. Just forget all about that stupid little girl. She don't love you." He added quietly, "Not like I do."

Gray tried to focus on his words, but they were distorted, as if Ace was talking under water.

"You all done here, son. Why don't y'all face that and come with me to Canada."

"Canada? I can't—"

"Shh. Just think about it. We could live in the wilderness, nobody botherin' us. Little cabin in the woods, just you and me. We could go right now. Tonight."

Gray turned to look at him. His eyes were on fire, burning with …what? "Ace, what are y'all sayin?"

"I'm sayin' I love you, man."

Gray watched the full, dark lips move closer, felt the iron-hard arms pull him tighter against his chest. Then Ace was kissing him. Slowly, his tongue rough but gentle in his mouth. He jerked away. "Ace, come on, this is too weird. I can't—"

"Yes you can. You need me, Gray, just like I need you. Ain't nobody ever gonna love you the way I do. Y'all should know that by now." He tightened his grip. Gray lay in his arms, too dizzy to fight, too disoriented to make sense of his whispered words. "You love me, admit it."

Suddenly there was a series of impressions. A door closing. Splinters of light crashing like stars around him. A gasp. A scream. *Hope. Hope!*

He tried to sit but his support was gone and the room was spinning again. He fell back to the floor and watched, mystified, as the scene played out in fragments before his eyes. Ace and Hope squaring off. Angry words. Shouting. A musk-scented shadow drawing near. A pretty, red mouth. A closed fist.

"Mama, no! Please, Mama!" Tears splashed on a background of color. Hands, his own hands, cradled his body for protection. "Please don't hurt me ... I'll be good ... please ... don't hurt me, Mama ..."

Far away a voice screamed. "What's the matter with him? What did you do to him? Look at him, he's all messed up. What did you do to him? *Whatinthehelldidyoudotohimhe'sallmessedup* ... And then there was silence.

Chapter Forty-Four

Dana rolled out her pie crusts and lifted them into the waiting plates with no more effort than it took to breathe. As she worked, her worrisome thoughts centered on her daughter. What could have happened to bring her running home again? Hope hadn't set foot out of the house since she'd shown up, wild eyed and hysterical on Saturday night.

Dana shook her head. That was the same way she'd come back from Buffalo. Terrified, but of what? She sighed. It must be something bad for Gray not to come after her.

She dumped a bowlful of apple slices into the pan, spooned her brown sugar mixture over them, and fitted on the top crusts. Sliding the pies into the oven, she turned and noticed Hope standing in the doorway, wearing the same dirty sweat suit she'd had on since Sunday. Her face was stripped of color except for the dark circles that rimmed her eyes. Pushing aside her worry, Dana forced a note of cheerfulness into her voice.

"Feeling any better?"

"No," she said softly.

Dana turned to the sink and washed her hands, praying for wisdom.

"Would it help to talk about it?"

Hope's eyes filled with tears. "I don't know if I can."

Dana put her arms around her daughter and guided her to a chair. "Let me make us some coffee."

Coffee. The magic potion by which low spirits were raised and reluctant tongues loosed, Dana always thought. She put the coffee maker to work, reminding herself not to pry. Hope was a grown woman and she must let her work out her problems in her own way. Moments later she set two mugs of coffee on the table and gestured toward the window.

"The leaves are falling early. It's going to be a cold winter, I'm afraid."

Hope's tears spilled over her lashes. "I'm afraid, too."

Dana reached for her hand. "Hope, what is it, honey? You look awful. And your father says Gray hasn't been to work in three days."

"Maybe he's left town by now."

"Of course he hasn't left town."

Hope took a deep breath, followed by a deep swallow of coffee. Dana could see she was struggling with her urge to confide in her.

"What happened, Hope?" she prodded.

Hope sucked in a breath. "We had a fight Saturday night. I went out to a party, but when I got there I couldn't enjoy myself. I just wanted to be home with Gray. So I left." She took another swallow of coffee. "But when I got back home he was … with someone."

"Oh, Hope. I can't believe that."

"It's true."

Stunned, Dana tried to take it in. Another woman. She wouldn't have thought Gray capable of it. Her heart broke for them. As bad as things had been between her and Ted over the years, thank God it had never come to that.

"I don't know if I can forgive him."

"Do you love him?"

"Yes," she whispered.

"Then you have to forgive him, Hope." She squeezed her hand. "Love isn't easy and it doesn't come cheaply. Sometimes you have to sacrifice some things for others. Like your pride."

"Like you did?"

Dana's cup paused in mid-air. "What do you mean?"

Hope drew a shaky breath. "After Jared died you stayed with daddy because you loved him. Even though it meant you got stuck with me."

She set down her cup and looked at Hope in disbelief. "I never felt that—"

"Of course you did. I killed your son. It couldn't have been easy living with me all these years. I knew you hated me."

Dana fought tears. "Honey, you couldn't have thought that."

Hope turned her head, but not before Dana saw the anguish in her eyes, the pain that had been veiled for almost a decade. "What you did that day was foolish and immature, but it wasn't murder. Heavens, I blamed myself more than I ever did you." When Hope collapsed in tears she pulled her to her breast. "You were my only sister's child. The child of the man I loved. I loved you. Losing Jared didn't change that."

"It didn't?"

She was like a child, clinging to her mother for reassurance. Dana wiped at her own tears, overcome with sorrow for all of the wasted years. How could she not have seen, not have known how Hope felt?

"Of course not."

Hope gave her a tremulous smile. "Mom," she whispered. "There's something else."

"What, honey?" Dana asked, bracing herself.

"I think I'm pregnant."

Dana tore herself from Hope's embrace and held her at arm's length. "Oh, Hope." She made a last swipe at her tears, unable to hide her pleasure. "Does Gray know?"

She shook her head.

"Are you happy about it?"

"I don't know. I wasn't happy at first. I lied to Gray because I didn't want to deal with it. I told him I had my period, like that would make it go away. But now ..."

"Now you have a decision to make."

Hope nodded.

Dana stood, once again brusque and in control. "First thing's first. We'll call Doctor Marks and see if he can get you in this afternoon." She moved to the phone, then remembered that her daughter was an adult. "If you feel you're ready."

Hope nodded again. "I'm ready."

Chapter Forty-Five

At two o'clock Hope walked out of the doctor's office, stunned but relieved. Strange, the fear and sickness she'd lived with for a month would disappear rather than intensify now that she knew for sure.

I'm going to have a baby ...

She climbed behind the wheel of her car and sat for a moment, running her fingers over her middle and trying to decide what to do next.

She pulled out of the parking lot and cruised back through town, taking a left onto Jack Hollow Road. She'd tell Gray first. If she could find him.

She drove up the winding road, trying to sort herself out. She wouldn't tell him about the baby until she knew where they stood. She shuddered, chilled despite the bright afternoon sun. The memory of Gray locked in an embrace with Ace would haunt her until the day she died. But whatever that was about, she couldn't believe it started with Gray. He was too ardent, too prolific a lover to have been faking it all this time. That the physical pleasure he took in her body was real was the only thing of which she was certain.

She reached the top of the hill and saw the driveway was empty. Yankee raced to the car, howling. It was obvious the dog hadn't been fed and her hopes plummeted. Maybe Gray really did leave town. In any case, he must be in tough shape if he didn't even remember to feed his dog.

Inside, she filled bowls with food and water and set them before the dancing hound. Taking a walk through the house, she saw that the bed was still made, the cans of paint sitting open where he left them. She felt a stab of remorse and quickly closed the door. If only she'd stayed home that night they'd still be together now. What a fool she was! She'd been terrified of losing her freedom, but what good was freedom without love? She locked up the house, knowing where she had to go next.

When she didn't find his Jeep at the Mt. Bishop Motel, she breathed a sigh of relief and slowly cruised through town, shivering again as another memory came—Gray huddled on the floor, crying and begging her not to hurt him. She'd always counted on Gray to keep her grounded. Now she didn't know what to think.

After an hour of searching, she spotted his Jeep parked behind Big Mike's, a bar on the outskirts of town. Pulling her car in beside his, she drew a breath to calm her nerves and walked inside.

It was dark, smelling of stale beer and dirty sneakers. She stood in the doorway, peering at the misfits who sat at the grimy tables.

"What do you need, kid?"

The bartender was big and dirty, his tone betraying annoyance.

"I'm looking for someone," she said, brushing past him.

He reached out a meaty hand and grasped her arm. "Hang on there, little girl. Unless you got some ID, you ain't looking in here."

She angrily pulled her arm free. "Look, I'm not going to drink and I'm not going to stay. I just want to find my husband. I saw his Jeep outside."

He folded his arms across his chest. "What's he look like?"

"About five foot eight, blond hair."

"Yeah, he's here all right. Been just about living here for the past couple of days. You'd be doing us both a favor to take him home." He gestured toward the rear of the bar.

The moment she saw him, Hope knew what the bartender meant. Gray sat with his head in his hands, the picture of defeat. Pulling in another breath, she walked toward him. "Gray?"

He looked up, then quickly turned away. "Get outa here, Hope."

She sat down beside him. "Why?"

"Because I can't face you."

"You're going to have to face me sooner or later," she said softly.

He took a swallow of beer, still not looking at her. "I guess probably y'all have been to see a lawyer by now."

"About what?"

"About gettin' me the hell outa your life. I don't know exactly how it works, but I wanna let you know I'm willin' to bow …" he swallowed, took a breath. "Bow out graceful. Y'all can have everything."

"Is that what you want to do? Leave?"

He faced her, eyes brimming with tears. "No."

"Come on," she said, reaching for his hand. "Let's go home."

"Hope, I can't stay here now."

"Why not?"

"Because I can't face you!" He said it loudly. The people at the tables turned to stare for a moment, then returned to their own misery.

"Gray, you weren't yourself that night, anyone could have seen that."

He put his head in his hands. His shoulders shook as he sobbed. She hugged him. "We can get past it. If you still want us."

"I want us, baby, but not like we been. It ain't no good, me sittin' around nights wonderin' where y'all are at. It's killin' me."

Her fist impulse was to blurt out the news about the baby, but she held herself in check. "Things are going to be different now." She smiled, hugging her secret close to her heart. "Our life is going to be beautiful."

He pulled her close and held her, clinging to her like a drowning man clings to driftwood. "Hope, baby. Do you think you can ever forgive me?"

"I already have. Now let's get out of this dump."

Back home she helped him to bed and went to take a shower. When she returned he was asleep. She climbed into bed and pressed her body close to his. "I love you, Gray Baldwin," she whispered. "I'm going to love you as long as I live."

The next morning Gray was in the shower before the alarm went off. He appeared in the bedroom wrapped in a towel and sat down beside her.

"I wish I could stay home with you today."

She chuckled. "You'd better show up at work or my dad'll fire you."

Pulling on her clothes, she drove him into town to get his Jeep. When she pulled into the lot at Big Mike's, he took her hand. "Hope, there's so many things I been thinkin' about the last couple of days.

So many things I wanna tell you."

"Me too."

He kissed her. "We'll talk about it tonight, about everything. Talk all night if we have to."

She looked into his eyes and for a terrifying moment she couldn't see the future. Some impulse inside her urged her to tell him, to blurt it out, but it wasn't the time, and so she smiled. "It's a date."

He kissed her and then she watched him get into his Jeep, once again overcome with a fear she couldn't name. "Gray?"

He turned back.

"Love me?"

He returned and gave her a last kiss. "More than life, babe."

When he drove away, she walked to the pay phone in front of Big Mike's, dropped a quarter into the slot and dialed the number she'd looked up the night before. The phone rang twice before he answered. When she heard his voice, her stomach reeled and she quickly hung up the phone. She'd hoped he'd left town.

Driving to the bank, she carefully thought out her course. The damage that had been done would heal with time. All that remained was to remove the one threat still in place. When she'd made her withdrawal, she drove to the Mt. Bishop Motel. She sat in her car outside his room, heart pounding. Whispering a prayer for courage, she got out and walked toward the door marked 26. She'd get rid of Ace Javitz, whatever it took.

Chapter Forty-Six

Ace lay in bed, broke, uptight and knowing he needed to make a decision. He couldn't hang here any more. As it was he'd have to run out on the bill for the last two nights. Where the hell was Gray?

He sat up, shook his last cigarette from his pack and lit it. He'd walked up that damned hill twice, only to be run off by that damned snarling beast. He thought Gray would have called him by now.

He went over it again. The timing seemed perfect. Who'da thought she'd come home early? And Gray freaking out. It took Ace the whole night to settle him down, with her running off, leaving Ace with the whole, stinking mess. Typical woman.

He slid his hand beneath the pillow and pulled out the gun. He paid too much for it, but what could he do? A man never knew what beast he might come across out in the wilderness, human or animal. He shook his head. Wherever Gray was hiding he hoped he'd come out soon. Ace couldn't wait around. He'd have to go today, with or without Gray. He puffed on his cigarette, watching the thick, dark rings rise and flatten against the ceiling.

Stubbing out his cigarette, he pulled the last of his cash from his pocket. Eight bucks. He'd pick up a pack of smokes and see what kind of breakfast three dollars would buy at the diner. With any luck the redhead would be working. She always cut him a break.

He rolled out of bed and pulled on his jeans and a tee shirt. He was about to open the door when he heard a soft knock. He flung it open, expecting to see Gray standing on the other side, but it wasn't Gray. It was her.

His eyes moved over her in contempt. "What the hell you want?"

"I want to talk to you."

He was tempted to slam the door in her face. But he needed to know what was up with Gray, and she was his best chance of finding out so he stood aside and let her in.

Inside, she drew herself up and faced him. "I want you to leave town."

"Ain't nothin' I'd like better."

"Then why don't you go? There's nothing here for you."

"I'm goin'. Just as soon as y'all tell me where Gray's at."

"Gray's not going anywhere with you."

"He's goin'," Ace said firmly. "Told me so himself." He moved threateningly closer. "Unless y'all did somethin' to change that."

She pulled a bank envelope from her pocket and handed it to him. "This changes it. Take it and go."

He eyed the envelope, then folded his arms across his chest. "Keep your damn money. I ain't goin' nowhere till I talk to Gray."

"He doesn't want to talk to you!" She shoved the envelope in his face. "Nothing you can say will make a difference. Just take the money and leave us alone."

He smiled, high on the scent of her fear. She was lying just as sure as he was standin' there. Why else would she be trying to pay him off?

"I known Gray Baldwin a long time. Long enough to know what's good for him, and lady, you ain't it."

"Why don't you let him decide that?"

"He already decide it. Told me so himself."

She tucked the envelope back in her pocket. "All right, Ace. For his sake I didn't want to send you away empty handed, but if you won't listen to money or reason, listen to Gray. In fact why don't you come up tonight and celebrate with us, he'll tell you then where you stand."

Her smugness caught him off guard and his confidence wavered. "Celebrate what?"

A smile of triumph spread across her face. "The one thing I can give him that you can't. I'm going to have his baby."

It started slowly. A shadow of doubt, a slight tremor in his hands. It built to a fury, slowly licking at his insides, until he was consumed with it. Rage. She stood there smiling, laughing at him.

"Bitch," he whispered.

"You're out of cards, Ace. He won't go anywhere with you now. He'll stay right here with me where he belongs." She started toward the door, and then turned back. "Tough break, huh?"

Trembling, silent rage. Blinding rage. One hand doubled into a fist as the other crept beneath the pillow. She grabbed the door knob.

Don't, man. Just let her go... But already his fingers were closing around the gun, taking comfort in its cold, hard, power. "Hey," he said softly.

She turned back.

"I just wanna say... Congratulations, baby."

He lifted the gun, waiting only for the satisfaction of seeing the terror on her face before he fired.

He grabbed his duffel bag from the dresser and ran to the door, stopping to lean over her crumpled body. Damn. Still breathing. He lifted the gun and pointed it at her face. Outside he heard voices, footsteps coming closer. Glancing out the window, he saw two women scurrying around, knocking on doors.

He shoved the gun down the front of his pants, dug the bank envelope and car keys from Hope's pocket, and fled, calm, cool, unruffled, until he reached the village limits. Then he slammed his foot down on the accelerator and thundered toward the highway. He checked the rearview mirror a dozen times. Seeing that no one pursued, he smiled. An almost demonic bliss possessed his entire being. He'd hit her clean in the head. She wouldn't be breathing long.

Chapter Forty-Seven

It was a relief to have Gray back at work. Ted was getting too damned old for the lifting and toting. Fifty-one, and feeling every hour of it. He set down his drill and rubbed his shoulders. What was he doing while time was creeping up on him, stealing his youth away?

He climbed up to the roof and checked the tile he laid the day before. Everything looked good. That afternoon he and Gray would install the gutters and tomorrow, with any luck, he'd be back in the office where he belonged.

His eyes traveled to where Gray hung the last of the vinyl siding. He looked pale and much too thin. Dana seemed to think he and Hope were going to be fine. Lord, he hoped she was right.

He worked in silence beneath the bright October sky, lost in his thoughts until he noticed the police car pull in the drive. He sat back on his heels and watched as Fran Piercy and Bill Moran got out and walked toward Gray. Gray tensed as he greeted them and Ted could tell by the rigid way he stood that he was hearing bad news. He pushed down the knot of worry in his stomach. Something to do with Ace Javitz, unless he missed his guess.

Gray slumped against the side of the house. The combination wail and scream that came from his throat carried fifty feet across the yard and sent Ted scurrying down the ladder.

"Fran, what is it?"

"Ted, I'm sorry as hell." Fran looked at him and then let his eyes drop away. Gray was still making the sound and Ted felt the knot of dread become a rock-hard fist. "It's bad news. Your daughter's been shot."

The rest of his words were heard through a white, numbing fog. Something about a maid and the Mt. Bishop Motel.

"Your wife's already on her way to the hospital. You'd better get over there as quick as you can."

Gray's voice cut through the fog. "Is she alive?"

Bill Moran's pause seemed to last a lifetime. Ted listened to the absolute silence of it, praying he wouldn't be sick.

"She was breathing when they put her in the ambulance, but it looked pretty bad."

•

Dana stood just inside the emergency entrance. She collapsed against him, a mass of tears and words he could barely decipher.

"Oh, Ted. Oh God, Ted."

"All right, honey. Try and calm down."

"They want information. I can't remember her date of birth. I can't remember anything at all. Oh, Ted, how could this happen to our baby?"

For Dana's sake, and for Gray's, Ted pulled himself together. He guided them to the waiting area and then went to the desk to fill out the paperwork. The nurse gave him a sympathetic smile. "She's in surgery, Mr. Hanwell. The doctor will talk to you as soon as he's through."

He returned to the waiting area and sat on the couch beside Dana. They sat, hands locked together, not speaking. Gray sat in the chair opposite, head bent over his own tightly clasped hands. It might have been hours or moments that they sat there. Time seemed to become a vacuum, a meaningless series of small black sweeps across an ominous white dial until the surgeon appeared. They followed him through the corridor and into another airless room and waited as he closed the door behind them. After another eternity he took the chair opposite them. When he finally spoke, it was to Gray. "Mr. Baldwin, we did everything we could."

The words tore a ragged breath from Gray's chest. Dana cried out and Ted caught her hand in a vice grip, numb except for the agony ripping through his lungs. It could have been any one of them that asked the question. For all Ted knew, the whisper might have passed from his own lips. "She's gone, then?"

The doctor sighed. "She was shot in the head at close range with a .52 caliber handgun. The bullet passed right through. If it's any comfort to you, she didn't feel a thing."

No one spoke. Ted sat, watching the pictures in his mind.

Georgie holding a tiny pink bundle. *Isn't she beautiful, Ted?* Hope at two, clutching the moon, smiling at him. *Love you, Daddy* ... At eight, wearing a pair of too large shoes and a second hand cocktail dress. Birthday parties, her arms wrapped around his neck. Graduation. Crumbled against him the day he'd gone to Buffalo to bring her home. Her wedding day. *I love you* ...

The doctor was speaking again.

"We've placed her on life support, but again, it's entirely your decision. She'll never regain consciousness. It's solely for the sake of the fetus. I want to make that clear."

Gray's eyes locked with those of the surgeon. "What fetus?"

The man's glance moved to Dana, and then back to Gray. "Mr. Baldwin, your wife is six weeks pregnant. I assumed you knew."

The sound came again from deep within him.

"The baby," Dana said. "It's unharmed?"

"As far as we can tell. There doesn't appear to be any reason she couldn't carry it. If you want it, that is."

Time stopped again as all eyes turned to Gray. "I want it."

After the consultation Gray went to see her. Dana started to follow, but seeing Ted wasn't coming, she stopped. "Ted?"

"Dana, I can't."

She took his hand in hers. "Alright," she said softly.

As the knowledge of what he'd lost at last overcame him, he slumped beneath the weight of it, clinging to his wife, the only thing he had left. When he heard the sound of his name, he released her. Bill Moran approached him cautiously. "Ted, I'm just sorry as hell. If it helps, they got the bastard."

"They did?"

"Chased him clear across the county line. Bastard ran right through a road block and down into the ravine. The car caught fire. Son of a bitch sizzled like a slice of bacon."

Ted nodded and swallowed the bile that crept up his throat. His voice came out a choked whisper. "Good."

Chapter Forty-Eight

She was going to come back to him. It was just a matter of time. Gray sat beside Hope's bed on a gusty November evening, ignoring the equipment that monitored her, and thought how much better she looked. The glow had returned to her cheeks and her hair curled softly where it stuck out from beneath her bandages.

He turned back to the tabloid in his lap and scanned the table of contents. "Listen to this, babe. Y'all will get a kick outa this. Mother of three gives birth to elephant boy."

He read through the article, stopping to hold the picture in front of her closed eyes. "Would you look at the size of that boy's nose. How do you think they made it look so big?"

Closing the magazine, he set it on the table beside the enormous bouquet of flowers he'd brought. After a quiet moment, he said, "I finished layin' the carpet in the livin' room. Decided to go with green. Looks real nice, but if y'all don't like it, we can change it. Oh, and I finally finished paintin' that bedroom. I didn't think I'd like it at first, but more I think about it, y'all were right. Beige would'a been boring."

He lifted her hand and planted a kiss on her fingers. "I been thinkin' about that bedroom next to ours. Thought maybe we'd put the baby in there, bein' it's closest. I picked up a can of yellow paint. If you don't like it, we can change that, too."

He sat, holding her hand and looking out at the snow. He told her about the drywall job he was hanging, and about the new house that was being built on their road. About the crib Dana dug out of her attic, and how he and Ted repaired it. "I know your daddy ain't come to see you, baby. I hope y'all aren't thinking' he don't miss you, 'cause I know he does, it's just," he lowered his voice, "these doctors made him lose his faith. He don't know y'all are gonna get better. But you are, aren't you?"

He peered into her face, struggling against the doubts that sometimes came. "Hope, I know how tired you are, but I wish you'd open up your eyes and look at me." We waited, anxiously watching her face. He squeezed her hand, offered up a silent prayer. "Alright, darlin'. Y'all don't have to if you can't. But soon, okay? And when you do, you're gonna see a man that loves you more than life." He kissed her cheek. "I gotta get outa here now, maybe go get somethin' to eat. Your mama sends more food than a man could eat in a year. So don't you worry none. I'm doin' just fine."

He lingered, giving her one moment more.

"Maybe I'll start workin' on that bedroom later tonight. I'd like to see how it looks with the crib in it." He kissed her one last time. "Good night, baby. I'll see y'all tomorrow."

The nurses smiled at him as he was leaving, sad, pathetic smiles that said he was wasting his time. Smiles that said Hope was never coming back. He turned up the collar of his jacket and walked from the hospital. They didn't know Hope like he did. They didn't know a damn thing.

Chapter Forty-Nine

A week before Christmas Dana trudged through the mall, trying to work up some enthusiasm for the holiday decorations, Victorian this year. She gazed into the store windows, barely seeing the life-sized Dickensonian characters that last year would have charmed her. But last year life had been good.

Her shopping list was small: an air hammer gun and a bathrobe for Ted, a tool box and a sweater for Gray, a Tickle Me Elmo for Quincy, assorted tokens for the paperboy, the hairdresser, and the mailman. She purchased the items and checked them off, soon finding herself at the bottom of her list. Done, but not ready to go home. Ted was working late and she couldn't bear to be alone in the house, couldn't bear the Christmas tree that mocked her from its corner in the living room, the plates of gingerbread boys no one would eat. Next year, she reminded herself. Next year there would be something to celebrate. Next year there would be a baby.

She stopped at the perfume counter at J. C. Penney, thinking something new might lift her spirits. One by one she removed the caps from the perfume bottles. Obsession. Patchouli. White Musk. Her hands shook as she set the bottle back on the counter. The salesgirl gave her a questioning glance. Dana covered her mouth to stifle a cry, to hold at bay the memories she had uncapped. She picked up the bottle again and took another sniff. "I'd like to buy this," she told the salesgirl.

"It's a nice choice. Very soft, feminine."

"How much?"

"Twenty-seven fifty. A terrific price for such a—"

Dana set the money on the counter and carried the perfume from the store. She hadn't been to the hospital since the day of the shooting. Somehow it would have seemed like betraying Ted. They'd both agreed not to hope, not to think of their daughter as alive. But Dana couldn't seem to stop herself. She pulled her car from the mall parking lot, steeling herself against her memories as she followed the signs to the hospital.

The woman behind the desk informed her Hope was in room 316. Taking a deep breath, Dana stepped from the elevator. She stopped just short of the door to Hope's room, surprised to hear laughter. Curious, she peeked inside. Gray stood beside the bed and Morgan Foster sat in the chair, laughing as she painted Hope's fingernails. Noticing her in the doorway, Gray's face broke into a smile.

"Hey," he said, placing a hand on Hope's shoulder. "Look who's here, baby. It's your mama."

Morgan dabbed at Hope's fingernails one last time and stood. "They don't keep her nails up," she explained. "Won't let her wear anything but clear. She'd hate that they let them get like this." When she averted her gaze, Dana knew the service had been performed more out of kindness to Gray than to Hope.

Lord help me, she thought, drawing nearer to the bed.

Instead of the nightmare of wasted life she'd expected, she saw a face completely at peace. "Oh!" Her breath caught. "She looks beautiful."

God help her, if it hadn't been for the life support equipment, she herself might have believed Hope was merely sleeping, that at any moment she'd awaken, smile. She sank down into the chair, unable to tear her gaze from her daughter's face.

"Go ahead," Gray urged. "Talk to her."

It was the hardest thing she'd ever done.

"Hello, honey," she began. She sank into an awkward silence, then remembering the perfume, reached into her bag. "I've been to the mall, and I got you a Christmas present." She pulled out the box. "It's early, I know, but I want you to have it now."

Her hand began to tremble. Gray reached for the box, pulled out the bottle, and loosened the cap. He took a sniff, then held the bottle beneath Hope's nose.

"It's your favorite perfume, see?" He placed a drop on her throat and another behind her ear. "White Musk."

Morgan cleared her throat. "I should go. Quincy's probably

driving my mom crazy. Good to see you, Mrs. Hanwell." She turned to Gray. "I'll call you later."

When she left Dana made small talk with Gray. He included Hope in the conversation as if it were the most natural thing in the world. Dana took her daughter's hand, trying again.

"They sold the old house on Walker Street last week. Do you know which one I mean? The big green one you always thought was haunted. It was quite a surprise, after all these months. They met the asking price to the dollar." Her voice trailed away. She looked out the window and saw that a Christmas tree was being erected on the hospital lawn.

"Your father and I put up the tree yesterday. What a job! He didn't want to bother with it this year, but I made him. Christmas wouldn't be Christmas without the tree, I told him." She knew she was rambling, speaking more to herself than Hope, but she couldn't seem to stop. "I broke the angel, can you believe it? Remember how you and Jared used to fight over who would put the angel on the top?" Tears rolled down her face. "I'd never let either one of you touch it because I was afraid you'd break it, and here I went and broke it myself." Gray moved to her side and gently touched her shoulder.

"I'm sorry," she choked.

"It's alright," he said. "It's hard at first."

She stood and collected her coat and purse, managing a smile. "I'd better go."

"Alright," he said. As she was leaving, he called out to her softly.

"Dana?"

She turned back.

"Thank you."

Driving home she felt buried under a weight of sorrow as deep as a snowdrift. She'd always thought of herself as strong, but Gray was made of steel. She felt tears acing the back of her throat. She didn't know what was more sad, that Hope would never awaken, or that Gray believed she would. She shuddered, chilled at the thought of what would happen when the truth came crashing into his life.

Chapter Fifty

On Valentine's Day, Gray walked into Hope's hospital room laden with a dozen red roses, an unwrapped oblong box, and a small square package tied with a velvet ribbon. A nurse stood at the end of Hope's bed, making notes on her chart. She smiled when Gray set the packages on the table. "Would you look at this. I've been married three times and I never made out this good on Valentine's Day." She peeped at the boxes with curiosity.

Gray bent and kissed Hope's lips. "It's more than just that. Today's our anniversary. Been married a whole year, haven't we, baby?"

The nurse's smile quickly faded to the sad, pitying look Gray had come to hate. Pushing his anger down, he reached for the larger of the two boxes. The nurse drew closer, watching as he opened it and pulled out the silken night dress.

"Got somethin' for you, babe." He took her fingers and ran them over the fabric. "It's your favorite color, too. Pink." He glanced at the nurse. "Will y'all help me put it on her?"

She hesitated, no doubt thinking how much less convenient the night dress would be than the ratty hospital gown. "Let me call for an aide."

She pressed the call button and soon a stout, bored looking man appeared.

"Give me a hand, will you, Jack?"

She pulled the curtain closed and they eased Hope forward and removed the hospital gown. Gray saw that her breasts were swollen with pregnancy. He clenched his hands into fists, aching to lay his head against them and be comforted.

Once the new gown was on her and the equipment back in

place the nurse and aide left the room. Gray opened the smaller box and pulled out the necklace, a princess cut diamond set in a silver cross. He put it on her, arranging the pendant at her throat. "You look real nice, baby."

Taking her hand, he sat down beside her bed, for once having nothing to say. He was lost in the memory of her smile, the sun in her hair on their wedding day, how she'd come to him, smiling. He felt the knife blade of pain that came with remembering the day she'd pledged her love to him, asking only one thing in return.

"I'm sorry, Hope. I let you down," he whispered. "I wish I'd known what y'all were plannin' to do. I would have made him leave. Y'all didn't have to try to take him on by yourself."

At eight o'clock a shopping mall voice came over the PA system announcing that visiting hours were over but Gray couldn't bring himself to leave. He set his jaw. Let them try to kick him out.

"Hello, Mr. Baldwin."

Seeing the night nurse's smile, he relaxed. "Ma'am."

"Well doesn't Hope look pretty tonight. New gown?"

"Yes, Ma'am."

She flipped through Hope's chart. "I see the doctor found your baby's heartbeat this morning."

Gray's head snapped in her direction. "What?"

"Didn't they tell you?"

"No," he said, feeling his own heartbeat quicken. "They didn't."

"Right here." She showed him the scrawled message on the chart. "What is she now, about twenty-two weeks along?"

"I guess that's about right."

She smiled again. "Would you like me to try and find it for you?"

He tightened his grip on Hope's hand. "Yes, Ma'am. I would."

She left the room, returning moments later with a Doppler. "Now don't worry if I can't find it. I haven't done this very many times." She moved the Doppler around on Hope's stomach. "There it is. Do you hear it?"

He gripped Hope's hand as the sound filled the room. A beating heart. His child. Their child. It was too much for him. Tears spilled from his eyes and streamed, unchecked, down his face. The nurse pulled a tissue from the box on Hope's table and handed it to him, smiling again. A genuine smile. "Thanks," he said, not sure whether for the tissue or the smile, or for making his wife seem like a human being.

She put the Doppler in her pocket and studied him. "Do you talk to him?"

"Huh?"

"The baby. Do you talk to him?"

"Uhm, no."

"By now he's developed enough he probably recognizes the sound of your voice."

"Really?"

"Really. You should talk to him. Then you won't seem like a stranger when he comes out. Or she."

She made a note in the chart, adjusted a gauge on the monitor and slipped from the room, leaving Gray alone with her words. Wiping away his tears, he slid his hand to Hope's belly and kissed her. "Thank you, baby," he whispered. Pulling a rose from the vase, he laid it beside her on the pillow and quietly walked from the room.

By March Hope's abdomen had swollen to twice its size and she was positioned on her side most of the time. The nurse told Gray the baby weighed two and a half pounds, and that it was likely its eyes were open.

He sat by the bed, rubbing Hope's belly as he read from the books he brought. Nursery rhymes, *Goodnight Moon, Winnie the Pooh.* He left a CD player beside the bed, and when he tired of reading, he put in sing-a-long CDs and lullabies. He couldn't stop thinking of his baby's eyes, looking through a watery world, its tiny, sensitive ears listening for the sound of his voice.

On the last day of the month he and Morgan sat watching the ripples that moved beneath the surface of Hope's skin and trying to identify them.

"Look here. No, here. Do you feel this?" Morgan guided his hand to one of the bulges. "This is a foot."

Gray stared in awe at the moving lump. "You think?"

"Maybe." She moved her hand expertly over the mound. "No, wait, this is a foot. I think that one's a butt."

He laughed, then all at once turned serious. "Morgan, does it hurt her?"

"Hmm?" She tore her eyes from the bulge. "Does what hurt

her?"

"When the baby moves around. Seems like it would hurt some."

She smiled. "No. It's weird, but it doesn't hurt, exactly."

"Good."

She reached for his hand and gave it a squeeze. "Feeling your baby move inside you, it's the most awesome feeling in the world."

They sat for a moment in the comfortable silence of friends. Then he spoke again. "I gotta start getting' the room ready."

"I thought you had it ready."

"Only partly. I got it all painted and put the crib in, but I don't have a theme. Dana says a nursery's gotta have a theme."

"Mm." She nodded in agreement.

"What did y'all use for a theme in Quincy's room?"

"Odds and ends," she said. "Rummage sale specials. I couldn't afford to do it the way I wanted to."

"What would you have wanted to do?"

"I would have made it a safari. I would have painted a blue sky with clouds on the ceiling and put up animal wallpaper borders and a little trolley train running along a shelf all the way around the room. I saw it in a magazine and it was so incredible cool."

"Yeah, that's what I want. Somethin' incredibly cool." He smiled. "Will y'all help me put it together?"

The next afternoon they carried their treasures into the nursery and set them in piles on the floor. Crib sheets, curtains, a lion lamp. Enough gear for three babies, Morgan said laughingly. She glanced at her watch. "Wow, I didn't know it was this late. We were at the mall three hours?"

"Will your mama be mad?"

"No, but Quincy probably will."

He chuckled. "Hey, why don't we go and pick him up together? I'll take y'all out to supper."

"All right."

He indicated the pile of bags, the bright red train engine. "Do you think she'll like it?"

"Are you kidding me? She'll love it." She nudged him with her elbow. "Especially if she turns out to be a he."

"No, I was talkin' about Hope."

"Oh." She averted her gaze, but not before he saw it. The pitying look, the doubt. It hurt him, but not as much as it angered him. He hadn't expected it from Morgan. She was the one person in the world who believed, like he did, that his love would pull Hope through.

"Gray, what if Hope doesn't come out of it?"

"She will."

"I mean, I know she will. But what if she doesn't?"

He stared angrily into her eyes. "She will, Morgan."

•

Spring melted into summer and as the cycles of life rushed to completion, so did the tiny life inside Hope. On the seventh of June, Ted, Dana and Gray sat face to face with Hope's doctor in a tight, airless room. Gray fidgeted as the doctor studied the charts in front of him. Finally he set them aside. "She's in her thirty-seventh week now. The fetus is almost six pounds, fully viable. I think it would be wise to take it."

Gray felt the color drain from his face, but Ted and Dana only nodded.

"Very good, then. I'll set it up for tomorrow morning."

The impact of his words hit Gray like a freight train. Hope might not be awake tomorrow. He cleared his throat and struggled to find his voice. "Doctor? Could y'all hold off just a little while longer?"

The doctor hesitated. "The head's already engaged, Mr. Baldwin. If we let it go too much longer your wife could go into labor. I can't see any point in putting her through that."

"Gray." Ted touched Gray's arm. "I don't think there's any point in putting it off."

"Well I do think there's a point!"

"Gray," Dana said softly. "Please."

The doctor sighed. "I'll be going out of town on the tenth. We'll do it on the ninth. That's two days from now."

"Thank you," Gray whispered.

That night he knelt beside the crib and begged God for a miracle.

Chapter Fifty-One

The eighth of June dawned heavy and overcast, matching Gray's somber mood. Tomorrow was the day, and he was no more ready for it than he'd been seven months before. He spent the day at Hope's bedside, studying every detail of her face. At eight PM he smoothed the blankets around her and gave her a last, gentle kiss. *Tomorrow.*

"Baby, we're running out of time." His voice cracked. "Darlin', please. I know y'all can do it. Open your eyes and look at me." He peered into her face, willing her to respond. "Hope Baldwin, you look at me. Come on, now!" Overcome with sorrow, he rested his head against her breast, his final command a choked whisper. "Look at me ..."

"Gray?"

He sat up and passed his hand through his hair, not looking in the direction of Morgan's voice. "I thought y'all went to pick up Quincy."

"I decided to leave him with my mother. I thought maybe you shouldn't be alone." She laid a gentle hand on his shoulder. "Want to go and get a cup of coffee somewhere?"

His heart filled with gratitude. The thought of returning alone to his haunted house was more than he could bear. He cupped Hope's face in his hands for a moment, then slowly let his hands fall away. "Get some rest, baby," he said softly. "We've got a big day tomorrow."

He and Morgan went to a coffee shop near the hospital and talked until midnight. About Quincy. About Morgan's job at the diner. About anything but Hope. When the restaurant closed they reluctantly stood to leave.

As he walked out into the humid night air, Gray looked up at the moon and was filled with fear of the ghosts that would come to him when he was alone. Ghosts of Ace, of his mother, and of Hope. Mostly, though, he feared the loss of Hope.

As if reading his thoughts, Morgan spoke. "My mom's keeping Quincy all night. Do you want to come by the apartment for awhile, talk some more?"

He followed her to the small hovel in the alley behind Main Street and waited on the stoop while she rummaged in her purse for her keys.

"They ought to put a light out here," he said. "It ain't safe, a young girl coming and going at night."

She smiled. "I don't usually come and go this late at night. Here they are."

She unlocked the door and pushed it open and he followed her into the shabby living room, waiting in the doorway while she turned on a lamp.

"I'll go and make some coffee," she said.

When she disappeared into the adjoining room he took a look around him. The walls were badly in need of paint and the avacado-colored carpet was nearly worn through. He looked at the colorful blankets that covered the second-hand furniture and the checkered curtains in the window and was touched by her efforts to make the hovel into a home.

She returned to him carrying two cups of coffee and an ashtray. She set them on the coffee table and shook a cigarette from her pack. Gray reached for his lighter and lit it for her, then pulled a cigarette from his pack and sat down beside her. It was a long moment before she spoke. "Four o'clock, huh?"

He exhaled. "Yeah."

"Do you want me to come?"

"If you want to."

"I want to."

"All right."

They lapsed back into silence.

"Gray, are you scared?"

He turned to look at her. Her auburn hair glowed like fire in the lamplight and her hazel eyes were as round and deep as saucers. "Yeah."

She reached for his hand.

"Morgan, I don't think I can let her go." His tears came slowly. He was naked, vulnerable, too weary to hide them any more.

"Oh, Gray. I'll help you all I can."

A nod. A voice that would not speak. Two cigarettes crushed in an ashtray. Two cups of coffee growing cold. Two arms reached for him as two lips drew closer, soft, full lips. Not Hope's. But enough like Hope's that he could pretend, only for a moment, only once. He would only kiss her once. A whisper. His name, her lips. He'd only kiss her once.

Soft lips, soft hands, touching him, drawing him closer, drawing him in. A tongue, soft as a whisper in his mouth. *Oh, God. Not Hope. Morgan.*

"Morgan."

"Shh."

Hands, his hands, moving down her body. A kiss that wouldn't end. Skin, flesh, breasts. Round and large. Not Hope's. But enough like Hope's that he could pretend. Only for a moment. But like a dieter's cake, an alcoholic's drink, a child's first taste of ice cream, one taste left him aching for more.

"Morgan ..."

"Shh. Shh. Shh."

Lips and hands and buttons coming loose. Two cups of coffee growing cold on the table. Hands, not Hope's, finding his scars, touching him, offering comfort. Buttons and hands and lips and warm, soft softness. A tunnel. Absolute darkness where he could hide. Not Hope's, but enough like Hope's that he could pretend. He could hide. Only once. Only for a moment.

Chapter Fifty-Two

At five o'clock in the morning Ted shot up in bed, heart pounding, looking wildly around the room. He grasped hold of the ordinariness around him, taking comfort in it as he slowly made the transition back to reality. Good God, what a dream.

He was standing on the bank of a river, gazing across. Hope and Georgie stood on the other side. Their faces were identical, as were their translucent gowns. They stood watching, waiting, and then Georgie spoke. *Say goodbye, Ted. It's time to say goodbye.*

He got out of bed and stumbled to the bathroom. He shaved, showered, tried to block the dream from his mind and found he couldn't. It was unsettling, seeing Hope like that. He hadn't thought of his daughter as alive for months.

He slowly dressed for work. He'd go in for the morning, and then meet Dana at the hospital. They'd wait together for the birth of their grandchild. *My grandchild.*

It was a notion that filled him with joy and sorrow. Focus on the joy, he reminded himself. Today they would celebrate life. Tomorrow would be soon enough to mourn their dead.

Say goodbye, Ted ...

He retrieved the morning paper from the door step and sat down to a cold breakfast, knowing he wouldn't eat. He scanned the headlines before turning to the Sports section. He read the opening paragraphs three times, then set the paper aside and pulled on his shoes.

Say goodbye ...

Inside the cluttered comfort of his office, he poured a cup of coffee and sat down at his desk. He'd catch up some paperwork, maybe take a ride out by the new medical clinic later and see how the job was going. He pulled out the stacks of invoices and the ledger, opened it, stared at the columns. The figures swam before his eyes. Georgie's voice buzzed in his head, ever more insistent. *Say goodbye, say goodbye, say goodbye...*

•

He didn't even know what room she was in. He walked to the front desk and cleared his throat. The receptionist looked up with a smile.

"Can I help you?"

"I'm looking for a patient. Hope Baldwin. She's my daughter."

Her smile faded and there was no mistaking the pity in her eyes.

"Room three-sixteen."

Moments later he walked from the elevator. He paused to collect himself before heading down the corridor. It was ridiculous, after all these months. 301. 306. She wouldn't even know he was there. 310. 312. He was a damned fool to put himself through this. 314. And all because of a dream.

The room was filled with flowers. He hesitated in the doorway, gazing at the figure on the bed. He was afraid. God, he was afraid.

He took a deep breath and a tentative step. Then another. He looked at the pictures on the table, Hope and Gray, Hope and Morgan Foster. Hope and him. He looked at the vases of flowers— roses, painted daisies, chrysanthemums. He pulled a chair to the side of the bed and sat down. Then he looked at Hope.

His heart constricted. She wasn't garish or frightening, or any of the things he'd thought she would be. She was his child, his beautiful little girl. He laid a tender hand on her cheek. "Hope? Honey, it's daddy ... "

Chapter Fifty-Three

"Mr. Baldwin, are you sure you want to go in?"

Gray looked from the nurse's face to Hope's. "Yeah."

"You don't have to, if you don't think you can do it."

"I want to."

"All right. Then you'd better go and change."

He scrubbed his hands until they were raw, wondering why he couldn't feel them. He changed into the sterile gown and gloves they provided, then returned to the room and followed the gurney down the hall, feeling like he was walking in a dream.

Two steel doors opened, swallowed them up, and groaned to a close. He sat beside Hope, holding her hand, wishing he could feel her beneath the heavy gloves. He watched as they draped her lower body. A surgical nurse wheeled in a tray of instruments and he avoided the cold, hard scalpel. The surgeon arrived, and Gray heard voices talking from what seemed very far away.

"... had a good round at lunch time. Scalpel."

"... bogied the ninth hole. Sponge."

"... a nice, clean slice at the fourteenth. Suction."

"Looks good. We played that new course over the weekend, Eagle Run. A little more pressure... Beautiful."

"It's a boy."

He glanced up to see them looking at him, smiling.

A boy.

They suctioned the baby's nose and mouth and he let out a wail.

"Mr. Baldwin, would you like to meet your son?"

They laid the soft, wet parcel in his hands. He clutched the velvety, wet body to his chest and stared in awe at the clear blue eyes. He laid a trembling hand on the damp, white curls. A boy.

My boy.

It was a dream. As sure as he was sitting there, it had to be a dream.

The nurse spoke to him. "I'm going to take him to the nursery now and clean him up."

Gray reluctantly let him go. He waited in silence while they stitched Hope's abdomen and put away the instruments. He took her hand and whispered a last, gut-wrenching prayer, knowing it was now or never.

The surgeon gripped his shoulder. "I'll give you a moment alone with her before we call in the rest of the family."

He nodded. When the surgeon left, he gazed down into her pale, beautiful face and made himself face the truth.

"I guess this is it, baby." He smoothed the damp ringlets away from her face. "I was hopin' …" He swallowed. "I don't blame you, baby. I know you would if you could. So I guess we'll do it the other way, huh? I've run away from a lot of things in my life, I guess y'all know that. They'll think I'm takin' the easy way out, but …" his voice cracked. "I can't do it without you, babe. It's only half a life I've got."

He choked back tears of sorrow.

"Least we'll go knowin' there's a piece of us left in this ol' world. It's better this way. Your mama, she'll do right by him, I know she will. And your daddy. They'll give him a good life."

He pressed his lips to hers and kissed her.

"I guess it's time to go. When y'all get there, you sit tight and wait. I'll be comin' right along. I'll find you, baby, so you go ahead and sleep. And when you open your eyes again, you're gonna be lookin' at a man who loves you more than life."

A calm descended over him as he stood and walked from the room. Ted and Dana hovered in the doorway and Ted stopped him as he passed.

"Gray, are you all right, son?"

Morgan rushed to his side, crying. "Gray …"

He took her in his arms and held her close, softly stroking her hair. "Shh. It's all right."

She lifted her tear-stained face to meet his gaze. "Are you okay?"

"I'm fine."

She gave him a tremulous smile. "I saw the baby. He's beautiful, Gray. He looks just like you."

He held her for one moment more. "Him and Quincy, they'll grow up together. Be just like brothers, right?"

"Right," she whispered.

He gave her a squeeze and released her. "I wanna go and hold him again. And then I wanna be alone for awhile."

"Are you sure you're all right?"

"I'm gonna be fine."

Knowing there was only one place to go, Gray drove out to the gorge and parked his truck. It was early in the season and late in the day and only a handful of cars dotted the lot. He walked past the picnickers, packing up their coolers and children for the day. He walked slowly up the winding trail, not seeing the cut rock or the trees, not hearing the distant roar of the waterfall or the snapping of twigs beneath his feet. All he saw was Hope's face, eyes as blue as the sky, hair shining like gold in the sun. He heard her voice in the call of doves, in the stillness of the air that filled his lungs. *I love you, Gray.*

He trudged to the top of the path and leaned against the stone barrier. Gazing across the gorge, he thought about life and about the absence of life. He thought about his mother, his son, his wife, even Ace, all victims of life. His thoughts swirled like falling leaves, faster and faster until he was dizzy, spinning out of control. His laughter started as a sob torn from deep in his chest and grew until it gripped him in its fist and forced tears from his eyes. He'd spent his whole life wanting to believe in love, in miracles, wanting to believe he was not alone. Where was Gladdy Parker's Jesus now?

Tearing the silver chain from his neck, he hurled it into the gorge. Then he climbed onto the ledge and looked down in.

Chapter Fifty-Four

Ted picked his way up the winding trail, a man at war with himself. He was half angry, chiding himself for not letting the boy alone to grieve in his own way, but even more, he was sick with apprehension. His gut told him something had been wrong with Gray's eyes. If it hadn't told him so strongly he never would have followed him.

He stopped at a fork in the trail. Letting his instincts guide him, he chose the path that led to the top of the gorge. He paused to catch his breath before pushing himself upward. He'd been ten minutes behind at most when he saw Gray heading up the trail. Shading his eyes, he peered into the gorge, then lifted his gaze upward. His heart nearly stopped when he saw the lone silhouette standing on the upper ledge. "Oh, Christ." He broke into a run. "Christ Almighty, Gray, don't jump."

He approached quietly so as not to startle him. Each silent gulp of air was agony as he crawled toward the ledge.

"Gray?" he said, forcing his voice into submission. "What are you doing, son?"

He didn't look at him. "Go on home, Ted. This don't have nothin' to do with you."

Stepping closer, Ted grasped the ledge and swung his body upward.

"Ted, don't. I'm tellin' you, you ain't gonna change nothin'."

Ted sat with his legs hanging over the edge, sweating with the effort of not looking down. His mind worked slowly, carefully, figuring all of the angles. He had one advantage and he prayed for wisdom enough to use it. He drew a breath. "The night I lost Hope's mother I drove out to a warehouse on the edge of town. I sat there all night, a bottle of JD in one hand and a shotgun in the other."

Gray turned to him, his eyes as flat and lifeless as his voice. "You did, huh?"

"I thought about that girl and the life we had together. I didn't want to live without her."

He waited for Gray's response. When none came, he drew another breath and continued. "I didn't take my life, though, for the same reason you won't take yours."

Gray's lower lip quivered. He sucked it between his teeth and stared down into the gorge. "Why's that?" he whispered.

"Because I had a brand new baby at home that needed me."

Gray let out a choked sob. For a blood chilling moment he wavered on the ledge. "It ain't enough, Ted."

"Gray, sit down here a minute." He gave the ledge a firm pat. "I want to hear your reasons, and then I'll go if you want me to."

Gray looked at him again, but stood firm.

"Please," Ted urged. "Help me understand."

When he finally spoke, his voice was a strained whisper. "I been shoved around my whole damned life." He let loose a short, harsh bark of laughter. "Made the same mistakes time and time and time again." Raising his hand, he wiped at the tears that streamed from his eyes. "A lot I got I probably deserved, but there was a hell of a lot I didn't. I been God's whipping boy my whole life, my whole damned life I've spent walkin' in the shadow of a man I never even knew, payin' for my daddy's sins. I can't do it no more, Ted."

"Gray, you don't have to."

"She was the only thing that ever made me feel alive."

Ted sighed. "That's the way of life, Gray. It beats us down, then it turns around and gives us a reason to get up again."

"Yeah, well I been beat down. Hell, I been beaten since the day I was old enough to walk." His voice rose in anger. "All I wanted was one stinkin', lousy miracle! Was that too goddamned much to ask?"

Ted's voice came back softly. "She kept breathing, Gray. There's your miracle."

His face was still contorted with anger, but Ted saw that his eyes had softened. "What?"

"I've figured it from every angle and there's no other explanation. She had a hole in her head the size of a quarter. When they got her to the hospital there was no brain activity, no earthly reason for her to be alive. But she kept breathing anyway."

Gray sank to his knees and cradled his head in his hands. He began to moan, rocking back and forth. Ted reached out and touched his shoulder. "For life, Gray. For your sake and for the sake of that little boy back there, she kept on breathing."

The sun was fading and Ted could see shadows beginning to envelop the gorge. Gray was meeker now, visibly shaken.

"He's got an awful lot of things to learn. Who's gonna teach them to him, if not you?"

Silence.

"Hell, he hasn't even got a name."

"He's got a name," Gray said softly. "It's the same as yours."

"I'm honored."

"Theodore. It means gift of God."

"That, he is."

"Yeah," Gray whispered. "That he is."

They sat without speaking until the lights came on and bathed the paths in a hazy, almost surrealistic glow. Ted drew a last, silent breath. "It's getting late. Come on, let's go see that little man."

He waited, tense, feeling at one with air and rock and water until finally Gray eased his legs over the ledge and set his feet firmly back on the path.

• • •

M. Jean Pike

Photo by Sharon Burr

Abandoned buildings. Restless spirits. Love that lasts forever. These are a few of M. Jean Pike's favorite things. A professional writer since 1996, Ms. Pike combines a passion for romance with a keen interest in the supernatural to bring readers unforgettable stories of life, love and the inner workings of the human heart. She writes from her home on a quiet country road in upstate New York.

Printed in the United States
126258LV00001B/12/P